In Want of a Wife

Luella Linley

License

to

Meddle

BOOK 2

MEREDITH RESCE

In Want of a Wife

Book 2 Luella Linley – License to Meddle

Golden Grain Publishing

PO Box 880 Unley SA 5061

The National Library of Australia Cataloguing-in-Publication Information:

 A catalogue record for this work is available from the National Library of Australia

978-0-6489537-2-2 – Paperback
978-0-6489537-3-9 - eBook

Cover Art by Annie Millard Designs

Endorsements

"You can always count on Meredith Resce to put her characters into seemingly impossible situations, but then watch her weave her magic as she deftly extricates them to a satisfying ending. In Want of a Wife has just the right mix of romance, humor and "what next?!" to keep you turning pages well into the night."

Amanda Deed - author of the *Jacksons Creek Trilogy*

"Luella Linley has her matchmaking sights set on her daughter, Chloe. Luella shows Chloe's photo to Michael, her new tax lawyer and, much to her surprise, the young couple quickly claim to be a perfect match. It all seems too easy...

Michael and Chloe have reasons for faking their engagement, but real feelings, hilarious situations, and long held secrets toss a spanner into their carefully laid plans. Highly recommended for readers who enjoy fun and faith-filled romance stories that tackle real life contemporary issues."

Narelle Atkins – Author of Solo Tu

"A charming fake-to-real romance that honestly portrays life's genuine challenges with fictional fun."

Carolyn Miller – Author of Author of Regency and contemporary romance

"This is an intriguing romance and also a wake-up call to cherish our own values and allow others grace to do the same. I love it when Luella Linley's Regency romances converge with the sticky situations of her own very modern Australian family. Most of all, I love Chloe and Michael, and their good intentions to lead people astray while helping each other out. Put aside a good block of time for this satisfying read."

Paula Vince – Author of *Best Forgotten* and *Picking up the Pieces*

A note for non-Australian readers: Thank you for deciding to read 'In Want of a Wife'. I have set this novel in Adelaide, South Australia, and wrestled with the idea of whether I should adapt language and measurements to that usually understood by North American readers. In the end, though I have changed the spelling from Australian to US, I have retained the local Australian language. I hope you enjoy the local Aussie flavor. Below is a glossary of terms you may encounter that you may find unfamiliar.

Glossary of terms for non-Australian readers

Speed limit conversion: 60 km per hour = approximately 37 miles per hour

25 km per hour = approximately 15 miles per hour

Lollies – Candy/sweeties

Chips – Potato chips/crisps. Also chips refers to the thick cut fries served in café restaurants.

Pokies – A poker machine or slot machine, sometimes referred to as 'the one-armed bandit'. Many Australian pubs and clubs have a room full of slot machines and is colloquially referred to as the pokies.

Expiation Notice – South Australian traffic infringement notice outlining the offense and how to pay the fine.

Serviette – Napkin

Bathers – There are so many different names for swim-suit. Cosi, togs, bathers—really it depends on where you live. In South Australia we call them bathers.

Aussie Burger – Like an ordinary burger from the US, only it must have beetroot, egg, sauce (ketchup) and sometimes a ring of pineapple (the pineapple is optional).

Fringe – In reference to hair styles, a fringe is what is sometimes referred to as bangs. Though I can never quite figure out why anyone would call a fringe 'bangs'.

T-20 Cricket – A fast-paced version of cricket that is limited to twenty overs. It is played usually in two hours instead of the original cricket which takes five days for a match to be complete.

Hit for six – A Cricket expression which is like a home-run, hit over the fence. It is worth six runs.

Vegemite – Breakfast toast condiment loved by millions of Aussies, hated by anyone from anywhere else in the world. It's black and thick and salty, and perfect spread lightly with loads of butter. Warning—do not try it without an expert to show you how it's done.

Copper – Police officer.

Footy – Australian Football League.

Chook cage – Chicken coop. Hens and chickens are often referred to as chooks.

Chapter One

Chloe stormed through the front door, throwing her keys on the hall table as she stomped past. When they flew straight off and landed on the floorboards with a jangling clatter, she let out a chesty noise that could not qualify as either a statement or a groan, but communicated plenty by way of her mood.

"What's got your goat?" Dad called from the study, then put his head around the doorway. "You sound like a rampaging elephant."

"Seriously, Dad." Chloe wasn't in the mood to be teased. She was beyond frustrated having just worked back-to-back night shifts at the hospital.

"I take it you had a bad day at work?"

"My night shift was reasonably uneventful," Chloe replied. "It was the drive home that has me hopping mad."

"Cup of tea?" Dad asked.

Chloe nodded. Tea was the prescribed medicine for most stress related troubles in this house, and there was a good chance Mum had baked goods in Tupperware somewhere she could raid.

Chloe sat down at the kitchen table and dipped her spoon into the honey jar. She was trying to cut down on the number of sweeteners she had but today was an emergency. She scooped out a fully loaded teaspoon and inserted it with a plop into her cup of tea.

"That bad?" Dad put a container of chocolate slice on the table in front of her.

"I'm sorry, Dad," Chloe said. "I've just spent the night seeing to the needs of patients and then I get pulled over by a smug copper who treated me like I'm a repeat offender."

"That's not like you," Dad said. "You've never had a traffic infringement. You're usually a very sedate driver."

"Exactly! Pete is the one likely to get a speeding ticket, not me."

"You're a bit harsh on your brother."

"He doesn't try to drive carefully. I do."

"So, what happened?"

"You know that stretch of road in front of that small private school near Megan's place?"

Dad nodded. "You're hard pressed to even know a school's there, it's so far back from the road."

"I know, right?"

"They don't even have a speed reduction sign there."

"They do now." Chloe grabbed another piece of chocolate slice to shove in her mouth. "Fully equipped with a traffic cop who is literally parked there, reeling in ordinary law-abiding citizens with otherwise untarnished driving records." It was a wonder Dad even understood what she'd said, given the amount of chocolate slice in her mouth as she spoke.

"Your first speeding fine. Your mother will never let you hear the end of it."

"I was doing fifty-seven kilometers per hour. Dad! That is not speeding, and yet I have an eight hundred dollar fine and loss of seven demerit points for going thirty k's over the limit. That cop said I was lucky not to lose my license."

"Wow! When you fall from grace you do it in grand style."

"Dad! It is unjust! They put the school speed limit signs up on Friday and had the cops there on Monday. You never see kids on the road there anyway. Their parents always drive through the zone set way up the drive. This is extortion!"

"Your first speeding fine." Dad sat back in his chair and smiled. Or was he smirking—reminding her of the self-righteous lectures she'd delivered every time he'd scored one of *his* many fines?

"I don't think you're taking my situation seriously," Chloe complained. "I'm going to call Cam."

"I doubt he'll let you get out of it," Dad said. "He may be a cop, but he can't let you off a legitimate fine just because he's your brother-in-law."

"It's not a legitimate fine. It's a government fundraising rort!"

"So cynical. And you, a law-abiding citizen and all."

"You can make fun of me if you like," Chloe got up from the table and pushed her chair in. "I'm not going to pay this fine. I'm going to fight it."

"Good luck with that." He *was* laughing at her. Seriously. It was infuriating.

"Cam will help me."

"Mmm. I'm sure he will."

***

"I can't change a speeding fine, Chloe." Cam's voice came over the phone, infuriatingly calm despite the passion with which Chloe had used to describe her situation. "If you were driving above the signed limit you were breaking the law and there isn't anything I can do about that."

"But how can that be fair?" Chloe cried. "It was like they saw an opportunity to make a bucket load of money from fines and parked themselves in position."

"I'm not even in the traffic division," Cam said.

"But can't you ask some questions?"

"Not really."

"Don't you have cop friends in the traffic division who can sort this out?"

"Chloe, we are law enforcement officers. If you were driving over the signed limit then we have a right to pull you over and issue an infringement notice."

"But it's not fair!"

"You said that already."

"I don't want to pay the ticket. I don't believe it's right."

"You have the option not to," Cam said.

"What? How?"

"Turn your expiation notice over and you'll see on the back a place where you can tick a box that says you elect to be prosecuted."

"What? That sounds worse than paying a fine."

"So, pay the fine."

"But it's over eight hundred dollars and seven demerit points."

"Chloe! How fast were you going?"

"I already told you. Fifty-seven k's."

"In a twenty-five school zone?"

"A pop-up, surprise, twenty-five zone that wasn't there last week. Cam." She dragged his name out like a pleading child. "You have to help me get out of this."

"It does seem a bit unfair."

"I know, right?"

"Your only option is to have them take you to court and argue the case."

"But I don't know how." She was really sounding like a whining teenager now, but what could she do?

"Find a good lawyer."

4

Sure. Right. Of course. *Why didn't I think of that?* "Cam. You're being ridiculous."

"If you go to court and you lose, they may increase the fine, there will be a criminal conviction and you'll have to pay court costs."

"Cam!"

"It's not my fault, Chloe. That's how the system works."

"So what you're telling me is, I can't win."

"If you have a good lawyer who knows how to argue a case well, you might win."

"But lawyers charge bazillions of dollars and by the minute."

"It's your call, Chloe. Pay the fine, wear the demerit points and drive more carefully."

"I *was* driving carefully," Chloe mumbled after she disconnected the call. "I always drive carefully. This is rubbish! I'm not going to pay that fine."

***

Evelyn's heart thudded painfully against her ribcage. She had seen the gentlemen riding up the lane and recognized Lord Bradshaw as one of the riding party. The moment she saw him she turned tail and hurried back to her small, broken-down cottage. Had he seen her? Did he recognize her? Oh, she hoped not. What would he think if he saw her in this state of dress? How would he respond if he had seen her enter this ramshackle abode her father had allowed to fall to pieces? Those few short months where she had lived in another world—where her life had been that of a respectable companion for his elderly aunt—those were the days of happiness and hope. She had thought she might find a place in Lord Bradshaw's heart—that he would look past her humble home-life. But she had not had the opportunity to even broach the subject with him before her perfect world had shattered before her eyes. Her employer, Lord Bradshaw's aunt, had died suddenly. Evelyn had been dismissed without a reference or severance pay. The housekeeper had shown no sympathy for her situation and had her ushered from the estate before Lord Bradshaw had returned from London.

Oh, why had she allowed her expectations to rise up on wings of anticipation? Why had she been so foolish to imagine that her father's irresponsibility that had reduced him to ruin would not also affect her prospects? She had nothing. No money to call her own and no hope of respectable employment. She could not allow Lord Bradshaw to see her in this state. She must forget she had ever exchanged pleasant words with him.

Pleasant words? How inadequate. Fancy trying to explain those depths of feeling with 'pleasant words'. Louise snapped her laptop lid closed and stood up. Time for a cup of peppermint tea with some Manuka honey. The kettle had only just begun to boil when Louise's phone rang. She glanced at the caller ID and decided she'd better take the call.

"Fiona! You've just caught me on a tea break."

"Excellent. I'd hate to break your creative flow. Are you on schedule?"

Not even close, but that was not the right answer to tell her agent. "I'm moving along nicely," she said instead.

"Well, I hate to be the bearer of bad news, but we have some issues with your contract regarding the tax component of what you earn. IRS insist that the advance be taxed and everything you earn by way of royalty following."

"That's not fair!" Louise said. "I have to pay tax in my own country. I don't want to have to pay it twice. Why do we have to go through this exercise every time we do a contract?"

"You know government departments. They never let the right hand know what the left hand is doing."

"Last time I looked at an IRS form for international tax agreements my brain went into meltdown. The US tax jargon is different to what we use here in Australia, and I don't understand it in either country."

"Yes, I know," Fiona said, her tone sounding decidedly condescending. "That's why I've made an appointment for you at our Australian law firm. All you need do is go in and they will walk you through the contract and all the IRS obligations."

"Will that cost me?" Louise asked.

"Luckily for you our US office has a number of international authors, and they have realized that legal and financial tax obligations are a mine field if not worked out properly."

"You did tell me all this last time. Sorry. You know how it is. My mind is mostly in the 19th Century."

"Yes, I understand. My main task is to make sure you're on schedule with these next two titles."

"For the most part. I do get distracted when I'm worrying about paperwork."

"I'll email through the details of your appointment."

"Is it the same law firm I went to last time?"

"Same firm, different lawyer. Michael Sullivan is relatively new there and did his master's degree in the US at Yale."

"He's American?"

"No, he's Australian, but has lived in the States for a few years. He'll be the best person to help you navigate the international details."

***

Michael shuffled through the letters that had been sitting in the mailbox for the last three days. He had hoped his mother would check the mail every day, but like a lot of things with his mother, she simply forgot or was too depressed to be able to pull herself off the couch to check the mail, the use by date of the milk or even the toilet paper roll.

He shuffled through twelve envelopes. Two he was able to throw straight into the recycle bin—generic advertising for real estate agents and discount coupons that sold stuff no one really needed. Two letters for his mother, both from a bank—two different banks to be precise. When would these lending institutions develop some responsibility and stop trying to entice the vulnerable into credit cards they couldn't afford? He was tempted to ditch these in the bin as well, but thought better. Part of his mother's recovery involved her taking responsibility for her own financial decisions. But he would watch her nonetheless. He would like to think that she was impervious to temptation but feared she was not. He laid her two letters aside and that left eight envelopes he needed to attend to.

Why did everything have to arrive at once? He might have switched to having bills sent through email except he couldn't afford internet at the house, and he didn't want to have private papers being saved on his work computer.

"Mum! Are you home?" Where else would she be. She didn't have a car and she certainly didn't have money to catch a taxi. He doubted she'd be able to scrape up enough coins to even take a bus.

"Mum!"

"I'm in here." Still in bed, or was it she'd gone to bed early? Michael looked at his cheap imitation Rolex watch. It was only 6.30. Way too early for bed.

"Are you feeling all right?" He didn't turn on the light as the room was dark and instant brightness was cruel when one wasn't expecting it. "Mum?" She didn't move or turn to acknowledge him. She had slumped again.

"Have you eaten?" He sat down on the bed next to her in the semi-darkness and put his hand on her hunched shoulder. "Mum?"

"I'm not hungry."

"When did you eat last?" She had lost so much weight recently so he had to make sure she ate.

"Don't worry about me."

"Mum …"

"If I die, you'll be better off."

She had really slumped.

"I'm going to call the hospital," Michael said, taking out his phone and looking up the number in his list of favorites.

"I don't want to go to the hospital." Alison Sullivan roused and turned over. "Don't you go calling those people in here, Michael. I have a right to my own peace and quiet."

"Then you should eat something. If you're not ill, come and sit up while I make us some dinner."

Michael left the room. His mother knew he would make the call. He'd done it a number of times before when she became so low he feared for her safety and he would do it again if she didn't respond.

Having pulled out some vegetables—mostly old and somewhat wilted—Michael went about cutting them up with a mind to stir fry them and serve them with rice. He wasn't much of a cook, but when his mother was in this state he had to do the best he could. When he'd studied in the US for those three years he'd become the king of stir-fry. It was all he ever had time or money for as he was working his way through college. Thank God for soy sauce.

While he was waiting for the rice to boil, Michael began to go through his mail. Three utility bills, two of them presented in alarming pink and red tones—overdue. There was an invitation to the old scholars' reunion from St Peters College. That was amusing.

When he'd received a scholarship to the prestigious school he'd transferred from his ordinary high school in the low-socio-economic suburbs for his final two years of school. Even then he'd had to work at a fast-food restaurant to be able to afford the uniform and to fill the required book list. It had been tough adjusting his rough accent to hide the fact he was not one of them. There was no way he'd go to the reunion. Ten years after graduation and where was he? Back living in council housing with his single mother, trying for all he was worth to service a debt she'd run up while trying to satisfy her search for that pot of gold at the end of a slot machine. Stupid government should do something about these one-armed bandits that steal people's lives.

He let out an expletive as he saw the rice-water boil up and overflow the saucepan. Jumping up to attend to it he quietly apologized to God. He had his own bad habit of swearing that didn't fit well with his new-found faith.

"Mum?" He called out as he mopped up the mess on the stove. "Dinner's ready."

He hoped she would come. He was tired and didn't really have the energy to follow the procedure to get her professional help. As he placed the two bowls of stir-fried vegetables with rice on the table, his mother shuffled into the tiny kitchen and pulled out the tired vinyl-covered chair.

"Tomorrow I'll make a roast," she said. "And a nice pudding."

"That would be great," Michael replied. He didn't have the heart to mention there was no meat in the freezer and that he wouldn't have time to get out and buy some unless he went out tonight right after dinner. He was tired. A long bike ride to the 24-hour supermarket was not on his schedule for the evening.

"I'll take the car down and pick up what's necessary," Allison said.

"Mum. You know we had to sell the car."

"Well what was that flash machine you had parked out the front yesterday?"

"Mum!" It was exasperating always having to repeat things he'd explained so many times before.

"I saw you come home yesterday in a fancy silver car. I thought now that you had a job at that highfalutin law firm you'd have enough money."

"We cannot afford to keep a car with registration, insurance and running costs."

"But yesterday ..."

"I told you I need to hire a car every now and then to visit certain clients."

"It would be cheaper to own a small run around than hiring those luxury cars."

"I only hire for the day when I need it. The rest of the time I take a train into the city and cycle to the office. You know this."

"But surely now that you're a lawyer ..."

It was no use going over and over this. She just couldn't seem to grasp the magnitude of her gambling debts on top of the personal loans he had taken to get his fancy law degree. A good income was one thing, but paying interest on debt that was of no use to anyone was another. He would get them back in the black but it would take time. In the meantime he would cycle to work and skip an expensive gym membership.

Chapter Two

*L*ouise hated chasing about after silly paperwork. It messed with her writing mode. Honestly, tax departments in every country seemed designed to make life difficult. She was the one who did all the hard work, plotting and researching and crafting her work. Not to mention all the hard work she had to do to keep up a social media presence and planning a regular trip to the US to do book tours and go to writers' conferences. And now, not one but two tax departments wanted to take another slice of her pie. Not going to happen. At least if she paid tax in Australia there was some hope they may provide a health care package. What would she get if she let the IRS have it?

"Mrs Brooker?"

Louise looked up to acknowledge the receptionist.

"Mr Sullivan will be with you in a few minutes. You can go through to his office now if you like. Third door on the right."

Louise picked up her handbag and water bottle. She never went anywhere without her water bottle. One must stay hydrated even if the fluorescent orange drinking container didn't match with any professional ensemble. Louise entered the designated office and found just what she expected by way of furnishing. Ainsworth and Pembroke were an old and established law firm, known for their traditional values and old-fashioned ideals, so leather wing-backed chairs and wood-grain wall panels were quite within character. There wasn't much by the way of personal decoration in this office. A pot plant that looked as if it was taken care of by a professional plant person, gold-framed degrees on the wall—one from an Australian university and one from Yale. Very impressive. Other than the degrees with the name Michael Sullivan in calligraphy, there was one small photograph on top of the bookshelf. This was what attracted Louise's eye—something personal. It was one of those photographs that looked like it had been taken in a shopping mall, a young mother with a small boy on her knee. Both were smiling broadly. She was a beautiful young lady, though not much in the fashion department. It looked like she was stuck in the eighties.

"Sorry to keep you, Mrs Brooker." A young man breezed into the office and placed a file on his leather inlaid desk. "Michael Sullivan." He reached out his hand and shook hers warmly. "Nice to meet you."

Yes, I dare say. Billing out at sixty-five dollars every fifteen minutes, it would be a pleasure to meet any new client. "Nice to meet you too," she said instead.

The young lawyer pulled out his leather chair and sat down behind the desk, opening the file in front of him.

And now for all the technical legal jargon. She was in the hands of Ainsworth and Pembroke and trusted they would guide her through the murky waters of international tax agreements. Or more strictly speaking, she was in the hands of this fresh-faced young man— Michael Sullivan—and she hoped he had the experience to get it all right, because she would have no clue if he was doing it right or not.

"Now that you have signed all that paperwork I will lodge it and it should all work on its own," Michael said after half an hour of filling in paperwork, ticking boxes and entering tax file numbers.

"Thank you," Louise said as she got up. "Your son looks very much like you." Louise pointed to the photograph that had captured her interest before.

"That's because it's a photograph of me with my mother."

"She's a beautiful woman." *And she's your mother, not your wife. How perfect is this.* Just as dear Aunt Jane would say: a single man in possession of a large fortune must be in want of a wife.

"So, no family of your own then?" Louise asked.

"Not yet."

"Your wife not ready for children?"

"My wife doesn't currently exist, so I can't say how she might feel about it."

Perfect!

"I'm guessing you can't be more than 30, given your youthful looks. You'd have to be at least that to have completed all this education." She waved her hand toward the wall of academic certificates. "And you've spent time in America at Yale. That is quite an achievement."

Michael ducked his head. He apparently didn't want to discuss his age.

"Not that I'm suggesting you're too young to deal with my situation."

"I'm twenty-eight, Mrs Brooker, but I can assure you I've already dealt with the IRS and double taxation agreements a number of times. I had to deal with it myself, being an Australian and earning money while I worked and studied in the US."

"Oh of course. Mr Ainsworth would not be likely to employ someone who was not completely competent. I've been with this firm for all my legal issues for nearly fifteen years."

"Well, I don't want to keep you," Michael said. "As much as I'd like to take you over into the next billing increment, I'm sure you would appreciate my being efficient and economical."

"Yes, absolutely. Thank you so much." Louise stood up and looped the strap of her handbag over her shoulder. "Just one more thing."

"Yes?" Michael had come around from behind his desk and was standing nearby.

"I have a daughter about your age." Louise produced her mobile phone and opened her photo album app. "She is quite the looker and completely unattached. See?" She began to scroll through her photos and made sure the screen was well within viewing distance for the reluctant young man. "Would you be interested in going on a date with her?"

Louise caught him in eye-to-eye contact. The best way to get a direct answer was to hold that contact. The first one to break away loses. He was good. He must have played this game before because he didn't yield, though Louise sensed he would like to have.

"She looks lovely," Michael eventually said. "Thank you, I'm sure she is very nice …"

"But you're not interested?"

"Not right now. But I'll keep you in mind if I need a date at short notice."

Nothing ventured. Nothing gained. One day she would strike the right one. Look how things had turned out with Megan and Cam. That marriage was all due to her carefully organized meddling.

"Well, thank you once again for taking care of all this," she pointed to the folder Michael had tucked under his arm, then held out her hand to shake. My he had a strong grip. "And you think about it. My Chloe is a clever, successful young woman, not to mention quite beautiful. I'd be happy to set something up if you change your mind."

***

Change his mind. That was unlikely. But he had to give it to this famous author—she had an imagination, and she seemed like the sort who would persist when she'd set her mind to arranging something. *I wonder how her daughter feels about it?*

Michael wasn't sure if he should feel flattered that she'd selected him as a suitable candidate for her daughter or not. It was probably the money. Not the money he had, because he didn't have a dime, but the image of wealth he portrayed in this office. Ainsworth and Pembroke spoke prestige, money, power and security on just about every level. That was why he'd had to buy two ridiculously expensive suits. He might have been on the doorstep of destitution, but he had to make everyone who set foot inside Ainsworth and Pembroke believe he was rich, successful and competent. Well he was competent, and he would be successful. Time would prove that. Rich was another prospect altogether.

His office intercom buzzed and he came back around to his desk to answer.

"Yes Jeannette?"

"Mr Ainsworth would like to speak to you if you can spare fifteen minutes."

Michael looked at his watch. He only had to file Mrs Brooker's papers away and then he had an hour before his next appointment.

"Tell him I'll be five minutes."

Being relatively new to the firm, Michael always felt a level of anxiety whenever the boss called him into his office. He mentally went through the cases he'd been working on in the past few days and ticked off each one as having gone without incident or complaint—that he knew of.

"Michael. Come in. Sit down." Mr Ainsworth was always friendly, or at least that was the persona he wanted to advertise. Somewhere behind that smile Michael suspected there was a tough character, perhaps even mean. He had watched Mr Ainsworth argue cases in court and had been somewhat intimidated by his forthright and unrelenting manner. Michael didn't have confidence in the veracity of the friendly persona.

"How are you settling in?" Harold Ainsworth asked.

"Good." Michael couldn't help the long questioning tone that slid into the word.

"No need to worry," Harold said. "I haven't had any complaints."

Only when he felt the sigh of relief did Michael realize he'd been holding his breath.

"You may not be familiar with the workings of this company," Harold continued, "so I'd just like to go over them again for you."

Michael nodded. He was somewhat familiar, but Mr Ainsworth was the boss.

"You know that Ainsworth and Pembroke are a family friendly firm?"

"Yes, sir. I do know that."

"You know that we pride ourselves on traditional values."

Michael nodded.

"We stay away from divorce cases as much as possible, as we don't want to facilitate the breakdown of the family."

Michael felt his stomach clench. He'd read this information and had felt bad about it at the time. His mother wasn't divorced—she'd never married in the first place. Goodness knows where his father was. He didn't even know his name but remembered his mother had told him his father had been a married man she'd had an affair with. He was unlikely to acknowledge his illegitimate son, no matter how many scholarships he'd won. Michael had not discussed this with his mother in over fifteen years, and he certainly had not shared this information with the head of Ainsworth and Pembroke. His dysfunctional beginning bore no resemblance to the image this company prided itself on.

"And you know that we want to encourage by example strong stable marriages?"

Michael felt a lump forming in his throat. He had read this in the information booklet but hadn't thought it would ever be brought up.

"I believe you had written on your application that you were pursuing marriage?"

He had checked a box that had a statement of some sort. He would pursue marriage once he was out of debt and if he found someone he felt he could trust with his history. Probably not before. Mr Ainsworth was looking directly at him. Had that statement been a question? He gave a brief nod. No timeline was being discussed here.

"Good. I'm so glad, because we're having a staff retreat in a couple of weeks to celebrate the end of the year. The company is paying for all our staff and their spouses to go to the Gold Coast."

"I'm not married yet," Michael said. Not even close, considering the debt that still had to be cleared.

"That's fine. I will book separate rooms for you and your fiancée."

Fiancée? He hadn't said fiancée.

"If you could check with her to see that she's free, I'll make the reservations."

"I'm not sure…"

"What does she do for work?" Mr Ainsworth went on.

Moment of truth. Should he tell the boss about his actual relationship status, or … Chloe Brooker. Mrs Brooker's daughter. Unattached, beautiful, apparently looking for a husband. What did she say her daughter did for work? She hadn't, but two of the photos he'd been shown, Chloe was in scrubs.

"A nurse. Chloe is a nurse."

"Well tell Chloe I'm prepared to pay her for the week if she has to take leave without pay. The whole trip is on the company, and I'd really like to have the whole family there."

***

"Mum, I really need a lawyer." Chloe came over to her mother and lay her head on her mother's shoulder.

"Do you dear?" Louise replied. "I nearly got one for you today."

Chloe snapped her head up. "Really?"

"A lovely young man, highly educated, high-paying job. Works for Ainsworth and Pembroke."

"Mother! I don't need a husband lawyer. Just a lawyer who can help me beat this stupid speeding fine."

"Well I was going for both but as it turns out, he wasn't interested."

Chloe rolled her eyes. "You didn't show him my photo."

"Showed him the folder on my phone of all your photos."

"Mum!"

"Don't worry. He wasn't interested."

"You can't do that all the time."

"What all the time? I've only done it once before."

"For me. But you actually invited Cam over here to meet Megan. You're incorrigible."

"Stop your complaining. Look how well it turned out for your sister. She and Cam are married and happy."

"You know your mother," Dad said as he came into the kitchen. "She won't rest until you're all settled."

"You're no help, Dad. You know how she uses Jane Austen as a template for everything in life. This is not Longbourne—there are no gentlemen at Netherfield."

"Bravo, Chloe. You actually made an Austen reference in conversation," Mum said.

"How can I help it? You've played that blessed DVD so many times I can almost recite it."

"Glad to see I've contributed something to your education."

19

Chloe sat down at the kitchen table. "Seriously, I would like to beat the injustice of this speeding fine. How much do you reckon it will cost to hire a lawyer?"

"Wouldn't it be easier to just pay the fine?" Dad asked. "Cam told me there would be a good chance that the magistrate might increase the fine and then give you a criminal record."

"I. Was. Not. Speeding."

"But you were going above the signed speed limit," Mum said.

"That's not the point."

"Well I don't know what the point is," her mother continued.

"The sign should not have been there!"

Chloe could see she was not making a good case. Her parents had moved on to discussing her father's latest business venture. She needed a lawyer, but could she afford it on her small income? She was a nurse but at this stage she was only working for a nursing agency and the work was casual.

Frustrated, Chloe got up to wash the teacups. Her mother's phone, set on the cupboard next to the sink, rang. She picked it up and handed it to her mother. No caller ID so she couldn't satisfy her curiosity as to who was calling.

"Louise Brooker." Her mother always sounded so professional when she answered the phone. "Oh, hello Michael. Nice to hear from you."

"Who's Michael?" Chloe asked her father in a stage whisper. Dad shrugged his shoulders.

"Yes, of course. She's right here, as it happens."

Chloe's ears pricked up further. She was the only other 'she' who was there. Who was Michael?

"Yes, she lives here with us. Came home after her sister got married. They'd been sharing a house until that point."

"Mum!" Chloe frowned. "Who is Michael, and why are you discussing me in a phone call?"

Mum held up her hand and went on listening.

"Absolutely. I'm sure she would be happy to. We were just talking about you before, and she was saying how much she wanted to meet you."

Chloe gave her best what-the-heck-are-you-saying look, glaring at her, jutting her head forward.

"Just hold on a second, Michael. I'll put Chloe on and you can ask her yourself."

Chloe looked at the phone her mother held out to her as if it were a piece of slime.

"It's Michael."

"I gathered that much," Chloe said.

"The lawyer. You said you needed a lawyer." Her mother poked the phone another few inches closer. "Hurry up, Chloe. He wants to talk to you."

Whatever. Chloe took the phone. She was going to have serious words with her mother later.

"Hello, this is Chloe." Just like Mum, with a false sweetness she didn't particularly feel.

"Hi, Chloe. Michael Sullivan here."

"Hi. I'm not sure I've met you before."

"No, you haven't. I met your mother today and she told me about you. She said we might enjoy going on a date together. Are you interested?"

Oh, the moral dilemma. No way was she interested in going on a blind date, but he was a lawyer and that was just what she needed at the moment. Was it dishonest to say yes to a date and then spring legal questions on him?

"He's a lawyer," her father said from the watching crowd. "Just like you wanted."

Chloe shook her head at him and frowned in an effort to make him be quiet.

"I may be interested," she said slowly.

"Great. What about tomorrow night?"

"Sure. What time?"

"I can pick you up around seven. Do you want to go out for dinner or just for coffee?"

"Let's just try coffee to start." That way she wouldn't feel so bad about hounding him for free legal advice.

"OK. That sounds like a plan. Can you text me your phone number and address? I only have Louise's contact details."

"Sure."

"Great."

"Great."

This one-word affirmation fest could go on forever.

"I'll see you tomorrow night at seven," Michael said.

"I'll see you then."

Chapter Three

Because he'd hired a car for the day Michael had time to get home after work, take a shower and have a quick bite before going out.

"Why have you got a fancy car in the driveway?" Mum asked him.

"I had to hire it for the day. I'll return it tomorrow."

"I need to do grocery shopping. Can I take it out for half an hour?"

Michael cringed inside. The car wasn't insured for his mother so she couldn't drive it, and he only had an hour before he needed to leave to pick up Chloe for their 'date'. But his mother had not shown this much interest in shopping or anything at all in a long time.

"I'll drive you down but we'll have to leave now, and I only have an hour."

His mother had already picked up her handbag from the hall table. Goodbye shower and a quick bite. He hated wearing his suit outside the office. It was pretentious. And it looked ridiculous with him pushing a shopping trolley with his green reusable shopping bags. He tugged at the hundred-dollar silk tie and left it on the hall table. This would have to do as his casual shopping look.

His mother was in a particularly good mood. She loved riding in the European metallic silver sports car and he guessed she enjoyed getting out of the house. She was putting some expensive meat in the trolley. Not that he minded, but they had agreed she would pay for groceries from her welfare money while he took care of every other bill and the debt.

"Isn't your pay day next week?" he asked. He knew full well when her pay day was.

His mother kept pulling things from the shelf and putting them in the trolley.

"Mum?" She had just put in a large box of expensive chocolates. Not within the usual budget.

"If I can't have a treat once in a while, Michael, then I can't see the point of my having sacrificed for you to get your education."

She had been in the local pub feeding poker machines most of the time he'd been working extra jobs to help get himself through school, but he didn't say that.

"We agreed. I'm paying for everything except the groceries. Have you got the money for all of this?" He waved his hand over the pile of high quality and sometimes unnecessary products in the basket.

"Michael, you drive a car like that and you can't afford to give me a treat once in a while?"

Guilt surged through him. He had calculated a tight budget based on both their incomes and had only allocated a small amount for treats. He had planned to use this weeks' allocated funds on tonight's coffee date. But his mother had been in the doldrums for a number of weeks and he didn't want to dampen the current level of joy she was showing.

He quickly recalibrated his plans. It looked like he and Chloe were going to pick up a takeaway coffee from a drive-through and take an evening stroll in the park. The evening was going to be cool. He'd suggest she bring a coat.

As they got everything through the checkout, the major consolation was that he could look forward to some good meals in the coming week—if his mother stayed buoyant and was able to cook. He wasn't so sure he'd make much of it if it were left up to him.

"That will be a hundred and twenty-three dollars and fifty-eight cents." As the cashier recited the amount, Michael waited for his mother to use her card. He would cover the extra amount, hopefully no more than thirty or forty dollars.

"Michael?" His mother was looking at him, so was the cashier.

"I'll cover the extra. Use your card first," he said. He hated treating his mother like a child, but he couldn't allow her to continue to evade responsibility. That was how they got in this mess in the first place.

"I've had extra expenses this week. You pay this time. I'll pay next time."

Michael took out his credit card and smiled at the cashier, but it belied the fury that was welling in his chest. She'd done this to him before but he didn't have the heart to argue with her in front of strangers. He wanted to take the expensive chocolates and the gourmet pre-prepared chicken rolls, and several other luxury items, out of the bags. He could not afford to put this on credit.

Once he had the groceries in the boot of the car and they were both seat-belted ready to go, he spoke.

"What have you spent your money on this last week?"

"I've had a couple of expenses come up," she said without any sign of remorse. "You don't know how hard it is to live on welfare."

Didn't he? Wasn't that the story of his entire childhood?

"Mum, I pay the rent, the insurances, the utilities and the debt repayments."

"You've got the money. Why are you being such a stinge about it? I never get to buy anything for myself."

"I made a budget for you. We agreed you would pay the groceries and put some aside each week for clothes, household items you might want and some for going out. Have you been sticking to the budget?"

She didn't answer. He took a quick glance and saw her jaw was clenched. He didn't want to address this tonight. He had a date—which wasn't a date, more like an appointment to engage Chloe for a short performance.

Why did he have to perform for his boss anyway? He knew why. If Harold Ainsworth had even a notion of how he lived and how his mother traveled through life, he would find a way to end his employment. Of course, Michael could challenge any sort of unfair dismissal through the courts, but did he really want to go into battle for his job? Was he as smart as Ainsworth who knew the law and would make sure that whatever action he took was completely within the law.

***

"Chloe!"

That was subtle. Her father yelling through the house like she was a teenager getting ready for her prom. She wanted to yell back, but she was a 28-year-old medical professional, and yelling through the house was not her style. She was tempted though.

Chloe checked her makeup in the bathroom mirror, though why she bothered she could not say. She had no wish to be attractive to Mr. Michael Sullivan—not for the purposes of a relationship anyway. Getting him to find interest in her traffic infringement case was another issue. Would makeup make any difference?

The bathroom door opened and Mum stuck her head in the door. "He's here."

"I guessed when Dad started hollering my name."

"You look fine," Mum said. "Let's not keep him waiting."

Chloe zipped up her makeup bag and rolled her lips together to even the spread of lip gloss. He'd better be interested in helping her given the time she'd taken to get ready.

"Listen, Chloe." Mum blocked the bathroom doorway. By the look on her face, she could tell it was a mother-daughter chat.

"We don't want to keep him waiting," Chloe said, not really wanting to endure a relationships lecture.

"Can you be kind to him," Mum said.

"I'm always kind. Why, what's wrong with him?"

"There's nothing wrong with him, its just that … well, you know …"

"I don't know. Why wouldn't I be kind?"

"All of your equal rights fervor. You know. Don't bite his head off if he tries to be a gentleman."

Mum and her Regency gentlemen. So not the way of the world today. "I won't say a word." Unless absolutely necessary.

Chloe moved forward and her mother turned and led the way out to the family room.

"Michael, this is my daughter, Chloe." Mum stepped back and allowed the visitor to move forward.

"How do you do?" he said.

Chloe took his hand in greeting. His lawyer-looking hand that was smooth and clean, but still masculine and strong. Nice.

"Well I'm starving. Let's go eat." Chloe looped her handbag over her shoulder, watching her mother's face and waiting for the reprimand. It didn't come. What happened to her words of guidance on how to impress a young man—or at least a frown? She'd expected a frown. She shrugged.

"You kids have a nice time." Typical Dad. Chloe had been casual on purpose, but Dad didn't have to try to be clueless. It came naturally.

This time Chloe saw her mother's eyes go wide followed by a frown and an almost imperceptible shake of her head. A quick glance at her father and she saw him mouth the word "what?" He had no idea.

Michael Sullivan had said nothing, and Chloe was suddenly alert to his stiff silence. He'd moved to the door and was waiting for her.

"Don't wait up," she said. As if. She had no intention of staying out late, or staying over at his place, or anything that even hinted of forming an attachment. This was business—she hoped.

"Wow! Nice car." Chloe waited while Michael opened the passenger door of the silver sports car.

"Thanks." Michael closed the door. He was a gentleman. A quiet gentleman. This was when she would usually have spouted her independent woman spiel. Well she'd done it twice before when a guy had opened the car door for her, annoyed at the condescension displayed. With Mum's words still ringing in her ears, she kept it quiet this time. Besides, she wanted Michael Sullivan to help her so she didn't want to offend him right off the bat.

Tension mounted when Michael got in the driver's side and didn't say anything. Chloe wanted to roll her eyes but kept everything in neutral. This was going to be an awkward date. She hoped he was a better lawyer than he was conversationalist.

Chloe waited for him to start the car, but he didn't. He had his hands on the steering wheel and was looking straight ahead.

"Are you all right?" Chloe asked.

His lips were hidden and he nodded his head.

"Umm."

Chloe turned her head to look directly at him. It was a test of her self-control for her not to prompt him to speak. What was his problem? Had he seen her and decided she wasn't worth the effort? She was tempted to be offended. She wasn't that bad looking.

"I've got to be honest with you." At last, he put some words together.

"That's a good start," she said.

"I don't own this car."

Chloe shrugged. It was a great car, but it wasn't going to affect whether she would go on a date with him or not.

"I'd said we'd go out for coffee," he continued.

"I know, but I haven't had a chance to eat dinner yet. Do you mind if we go to a café and I'll order a pasta or something?"

Was that a shade of panic on his face? Good heavens, was he afraid of eating in public? Perhaps he was gluten intolerant.

"Can I tell you the whole story before we go anywhere?"

"I'd rather you told me the whole story over a bowl of pasta, I'm starving."

"I can't."

Wow. What was his problem?

"I can't afford it."

"Right." This guy was strange.

"Don't let the car and the job fool you, I'm on the edge of bankruptcy and I just don't have the money to pay for dinner."

"I'll pay for dinner. I don't believe in guys having to pay for my meal anyway, so let's just go and eat." *And let me find out if you're at least smart enough to argue a speeding ticket case.*

"Are you sure?"

"About dinner? Yes, I'm sure. There's a café not far from here that makes excellent pasta. Let's go there."

Thankfully, Michael must have decided that his deep dark secrets could wait as he started the car and moved out onto the street. Chloe gave the directions and they were pulled up out the front of the café within five minutes.

"I'll buy you dinner as well if you're hungry," Chloe said. "I hate to eat alone."

Her tall, dark and, might she say, handsome lawyer got out of the car. He was mysterious as well. Hardly uttered a word. Mum would be devastated. This was so not the man for her.

Michael opened the café door and stood aside to allow her through. *So* not the man for her. She hated the condescension when men felt the need to open doors and throw their coats around shivering shoulders. If she wanted to be warm she could be responsible and bring her own jacket. Be kind. She could be kind.

"Table for two, please." Michael spoke to the waitress and then followed as she led the way to a small table at the back of the café.

Please don't hold out the chair. He held out the chair for her to sit down. Any other man at this point would have received a long lecture on equality, but Chloe bit her tongue. Even if it hadn't been for her mother's lecture, she wanted him to argue her case in court. If the price was to suffer a few acts of chivalry, then she would pay.

Chloe sat down and took the menu from the waitress who was making goggle eyes at Michael and barely acknowledged her. What was so fascinating about Michael Sullivan? Chloe watched him for a full two seconds to do an analysis. Yep. He was handsome and looked sophisticated in the open-necked business shirt. But there was something about him that was confusing. His body-language should have said confidence and charm, but it didn't. He was troubled. Uneasy. Suddenly, Chloe was interested. What was going on in Michael Sullivan's life?

Chloe ordered the entrée serving of carbonara fettucine. She'd been here before. The full serve could feed a small village for a week.

"Do you want to order something to eat?" Chloe asked.

Michael had ordered table water but nothing else. He opened his mouth to say no.

"Make that a full serve and add a garden salad," she said to the waitress. "And could you bring two plates? We're going to share."

The waitress looked to Michael as if waiting for him to endorse the order. He smiled at her. "That will be all, thank you," he said.

"She's in love with you," Chloe said the moment the waitress was out of earshot.

"I doubt that."

"Then you can't read body language very well."

"Listen, Chloe, I'm really sorry about this."

"About what?"

"You having to order dinner for me."

"If it were the other way round, would it have been a problem?"

"What do you mean?"

"I mean, what if you were flush with cash and had taken me out on a date. Would you have expected to pay for my dinner?"

"Probably."

"But you have a problem when a woman orders and pays for your dinner?"

"I have a problem having asked you on a coffee date and turning up unable to even pay for coffee."

"Why are you driving an expensive car and dressed as if you've got loads of money but you can't even pay for coffee?"

He sighed. Actually sighed. There was a story here. She sat forward, elbows on the table, and locked him in her sights. She was here now and, no matter how bad the story was, she was going to hear it all.

Chapter Four

She was like her mother—forthright and no-nonsense. Did he like those qualities in a woman? So far, yes. A far cry from his mother who often suffered from depression, and the only time she was forthright was when she was trying to manipulate him. He was yet to decide whether Chloe was manipulative. So far it was: what you saw you got.

"I've asked you out under false pretences," he said.

"I've come under false pretences, so now we're even."

"Not even yet. You paid for dinner."

"Next time, you pay."

"Next time?"

She would consider another date given the disastrous start to this one?

"You want to confess first, or shall I?" she said.

Michael couldn't help the grin. She was open and funny.

"You go first. I doubt your ulterior motive could be worse than mine," he said.

She raised her eyebrows. Was she surprised?

"So, you haven't responded to my mother's shameless matchmaking attempts?" Chloe asked.

Michael grinned again. "Has she done this before?"

"You have no idea. I think she believes me incapable of finding a man myself."

"How many times has she set you up?"

"*Tried* to set me up." Chloe sipped her water. "Only once before, but I told her off *and* I forbade her from doing it again."

"And yet …?"

"You're a lawyer and I'm desperate for some legal help in fighting an injustice."

Michael raised his eyebrows in question.

"I was given an unjust speeding ticket and I wish to fight it in court."

Michael smiled. At least she was forthcoming at the start of the date *and* she'd paid for dinner.

"So, what's your dark secret?" Chloe waited while the waitress returned and placed the huge bowl of pasta on the table along with a basket of bread and two plates.

"I'll bring the salad in a moment," she said.

"So?" Chloe pinned him with her gaze again. "Why on earth would you respond to my mother's offer to set you up on a date?"

Michael waited for the salad to be placed on the table and for Chloe to serve out the pasta—on to both plates, he noticed. A good job too, as he felt bad about eating her pasta and probably wouldn't have served any for himself. This was going to be a long story and he didn't want any more interruptions.

Chloe had almost demolished her plate of pasta and two slices of bread while Michael had talked. His plate remained untouched. He couldn't hope to digest food while his stomach was in a knot of anxiety.

"So your boss is an old-fashioned stickler and you want to present a good image?" Chloe scooped the last fork of pasta into her mouth.

"It's more than that."

"How so?"

"He doesn't know about my mother."

"He can*not* discriminate against you in the workplace because your mother suffers from depression."

"And the gambling addiction."

"I thought you said she was recovered."

"I'm not sure she has."

"I'm sorry, Michael. That must be really hard."

He swallowed. It wasn't just hard, it was impossible.

"I still can't see why you need to worry about your boss. Your mother's illness has no bearing on your ability to perform your job."

"It's her marital status that's the problem."

"Your boss frowns on divorce?"

"He does, but Mum isn't divorced."

Chloe frowned at him. "Widowed?"

"I'm the result of an adulterous affair. I don't have a father, and my mother has never been married."

He watched closely for signs of judgment, but all he saw was a brewing anger in her face.

"What are you trying to tell me exactly, Michael? Because from what I'm hearing, it sounds like you're afraid to let your boss know who you really are."

"I've worked hard to get this job and I can't afford to lose it."

"If your boss is the sort of person who would sack a man because his background is dysfunctional, I'm not sure I'd want to be working for him."

"He's a good person, Chloe, and has treated me like—"

"Like a son?"

Michael nodded. He felt shame wash through him like a burning wave. She would leave now that she saw the whole ugly truth. He wouldn't even get to asking her for the favor. She got up but didn't pick up her bag. Instead, she pulled her chair around to sit next to him and put her hand on his arm. Michael bit his lip. What was this? Pity? Care? He didn't know what to make of it. He'd never made himself so vulnerable to anyone—ever.

"I think I understand." She was trying to catch his eye contact, but he avoided it. "How do you think I can help?"

Michael swallowed the ball of anxiety that had lodged in his throat. This had been a crazy idea. There was no way she would help him now that she knew.

"I shouldn't have bothered you. I feel really stupid."

Chloe gripped his forearm.

"You called my mother because you need help with something. I don't blame you for that. I need help for something too, that's why I agreed to the date."

"Yeah, but I haven't told you what I need yet."

"You've come this far, you may as well lay all your cards on the table."

Michael studied her hand still on his forearm. It was warm and it felt comforting, encouraging, understanding.

"Would you be my fiancée for a couple of months?"

He'd forced the question out but couldn't look at her. It was the most ridiculous question a man could ask a woman on their first meeting. She didn't answer. He waited for her to withdraw her hand, pick up her bag and walk out, but she didn't move. Her gaze was burning into the side of his head. Should he say something else?

"You need to help me understand your request a bit more, Michael, because fiancée usually graduates to bride and then to wife. I get the feeling that's not exactly what you're asking."

He took a deep breath and turned to meet her gaze. She wasn't angry. She wasn't offended. She was puzzled.

"Mr Ainsworth wants to take his whole staff and their partners for a week-long staff retreat to the Gold Coast."

"By partners, I assume you mean husbands and wives?"

"I'm the only single person employed at Ainsworth and Pembroke."

"Why didn't you tell him you were single?"

Michael sucked in a long breath through his nose and blew it out through his lips.

"Did you tell him you were engaged?"

"When I applied for the position, I didn't realize how fanatic they were about stable happy families, and I ticked a box that said I was pursuing marriage."

"But you weren't—aren't—pursuing marriage?"

"I'm in so much debt, I can hardly afford to keep my mother and me in council housing. I have no intention of trying to start a marriage that way. It would be disastrous."

"So, just tell him you don't have a wife, or fiancée, and go on your own, or take your mum."

"Are you kidding?"

"No. Not kidding. That's who you are— a single employee who is taking responsibility of his mother who is unwell. In my book that makes you a selfless and honorable man. From where I sit, those are the qualities that should make Mr Ainsworth award you employee of the month."

Michael was stunned. He'd never heard anyone say something so encouraging to him before.

"I mean, I don't mind helping you out," Chloe went on. "I wouldn't mind a trip to the Gold Coast and all, but I've got work—"

"Mr Ainsworth said he was prepared to cover your work if you had to take leave without pay."

Chloe stopped and looked at him.

"Did you already tell him about me?"

A wave of chagrin crashed on his head. What presumption. What had he been thinking?

Chloe removed her hand. It was bound to happen sooner or later. He was an idiot.

"I'm not sure I understand you, Michael, but correct me if I'm wrong. You really believe your boss won't accept you if you don't fit into the settled, married, house-owning, church-attending mold?"

"I attend church."

Chloe sucked in a breath. "And yet you're prepared to lie to your boss."

"I'm hoping you'll take on the title, just for a couple of months, so I wouldn't really be lying."

Chloe shook her head, her lips pinched.

"I'll help you fight your speeding fine."

"I was *not* speeding."

Michael put on his pleading eyes. Chloe stared back, her face a mask of—what? He couldn't make it out.

"Is this how you work your juries to win cases?" she asked.

"I'm not a criminal lawyer."

A few more seconds of silence. He could see the wheels of thought turning in her eyes.

"Let's get something straight," Chloe took her chair and placed it back on the opposite side of the table, then sat down. "If I'm going to take on this role, there are a few details that have to be agreed on."

Michael nodded. "Shoot."

"You will help me beat this unjust traffic infringement notice."

Michael controlled the smile that wanted to break out and just nodded his head.

"And you will not tell my mother that the engagement is bogus."

"What? Why?"

"Because you don't want to lie and so this will be for real."

"But I can't … you don't want … I'm not ready—"

"I'm not ready either, but this is what you want—to impress your boss."

Michael swallowed. Chloe had unearthed some deep things during this conversation. Father hunger being one of them. Should he just pull the pin on this scatter-brained idea and go get some therapy?

"I'm going to start planning a wedding, Michael."

He opened and closed his mouth three times.

"Don't look at me like you're a goldfish. If I go on this retreat as your fiancée, and I'm expected to mix with other women, they will want to know all about our wedding plans."

"I can't afford—"

"I won't book anything. I'll just start a Pinterest page with pictures and quotes, and stuff like that."

She was a whirlwind. Given what he knew about her mother, he should have anticipated this.

"And, I will be wearing my great-grandmother's ring."

This had gone to a whole new level of crazy.

"Won't your mother know it's your grandmother's ring?"

"No, my paternal grandmother gave it to me. Mum won't recognize it."

"Why do you want to make your mother believe we're really engaged?"

"Because I want to teach her a lesson in meddling. When I announce we're engaged and I'm going away with you, she will freak out and back pedal like you won't believe. I'm hoping to cure her of her matchmaking fetish."

"Hardly a fetish. She's only tried twice."

"Not counting my sister, whom she managed to set up and follow through, until she arranged a wedding."

"She's a force to be reckoned with."

"That she is. And speaking of mothers, what are you going to tell your mother?"

Michael felt like he'd been hit with a brick. He couldn't tell his mother. She wouldn't be able to cope.

***

This couldn't be right. Liam dismounted from his horse and scanned all directions. There were only hedges and fields and this run-down dwelling that could not be called a cottage, let alone a house. Should he go back to the vicar and ask again? Liam was deflated, having eagerly followed the directions the Reverend Adams had given him. Where was Miss Evelyn Dixon? Why had she just disappeared from Bradshaw Manor? Why was he pursuing her anyway?

He had followed the Vicar's directions to this place, so he might just as well ask the occupant of this hovel if he knew where Miss Dixon's family lived.

The door looked as if it might fall from its hinges, so he only tapped lightly. One moment. Two. Ten. He could hear there was someone within. Why didn't they answer their door? He tapped again.

At last. The sound of someone releasing the latch and the old, weathered door opened.

"Miss Dixon!" She looked dreadful. "Are you unwell?" What a stupid question. He might just have said, 'you are pale, and your eyes are dull, and your hair...'

"Lord Bradshaw." Her usual warm smile was absent.

But what was she doing here in this disgusting, vermin-infested, place?

"I was looking for ... that is to say ... the vicar said I might find you here."

She nodded.

"Are you well?" Are you well? Are you unwell? Make up your mind. At least this question was within the prescribed list of polite questions. But she had probably taken offense at his first attempt. And she did look unwell.

Nice work Bradshaw. That was as smooth as a country road after rain. At least her hero was determined to search out the love of his life. Louise sat back and stretched.

Chloe had returned from her date with the lawyer and had said nothing. She shouldn't have been surprised. That Chloe went in the first place was the shocker. It was her determination to fight the speeding fine that was the motivating factor.

Time for a cuppa.

"Tea?" She said the word as she walked past Russell's office.

"Yup. Be two minutes."

Louise had the kettle boiled and teacups ready when her husband entered the kitchen.

"I'll have chamomile today," he said. "This job is crazy. They want their plans redrawn by tomorrow morning. No pressure."

Louise put in a chamomile teabag for Russell and a ginger tea for herself. She could use a bit of zip.

"How's your work going?" Russell took the steaming cup from her.

"I sometimes wonder if these characters are going to connect with the readers."

"You always say that. It's just your initial stages of developing the story. Once it's all finished, it will flow nicely."

"Thanks, Darl." She gave him a smile over her ginger tea.

"What did Chloe have to say about her date with the lawyer? Is he going to help fight her speeding fine?"

"She hasn't said anything. Not one word."

"And you didn't ask?"

"I'm trying to act disinterested."

Russell smiled. "She's playing a game with you. She knows full well you're twisting yourself into a knot pretending you don't care, but desperately want to know."

"Do you think she would do that?"

"She is her mother's daughter. Mark my words, she's waiting to see what you'll do next."

"Well, I'm not going to play her game. If she doesn't want to tell me about her date, then I don't want to know."

Russell laughed. "I give you five minutes from when she gets home from work, and you'll ask."

"I will not, Russell Brooker. Don't you be so smug. You want to know as much as I do."

"I'd be interested to see if she can get out of this speeding fine. I'm guessing you're hoping for something more in the line of love and marriage."

"I only want what's best for my children."

"Getting out of an eight hundred dollar fine would be best at this stage. I'm inclined to agree with her—that speed trap wasn't really fair."

"To be honest, I doubt Mr Sullivan would take kindly to being used like that."

"You don't think he'd be flattered that your daughter agreed to a date with ulterior motives?"

"No, I don't."

"Let that be a lesson to you. Leave her to find her own life partner."

Louise didn't reply. She hated it when her husband was right.

Chapter Five

Chloe searched the hospital directory to find the psych department. It was a long walk from where she worked in A&E, but she wanted to do some research. Michael had told her about his mum, her depression and that he suspected she'd relapsed in her gambling addiction. From her own research online, she knew relapse was part of the journey to recovery, but it was a stressful part. Especially for poor Michael. Poor Michael. She felt sorry for him, and it wasn't just because of his mother's situation either. He was desperate to find acceptance in his boss's world. She was sure that wasn't healthy either. He should own who he was—dysfunctional background and all. He should be proud of the man he was, having fought for his education and having stuck by his mother through the worst of times. Chloe was proud of him, and she'd only known him two days. And he was her fiancé. Temporary fiancé, but she was going to commit to the part while it lasted.

Chloe exited the lift and walked down the hall to the reception area.

"Can I help you?" The receptionist looked up at her and smiled warmly. That was a good sign. One wouldn't want a cold and disinterested receptionist greeting people who were struggling with anxiety and depression.

"I'm wondering if you have any information on depression, specifically depression related to addictive behavior."

"There are the brochures on the stands over there." She waved her hand in the general direction. "There are links to various organisations you can search for more information, but if this is a serious condition, you should get a referral and see one of our doctors for a proper diagnosis and treatment plan."

"I'm just doing some research for a friend." Right. The old it's-not-me-it's-my-friend line. Was she looking at her strangely? Suspicion, pity, concern?

"You work in A&E?" Probably the scrubs and ID card hanging around her neck gave it away. She nodded. "You know how to refer to the specialists. Have your friend come in if you're worried."

"I will, thanks." She wouldn't. She didn't know Mrs Sullivan, and she didn't want to appear condescending to Michael. He needed encouragement, not pity. Chloe went to the information stand and collected several brochures that promised to have useful information.

"Thanks." She waved to the receptionist as she walked back to the lift. She was only the temporary fiancée, and Michael seemed uncertain that she should meet his mother at all. Chances were she would never need to use this information, but it was better to be prepared in case something came up.

Now she'd finished work she prepared to face her parents—her mother in particular. She'd only greeted them in passing the last couple of days, as she'd had a late shift followed by an early. It was surprising her mother hadn't yet cornered her and demanded a report of the date.

"Hey Dad." She stopped by his office and leaned on his door jamb. "How was work?"

"Good. Not too busy, thankfully. How was your day?"

"Frantic. Can't stop to talk now. I've got more revisions to make and the client is demanding."

43

"OK. I'll catch you later."

One parent down. No probing questions.

"Hey Mum. How's your story coming along?"

"I'm not entirely happy with it, if I'm honest."

"Have you got Evelyn and Liam together yet?"

"Liam is turning out to be a bigger snob than I'd like."

"Well, you're the writer. You can make him behave how you want."

"He's just turned his nose up at Evelyn because he's realized how bad her background is."

"I thought her father was a gentleman?"

"A gentleman fallen from grace and destitute."

"Well, sort him out."

"Easy for you to say. You know how these titled characters wear their position like a crown and look down on the lesser people, particularly if there's scandal involved."

"Mother, you're in charge of these people. Give him a change of heart."

Chloe moved on down the hall to her room. Wouldn't it be great to be an author in charge of people and able to manipulate them to make their lives work out? Chloe threw her work bag on the chair and flopped onto her bed. After having got home at midnight last night, and having left at six this morning, she was beat. She closed her eyes and thought about Michael. They'd agreed to an engagement which they would announce on Saturday after they'd been out to dinner again. Mum was going to freak. Chloe smiled just imagining the things she would say.

Which reminded her, she must get the ring. She got up and closed her bedroom door, then went to her closet. It was in a box of mementos somewhere. There were several boxes high up so she pulled a chair over to help her reach. It was in the last box she pulled down, of course. Her nanna had given it to her in a small green velvet ring case. Chloe wasn't much of a jewelry girl and had put it straight in her mementos box. Now she opened the box and studied the ring. It wasn't really her style, but it was a diamond set on a thin gold band. It would do the job and she would tell Mum it was a family heirloom, because it was. Mum had never seen it and Dad wouldn't notice.

She snapped the lid of the ring case shut and put it in her handbag. She must remember to bring it when they went out tomorrow night. Right now, she needed to catch up on some sleep.

***

Should he tell Mum or not? On the one hand, if he told her he had a girlfriend and they'd decided to get engaged, he was fairly sure Mum would be ecstatic. She had hinted at the idea for years—hinted, cajoled, nagged. He'd always put her off citing the debt as the major obstacle to love and marriage. Was that cruel? Letting her feel the weight of the consequences of her gambling addiction? If he told her about Chloe she would have something to focus on and be excited about.

So that was the major reason why he should not tell her. It was only temporary and once they broke up, Mum would be devastated. This could undermine her mental health. What to do? Would the couple of months of joy and anticipation be worth the predictable slump in spirits that would occur once she knew the wedding was off?

No. It was better she didn't know.

"I'm going out tonight." Michael was dressed in his jeans and cheap t-shirt.

"Where are you going?" Mum was alert for a change.

"Just going out with a friend for dinner."

"Which friend?"

"Just someone I met through a client."

"A girl?"

Moment of truth. Perhaps the idea of a girlfriend would be enough to satisfy her curiosity without raising her hopes too high.

"Yes, Mum. A girl."

"I'm so glad, Michael. You don't know how much a burden it has been knowing that I've been the reason why you've locked yourself away from getting to know people."

"I'm just going out to dinner. Nothing to get excited about."

"But it's a start. And she must be pretty special for you to consider breaking your principles."

"Just a date, Mum. That's all."

The look on her face provoked ambiguous feelings. She looked so eager, but if she knew the truth …

"You need this." Mum smiled at him. "Something to take your mind from responsibility and constantly pinching pennies."

"I can't take my mind from responsibility, you know that. We're on the verge of bankruptcy and if I can't pay off all that debt and have to declare, I may lose my job. I won't ever be able to buy a house."

"You can't lose your job because of bad financial luck, surely?"

"It wasn't bad financial luck, Mum." He watched her face fall. "Look, I don't want to talk about this now. I'm going out. Why don't you watch a romantic movie or something?"

"I'd prefer to dream about your romantic future and the possibility of grandchildren."

There was no talking reason. There was no avoiding it. She wanted a future for the family—as did he. But he could not build a family or future if he didn't clear the debt. And he couldn't clear the debt if he didn't have a good paying job. And Ainsworth and Pembroke took a dim view on family dysfunction.

"Have a good night." He shrugged into his jacket, picked up his house keys and wallet, and went out the front door.

The night air was magnificent. Late spring brought beautiful warm days followed by mild evenings. Perfect for a walk along the riverbank. Was Chloe special? That remained to be seen. But she was a good sport. Of course, he had some work to do researching the circumstances surrounding her speeding case. Still, she had been respectful and kind when he'd told her about his past and family situation. No judgment, only care. He was looking forward to seeing her again.

He hadn't hired a car. Chloe told him to save the money and had offered to pick him up. What would she think when she saw where he lived? It was a council housing estate. There were many people in his neighborhood who did their best to keep their yards and porches neat and tidy. But there were just as many who either did not care or were unable to do simple things like mow the lawn or clear the hard rubbish from their front yards. He didn't judge. While he was studying in the US, his mother had no ability to take care of the property. At least now he put outdoor chores on his schedule two Saturdays a month. It wasn't fancy, but it was tidy.

Seven o'clock on the dot. Chloe pulled up in front of his house driving a small yellow hatchback. He opened the door.

"Hi." Hatchbacks were not designed for tall men but he did his best to fold into the passenger seat.

"Sorry. This car is nothing like yours."

"Not mine, remember." He clicked the seatbelt into place.

"Right. But it is the car you'd drive if you could afford it."

"Probably not. It's too ostentatious."

Chloe laughed.

"Well it is," Michael said. "Why drive a car that is showing off?"

Chloe pulled her car away from the curb. "Firstly, I was laughing because you used the word ostentatious, which in itself is ostentatious—"

"Fair call."

"And secondly, the reason you hire those ostentatious cars is to show off, isn't it?"

She had him there and it grated.

"The firm expect a certain image when they engage with clients."

"So, if you drove a late-model mid-priced car what will your clients think?"

"We've only been engaged for two days and already you're picking a fight?"

She laughed again.

"Hardly a fight," she said, "and hardly engaged."

"What would you call it then?"

"A robust discussion and a temporary working relationship."

Michael couldn't help the smile that rose. "You should go into law. You could argue your case perfectly well without my help, I think."

She cast a worried glance in his direction.

"Eyes on the road," he said. "You don't want to lose your remaining demerit points."

"Are you telling me you want out already?"

His lips tugged up either side. She was desperate to keep him representing her case.

"Michael?"

"Don't worry. I need your help as much as you need mine. I'm just saying your robust discussion could rattle an unprepared defense."

"Too much?"

"You're not the demure, submissive, Stepford-wife usually favored at Ainsworth and Pembroke."

"They favor Stepford-wives?"

"Probably not that bad but in that general direction."

"Help me out here, Michael. Are you telling me that the values favored by your boss include a quietly spoken wife who stays home and brings up the three children, serves on the PTA and sings in the church choir?"

"You sound like you don't like the idea."

"You're kidding, right?"

"What about that plan don't you like?" Michael asked.

"Three kids."

They both burst out laughing.

"Don't panic," he said. "We can have this argument in full color in a couple of months and then have a classic reason to break up."

"I guess. You need some plausible reason why it doesn't work out between us."

Chloe pulled the car up at the chain restaurant they'd chosen. Not too expensive since it was Michael's turn to pay and his budget was set.

"I brought the ring." Chloe plonked it on the table between them as soon as she was seated.

"I assume you don't want a full proposal."

"I do. Are you kidding? How often does a girl get engaged?"

"In your case, hopefully only twice."

"Are you going to go down on one knee?"

"This is only a temporary arrangement, remember?"

"What am I going to tell the other Stepford-wives when they ask me how you proposed?"

Michael smiled. "You're relentless."

"I'm just saying."

"Then you'll need to wait as I haven't thought of a proposal speech yet. Let's eat dinner, and maybe I can surprise you when we go for a walk along the riverbank."

"Sounds romantic."

And it did—sound romantic. The stupid thing was he was liking her more and more as the time progressed. It was a good job they had an excellent argument brewing or he would begin to get attached.

***

This *was* romantic. They'd talked and laughed and enjoyed the no-frills food they'd ordered. And now they were walking along the banks of the River Torrens enjoying the walking paths and gardens that were lovely, even in the artificial light from the solar-powered streetlamps. Despite their differences of opinion on how Michael should relate to his boss, Chloe was enjoying his dry wit and intelligence. And he seemed to be enjoying her company too.

"So, Chloe ..." He stopped walking, so she stopped as well. Then he stepped onto the path in front of her.

"Yes, Michael?"

He took her hand and dropped down on one knee. She should laugh, but she couldn't. The dimly lit gardens, on a balmy spring evening, his handsome face looking up at her—it was spellbinding.

"Will you marry me?"

Warmth infused her entire being. "Yes. Of course."

He stood and let go of her hand while he brought out the ring box, flipped it open and carefully lifted out the diamond ring. Then he took her left hand and slid the ring on her fourth finger. It was a little too big. She hadn't thought to try it on prior but at least it wasn't too small.

"What do you think?" Michael asked.

She didn't answer but threw her arms around his neck, bringing her face into kissing position. He responded with no hesitation, wrapping his arms around her waist, and bringing his lips down on hers, warm and gentle, for several breathless seconds.

He drew back his head but kept his arms securely around her. Chloe's heart was hammering away at an unreasonable rate, and every nerve of her body was pinging with energy. She didn't even try to prevent it as he came in for a second round of mind-numbing, exhilarating kissing.

She had lost her mind. By the look on his face, he'd lost his as well. They were passionately ensconced in each other's arms and she only drew back far enough to be able to gauge the look on his face. Michael's mouth opened and closed several times like earlier in the evening. This was obviously his way of trying to say something when intelligent thought refused to connect with his tongue.

Chloe took a deep breath. "Wow, Mr Sullivan. That was a convincing performance. I'll have those lawyer wives in a puddle of tears when I tell them about this."

"Your performance wasn't so bad either," he said. "You should go on the stage."

"I'm sorry to tell you but that was hardly acting. And besides, you asked me to marry you when our agreement was temporary fiancée."

"You said 'yes'."

"That was the only answer I could give. Are you sure you didn't sit at home and plot this proposal?"

He smiled and loosened his hold. "If I'd planned it, I would have organized someone to video the occasion for posterity."

They resumed walking along the path after Chloe had slipped her hand under his arm—it was the natural thing to do. After several minutes of walking in companionable silence, Michael took her hand in his and laced his fingers through hers.

"This is some proposal night, Michael," Chloe said. "The next one has a lot to live up to."

She felt him tense a little and he let go of her hand.

"Yeah, you're right. I better keep this in perspective."

"I like holding your hand."

"But we don't have an audience to perform for, and our agreement was temporary."

"We won't have any trouble breaking up. I've got a few arguments already lined up that I know will do it."

"What? Like where I live?"

Chloe stopped. He was sensitive about his home life. "That's not what I meant."

He shrugged. "I know I'm no great catch, and I wouldn't blame you if you used that as the reason to break up."

"Well, for a start, that idea never entered my mind. If you would introduce me to your mother, I plan on getting to know her and seeing if there is a way I can support her in her efforts to recover."

"I'm not going to introduce you to her. She would be devastated to learn that I'd lost my chance at happiness."

"You could tell her the truth."

Michael frowned and shook his head, then quickened his pace as they looped back towards the place where Chloe's car was parked.

"You're right, it won't take us much to break up," he said.

"Michael."

"But we agreed a couple of months."

Chloe didn't say anything else. Fine. If he wanted to be all antsy and defensive, it was just as well, because that other Michael—the

52

warm, passionate, romantic Michael—could easily cause her to forget who she was.

***

"How did your date go?" He knew that his mother would suddenly find interest in life with the idea of a possible family expansion.

"It was excellent." The look of pleasure that came over her face hardly matched the way he felt about it.

"Will you be seeing her again?"

"Very likely." Very likely, as in they had made a date for the weekend. Was he looking forward to it? Was the sky blue?

"Will you bring her around to meet me?"

Michael pursed his lips but didn't say anything.

"Is she too good for the likes of me?"

"No. She's asked to come, but I don't want you to get attached when it might not work out."

Mum stopped her interrogation. If her thoughts were anything like the ones running through his head, she would be wrestling with the desire to launch into happiness while fear of hurt barked at her heels. What was he doing? He couldn't afford a relationship of any sort. He wanted to please his boss but was Chloe right? Was this something to do with his latent desire to have his father recognize him, accept him, be proud of him? Obviously there was something of this nature because engaging Chloe in this charade was ridiculous. And exhilarating. She was breathtaking—literally.

Mum retreated into herself and Michael was sorry to see it.

"Let's just see how things develop."

Her eyes immediately lit with hope.

"But don't get too invested. I don't want you to get hurt."

"I promise I won't, but I would love to meet her."

Michael shouldered his backpack and secured his helmet. "I've got to go, Mum. I'll see you later."

He mounted his bike and set out, glad of the physical exertion required to negotiate the rises. He thought over their time together last night. Bolts of passion followed by the soggy blanket of his insecurity. Highs and lows in rhythm with the landscape he traversed.

By the time he got into the office, he had allowed the positive aspects to dominate. He quickly showered and changed into his suit and was at his desk five minutes before the day started.

The first email he opened was from the office administrator asking for confirmation about whether Chloe would be able to make the staff retreat. He flicked away the response. There was no doubt that Chloe was eager to take a break at a five-star beach resort, and given that all expenses were covered and that Harold had agreed to pay her for the week, there were no obstacles.

As he was scanning the list of emails, a text pinged on his phone. Chloe.

Thanks for last night. I had a great time. I've asked Mum if we might have dinner with them on Saturday night. She pretended to be nonchalant. Do you want to tell them, or shall I?

Michael closed his phone. He had to think on that one. He didn't understand why Chloe wanted her parents to think this was real. But then, she didn't understand why he needed Harold to believe he was engaged. The intercom buzzed.

"Morning, Rosanne."

"Your nine o'clock is here."

"Great. Send them on through."

Time to work.

Chapter Six

How was she supposed to respond this? She had eaten at Bradshaw Manor many times when employed as the Dowager's companion. It had never been a free and easy affair given she occupied that difficult social position that was neither lady nor maid. The companion was too high up to eat in the servant's hall, but not high enough to speak freely with others at the table.

But this letter, written in Lord Bradshaw's hand, wrote expressly to invite her to tea. After his display of disdain last week, Evelyn was tempted to throw the invitation in the fire. Who did he think she was? If he thought she would suddenly fawn sweetly in obligation, he was very much mistaken. Her father may have gambled them into a state of destitution, but she was still a lady at heart. And she had her pride.

"Will you go?" Father had picked up the paper from the simple kitchen table.

"Do you think I should?"

"You are better than this." He waved his hand around the shambles they currently called home.

"To hear Lord Bradshaw speak, I would suggest not."

"Evie. Don't let your bitterness prevent you from taking an opportunity."

It was good advice, though Evelyn had lost faith in her father's ability to make sensible decisions. And she was yet to be convinced that taking tea at Bradshaw Manor was a good opportunity. It may just be Lord Bradshaw's way of soothing his conscience at the way she had been dismissed.

The alarm sounded on her phone and Louise got up from her desk. Chloe had invited Michael Sullivan to dinner but she still wasn't home from work. It was time to put the vegetables on to roast.

Louise wanted to be delighted with this outcome but there was something fishy going on. Chloe was not that easy to please, and she'd only been on two dates—the first one was a set-up. Louise had not asked about either date, but that was only because Russell had challenged her that she would not be able to resist. She *had* resisted asking with a good performance of nonchalance but it was killing her not knowing. Chloe had not offered any information except that Michael was coming to dinner this evening. Could she have hit the target twice in a row? Megan and Cam seemed to be happy and settled as a married couple. Her meddling had paid off in their case. Was it possible that Michael Sullivan would be her second success at matchmaking? It was too easy.

Louise got all the vegetables out and started to peel. Not her favorite job, but when hands were busy it was an excellent time to plot. She should be focused on Liam and Evelyn. Their story was the one that would pay the bills. But she couldn't help thinking about Chloe and Michael. Hiding her enthusiasm was tiring.

The time flew by as Louise got caught up in all the food preparation.

"I'm home." Russell came into the kitchen, planted a kiss on Louise's cheek, and loosened his tie. "Smells great. What's for dinner?"

"Russell, you know that question is the single most annoying question you can ask."

He grinned. "I know. That's why I ask it."

"Well, your daughter has invited a young man to dinner, so you'd better get ready."

"The lawyer. Right. Do you think I'd better keep the tie?"

"Don't be ridiculous. It's a casual dinner. Just don't wear track pants."

Even before Russell left the kitchen, Chloe arrived.

"Smells divine, Mum." She also gave a peck on the cheek. "What do you want me to do?"

"It's your dinner. How do you want to set the dining room?"

"Let's go with the contemporary setting."

"Fine."

"I'll just get changed first. I don't want to sit down to dinner in scrubs."

The hour was approaching and the flurry in the kitchen increased, along with Louise's anticipation. Was Michael the right man for her daughter? He seemed nice, but Chloe's amiable cooperation raised a red-flag. Louise finished slicing the sourdough bread and put the knife on the sink. Nothing was set in concrete. It was only a couple of dates. Time would tell.

***

The nerves were out of control. Michael stepped off the bus and began to walk the few blocks towards the address Chloe had given him. She was going to tell her parents about the engagement. He wanted to say bogus engagement, but it wasn't. He had proposed, she had accepted, she had a ring, and they'd kissed. Boy, had they kissed. When they eventually got around to having their massive breakup fight, he was going to be heartbroken. His boss and entire office staff would believe it because it would be real. And all this in under a week. He would not have believed it could happen like this, except it had. Chloe Brooker was intoxicating. She encouraged him, accepted him, scolded him, lectured him, and judging by last night's performance, loved him. But that couldn't be right. Love didn't grow in such a short period of time. But something had grown, and whatever it was, he was on edge because he'd never faced potential parents-in-law in his life.

He rang the doorbell and waited.

Chloe answered. Thank you, Lord. "Hi. Hope I'm not late."

"You're just in time." She stepped close and kissed him—on the mouth. "I'm glad you came." She grabbed his hand and tugged him inside.

"Wait, Chloe." He pulled her to a stop and she turned to face him. "Are you sure about telling your parents?"

She held up her left hand with the ring sparkling on it. "I'm going to Queensland, and right at the moment I'm enjoying getting to know you. I can't see any reason not to proceed. You never know where it will lead."

She started to move, but he pulled her to a stop again. "Wait. You know where this will lead. It has to end. I can't afford—"

"—to get married. Yeah, yeah. I know. I'm not worried about it at present. Come on."

She pressed on, still holding his hand. He followed and hoped he didn't look as reluctant as he felt.

"Hello Michael." Louise Brooker was all smiles as she wiped her hands on a towel and stepped forward to shake his hand. "Is it all right if I call you Michael?"

He nodded. "Hello again, Mrs Brooker."

"Please, call me Louise."

He nodded.

"Glad to see you took my advice." She smiled and he smiled back. This—meeting one week and getting engaged the next—probably wasn't the advice she had intended.

"This is my husband, Russell," Louise continued.

Michael had met him briefly the first time he'd picked Chloe up, but he paid closer attention this time. Chloe's dad was middle-aged and stood about his own height. He held out his hand in greeting.

"Nice to meet you properly, Michael." Russell's grip was strong, and his expression was one of welcome. Michael warmed to him immediately.

"So, you're a lawyer." Russell waved Michael towards the lounge and indicated he should follow and sit down.

"I'll help Mum finish dinner," Chloe said.

Michael sat down but wasn't comfortable enough to relax. "I'm going to help Chloe fight her speeding case."

"I wasn't speeding." Chloe's voice reached them from the kitchen, and Michael couldn't help but smile. She was determined.

"What are you going to use as a defense?" Russell asked.

"There are a number of things we can look at. I need to do some research, but I think the most promising will be me looking up council by-laws about giving the constituents satisfactory notice when changing a speed limit or any other law."

"Yeah, you'd think they would have a certain amount of time where they would have to advertise the proposed change and then a grace period before they start issuing fines."

"I'm almost sure there will be something of the sort in the council by-laws. I just need to look it up and get the evidence of when the signs were installed and the fine was issued."

"Thanks, Michael. I appreciate you taking the time to help our girl out. An eight-hundred-dollar fine is a significant amount of money."

"Dad. You're not talking money with our guest?" Chloe came into the room and sat down next to Michael. She took his hand and laced her fingers through his. He knew she planned to announce their relationship to her parents but hadn't known how she would do it. By the look on her dad's face, this public display of affection was sending a message.

"So, is there something you want to tell us?" Russell's eyes were focused on their linked hands. Was he upset? Would he approve?

"Yes, Dad, there is, but let's wait until Mum comes in."

"Before dinner?" There was suspicion in Russell's tone.

"Yes, before dinner."

"Louise!" He was obviously comfortable to holler in the house and impatient to know details.

"What?" She shouted back.

"They always shout back and forth between the rooms." Chloe squeezed his hand.

Russell didn't answer his wife and a few moments later she appeared in the doorway. It only took a second for her to see how close Chloe had tucked herself against Michael on the couch, and her eyes zeroed in on the linked hands. The smile on her face was brilliant. She approved. Michael felt relief wash over him.

"So, what do you want to tell us?" Russell asked. His opinion was still not apparent.

Chloe held up her left hand and flashed the ring first in Louise's direction and then towards her father. "We're engaged."

Louise's face was a mask of shock. Russell's was still blank, not so easily read.

"Mum?" Chloe sat forward, but still held his hand. "Aren't you going to say congratulations?"

This was cruel. They'd only known each other a week, and no parent would be expecting an engagement in such a short time.

"Perhaps they need a little time to process," Michael said.

"Yes," Russell agreed. "And I'd like to talk to you after dinner." Michael felt Russell's gaze pierce him. His heart dropped. This was not the way to win a father's favor. Even if it was only temporary, Michael still craved his acceptance and approval.

The tension over dinner was like a stalking tiger. Chloe chatted and laughed and pretended her parents weren't in a knot of anxiety, but Michael could feel the angst. When Russell suggested he should go for a ride with him to deliver some papers, Michael was eager to go.

"Russell. Do you have to go out when we have someone over to dinner? Can't you deliver the papers tomorrow?" Louise said.

"No. I need to go tonight, and I'd like the opportunity to spend some time with my new son."

New son? Michael felt happiness and worry get up to start a fight. Would Russell really accept him as a son? What would happen when he and Chloe broke up?

"Coming?" Russell had the car keys and a cardboard tube that obviously held plans.

"Do you mind?" Michael asked Chloe but watched for Louise's reaction as well. Chloe watched her father, and Michael saw a message pass between them.

"It's fine. I'll help Mum clean up the dishes and we can have coffee when you get back."

He half expected Chloe to lean in and kiss him goodbye, but she didn't. Russell wasn't pleased and apparently Chloe knew it.

"Don't be long." Louise was the only one who didn't seem to understand the subliminal messages that were being passed back and forth.

Russell drove a late model SUV. It wasn't flashy but it was sturdy and serviceable and sensible. In many ways it was more comfortable than the expensive European cars he often drove. The atmosphere was thick, but Michael couldn't think what he should say.

It only took until Russell had the vehicle on the road before he spoke.

"So, Michael. Tell me your version of events."

He knew. Chloe thought he was clueless, but Russell was more perceptive than all of them.

"I should have asked your permission."

"You should. And you can, if you want. But do you really want my permission to marry my daughter?"

"I really would, but then I think you already know this isn't real."

"I'm not sure I know anything of the kind. I figure something is going down, other than a real engagement, because Chloe doesn't just go on a date and then turn up engaged five minutes later. That, and the fact she's wearing my grandmother's engagement ring."

"She didn't think you'd notice."

Russell hummed two short notes.

"So why don't you tell me what's really going on, and why?"

Michael sat back in the seat and let out a breath. He was relieved.

Russell Brooker was a good man. He didn't flinch once during the telling of the story and showed no sign of rejection when Michael told him about his family background.

"Let me ask you something," Russell said.

Michael nodded. There was no chance he would try to hide anything now that Chloe's dad had figured out this much.

"How did you get into so much debt?"

"I didn't realize how bad it was. I took student loans and a couple of personal loans to get me through college and planned to get them paid off as soon as I started work. But when I returned from America, I discovered that my mother's pokies addiction was not just extra grocery money, but she'd been conned into taking high-interest loans from some unscrupulous loan sharks. I took out another personal loan to pay these out. The banks weren't interested in helping, since I was only just employed, and so there is high interest on all the loans. But I have a plan to pay them all off. Mum has agreed to do her part—economising."

"How long do you project it will take?"

"If we stick to the budget, around ten years."

"I'm assuming a wedding, wife and children are not in your budget."

"There's no way I could afford it. I told Chloe this when I first disclosed the terms of the arrangement."

"But when you proposed to her, it took off further than you figured?" Russell asked.

"It did."

"So that brings me back to my original question: do you really want my permission to marry my daughter?"

Michael swallowed. He did want it, but he couldn't follow through. Not in the next decade anyway.

"I'll tell you what," Russell had pulled the SUV over in front of a house, "I'll just drop these plans inside to the client, and then I have a proposal for you."

Michael watched, his nerves chasing around in his stomach, waiting for Russell to deliver the plans. When he got back in the car, he didn't say anything until the car was back on the road.

"Why don't you come with me to the footy next Friday night?"

"What?"

"We have a home final, I have member's tickets, and the girls are fighting about who is coming. I'd like you to come. My son, Pete, is taking my son-in-law, Cam, with his spare ticket. Let's make it a boys' night out."

"Are you serious?"

"Don't you like footy?"

"I love it, but I've never been to a live game. I've only ever watched on TV."

"Your boss doesn't have a corporate box? Hasn't he ever let you have the tickets?"

"I think he does have a box, but I've never been offered the use of the tickets."

"Well, do you want to go?"

"Yes please, but—"

"But what about you and Chloe and the game she's playing with her mother?"

Michael nodded.

Russell shrugged. "I've found it's easier to let the girls figure out their own issues. I'm not one for meddling."

"So, should I tell Louise—about the nature of our arrangement?"

"That's up to you. I'm not convinced it's as much an act as you think."

"Chloe has knocked me off my perch, if I'm honest, but I can't marry her given my financial situation. And besides, I really should give us some time to get to know each other before making such a serious commitment."

"Well, it looks like you're going to have about three months to get to know each other. If your boss is such a stickler for old-fashioned values as you say, Chloe will become vocal about it before then. Don't be surprised if she takes him to task about equality while you're on the retreat."

"She wouldn't, would she?"

"I wouldn't put it past her. Do you have women employed at Ainsworth and Pembroke?"

"Just the receptionist and a couple of clerks."

"But no female lawyers?"

Michael shook his head. He'd noticed the imbalance in the company before but would never have said anything.

"Well, I can't promise she will be all compliant. That's not who she is."

"I still have to take her speeding case to court."

Russell laughed. "Take my advice and leave it until after your time away, then you'll have something to convince her."

"I don't want to blackmail her."

"I'm guessing by the way you describe your boss that you'll be getting separate rooms at the resort."

"Yes. Of course. Sorry, I should have said."

"Because we brought the kids up with Christian moral values, and though I'm aware no one today blinks twice at sleeping together before marriage, I wouldn't be happy with it. Just so you know."

"Thank you, sir—"

"Russell."

"Russell. How do you feel about my family situation?"

"How do you mean?"

"My mother has never married. I was the result of an affair."

"That's hardly your fault."

"What about my mother? How do you feel about her?"

"From what you tell me, it sounds like your mother has been paying for her mistake all your life. I'm glad to hear you've stood by her."

"Really?"

"I'm guessing it hasn't been easy. And you've supported yourself all the way through school. That shows a lot of character and responsibility. Good man."

Michael felt like his chest would burst. Russell knew the worst of it and yet he accepted him—accepted and approved. And he wanted to take him to the footy with all the men in his family. This was the best night of his life.

Chapter Seven

Mum had been awfully quiet for a long time, and Chloe was beginning to wince. It was a relief when she finally spoke.

"Are you sure you know what you're doing?" Mum put another load of plates on the sink while Chloe rinsed and placed them in the dishwasher.

"About what?"

"Chloe. You know full well. You can*not* go on a blind date one Saturday and then introduce the man as your future husband the next. What are you doing?"

"I thought you wanted me to marry him."

"Don't be ridiculous. I was just giving you the opportunity to meet someone nice and get to know him a little and see if you like him."

"I like him."

"Chloe!"

"Mother!"

"I'm pleased you like him, and that you've gone out on a second date, but engagement…?"

"Don't worry, Mum. Michael is a responsible, caring and hardworking young man. You picked a winner."

Mum frowned. Chloe ignored the prick of conscience. It was Mum's own fault for showing photographs around to random strange men.

They continued cleaning up the dishes, but Chloe couldn't think of anything else to say, and it seemed as if her mother, for once, was stumped.

"When do you plan on getting married?" Mum closed the dishwasher door.

"We have no plans about that yet."

"Well of course not. You only just met him. I'm not sure we should announce this right away. Perhaps you should give it a couple of months."

"Good idea." She would give it a couple of months, make sure she got her all-expenses-paid holiday to the Gold Coast, and had the speeding ticket sorted out. Then she would … would what? Announce they'd broken up? The idea was not appealing, though she should really be anticipating the day. How was it that she was enjoying this status of having a boyfriend/fiancé? Last week she had no idea of even looking. What a difference a week could make.

This was awkward. Should she just be honest with her mother? Probably, but Mum was the one who didn't think twice about setting her daughter up on a blind date with someone she barely knew. Let this be a lesson to her. Except Mum was not happy with her and it didn't feel good.

She'd just got the coffee cups lined up, the coffee percolating and had served out generous slices of her mother's carrot cake when she heard the men coming back. Her mother had been quiet for nearly twenty minutes and it was a strain Chloe was not used to. Mum was never short of something to say.

"It's going to be all right, Mum." Chloe picked up two plates of cake and took them to the dining room.

"I think you're rushing this and I wish you'd slow down." Mum came up behind her and put the other two plates of cake on the table.

Was this guilt fizzing in her stomach? Should she tell her the truth?

Too late. Dad and Michael were coming into the dining room.

"Excellent. Louise makes the best carrot cake." Dad sat down and indicated Michael should sit down as well. "Have you got coffee brewing?"

"Dad! You sound like a cave man. You could offer to make the coffee for us, since we've done all the cooking and clean-up."

"See, I told you." Dad exchanged a look with Michael and he grinned.

"Told you what? What did he tell you, Michael?"

Michael shrugged and then got up from the table. "Could I help make the coffee?" he asked.

"No fear!" Dad pointed his fork in Michael's direction. "If you crumble at the first sign of resistance you'll be in charge of coffee for the rest of your life."

"Dad!"

"Russell!" Mum's complaint came in chorus with Chloe's.

"Don't you listen to a word he says." Mum placed the coffee percolator on the cork mat in the middle of the table. "He's all talk."

Michael cast a grin in Chloe's direction, but she was not quite as willing to forgive.

"So, Michael and I had a good chat," Dad went on, unrepentant. "He's coming to the game with me next Friday night."

"What?!"

"Boys' night out. All my sons together."

"I was going to come with you." Chloe had been campaigning for the lone ticket ever since they knew their team would probably make the final.

"I don't have to go." Michael's offer was laden with disappointment. Even Chloe could hear that. "You can go with your dad and brother."

"No, it's all settled." Russell slurped a mouthful of coffee on top of the cake in his mouth. "I didn't want to favor one of my girls over the others so this way you girls can stay home, watch the game and order pizza. Girls night in, while I take the boys out all together."

This was insufferable. Why was Dad being so difficult to get on with? When he'd left the house, Chloe had wondered if he might grill Michael. Whatever happened, Dad seemed determined to provoke Chloe. He knew how she felt about equality. Chloe didn't mind doing her share in the kitchen but hated it when Dad or Pete sat back with their feet up as if it was their God given right to be waited on hand and foot. And now he was suggesting a boys' night out. That stung. She loved football every bit as much as Pete or Cam or Dad. But then she saw Michael looking at her. His posture suggested he was worried.

"Do you want to go with the guys to the footy?" she asked.

"Would you be mad if I said 'yes'?"

Chloe pursed her lips. She'd only known Michael for a week, but she could tell he would not go on this outing if she didn't approve. Was that the sort of girlfriend she wanted to be? Pete's new fiancé refused to go to the games and often made him stay home. Collette had no scruples about making Pete feel bad about his passion for football. Chloe thought she was a selfish … well, she didn't like the way she treated her brother. If she was mad at Michael for saying 'yes' to Dad's invitation, she wouldn't be any better than Collette.

"No, I won't be mad. I'm just disappointed that I don't get to go."

"Look at it this way," Dad said. "Megan wanted to go, your mother wanted to go—one of you was going to be disappointed. This way, you can organize the night how you girls want with no interference from us men."

Dad was so sexist sometimes.

Chloe didn't enjoy the cake and coffee as she would usually have done. It didn't feel good letting her mother believe a lie. But then it wasn't a lie, so much as the truth with only half the context. That was deep. Truth with half the context may just as well be a lie. And she felt bad about fussing over the guy's night out. Michael was not relaxed. She needed to talk to him.

"I'm going to drive Michael home." Chloe stood and went to the kitchen to get her bag and keys. When she came back into the dining room Michael had stood and was shaking her father's hand.

"Thank you, sir."

"Russell. Or Dad, if you prefer."

What was he thinking? When they'd first told him, Dad had been tense with an underlying aggression. Now he was inviting Michael to call him 'Dad'. Chloe grabbed Michael by the hand and began to tug him towards the exit.

"Thank you for dinner." Michael smiled at Mum.

"My pleasure," Chloe replied. She was being obnoxious, but her night had not gone well and she was annoyed.

"Do you want me to drive?" Michael asked once they got outside.

"Wow. You and Dad have had a great time, haven't you?"

Michael shrugged. "I don't mind driving. I have a license."

"You know what I mean."

"What? That you resist anything that looks like sexist gender roles?"

"Do you want a fight?"

Michael grinned. He was teasing her. Should she get out her women's rights flag or relax and respond to the joke?

"Your dad is teasing you as well. You know that, don't you?"

"How is it you're so thick with him all of a sudden?"

"He knows about our engagement."

"Did you tell him?"

"No, he knew. He recognized the ring."

Chloe stopped and looked at him. "Dad? Recognized the ring?"

"You don't give him enough credit. He's not Homer Simpson."

The car beeped as Chloe unlocked the doors. This night was messing with her equilibrium. "OK, you drive." She threw the keys at Michael and caught unawares, he juggled them.

Once they were on the road Chloe resumed her interrogation. "So, Dad knows. What did you say to him?"

Michael touched his nose. "Secret men's business."

"Michael Sullivan! Do you want this engagement to end before we've impressed your boss?"

"Depends on whether you want that speeding ticket fought in court. I've already filed the paperwork."

"Are you blackmailing me?"

He reached across the console and took her hand. "Don't worry, I'll represent your case in court even if you dump my sorry hide on the side of the road. It's just that I had a talk with your dad and it was the first time I've connected with someone who spoke to me like a father."

"What about Harold Ainsworth?"

"That relationship is all based on conditions. I have to be the man he believes is the epitome of morality or I doubt I will last at the firm."

"But Dad…?"

"Your father knows it all—every last sordid detail."

"And?"

"He said I was a good man for standing by my mother."

"Yeah, he would. Dad's good like that."

"And he's given me permission to marry you."

"I thought you said he knew it was a scam?"

"He has this funny notion that I might really want to marry you."

Chloe let out a laugh that almost ended in a snort.

But Michael just kept driving. His eyes on the road. No response at all.

"You set him straight, I assume?" Still no response. What was that warm liquid that had started to seep through her veins? "Michael? What did you say to him?"

"I told him I was not in a position to get married."

"Because…?"

"Because of the debt."

"But if it weren't for the debt?"

Michael shrugged. "That's conjecture and not admissible as evidence."

Chloe felt the warmth climb into her face.

"This is not a court of law, Michael. Just humor me."

"We've only known each other for seven days, Chloe. That's too early to make professions of undying, eternal love."

"OK. But what about something a little less permanent, like a steady relationship?"

"It's too early—"

"Rubbish. I already know."

Michael turned his head in her direction wearing a deep frown.

"Eyes on the road!" Chloe let go of his hand and pointed forward. He turned his attention back to the traffic.

"What do you mean by that, Chloe?" he asked.

"Nothing."

"You know we talked about this. I can't consider being involved in a long-term relationship. And you know why."

"Yes, Michael. I know why. But look at the bright side."

"Which is?"

"Our trip to the Gold Coast will be entirely honest—from my point of view anyway."

Michael shook his head. He'd put both hands on the wheel now, and Chloe missed his touch. Why didn't he say something? That was as close as it got to putting her heart out there.

But he didn't say anything. Even when they pulled up out the front of his house, and she got out, he was distant.

"Aren't you going to kiss me goodnight?" she asked.

"You're all for equal opportunity. Why don't you kiss me?"

Fine. If that's how he wanted to be. She flung her arms around his neck and pulled his head down. *I'll show you, Michael Sullivan.* And she kissed him leaving no room for misinterpretation. She felt something for him. Something strong and irresistible.

Chapter Eight

Dad had gone early to pick up Michael for the game. Chloe felt funny about it. She'd only just got used to Cam as a brother-in-law and to see her father so ready to accept Michael as a son—and he knew—it was strange.

"Are you ready?" Mum came into the kitchen dressed in her footy colors. She was next level football mad. "Where's your scarf?" she asked.

Chloe picked up the red, blue and yellow scarf from on top of her bag and waved it in her mother's direction.

"Did you order the pizza?" Mum asked.

"Yes, and Megan is getting the ice-cream. Do you have other emergency snacks?"

"Check. This is going to kill my diet."

Chloe laughed. Her mother dieted as a regular habit, for a few weeks, and then she fell off the wagon.

"You just wait until you get to my age." Mum picked up a green-grocery bag that gave satisfying crackly-crinkly sounds. That was the sound of carbs and sugar in delightfully colored chip and lolly bags.

After loading the non-diet-approved snacks into Mum's car, they got in and set off.

"Did you ask Collette if she wanted to join us?" Chloe hoped her mother had forgotten but it was only fair they should ask Pete's fiancée, even if Collette was a snooty football-hater.

Mum shook her head. "I don't know what your brother sees in that girl."

"I thought your goal in life was to see us all safely married and producing children."

"Mmm."

Chloe still hadn't cleared the air with her about her engagement. She still wasn't sure how her mother felt about it, but given it was only short-term she guessed it probably wouldn't matter.

Megan and Cam lived only ten minutes' drive from home. Chloe had lived with her sister for a number of months before Megan and Cam had married. They had a big screen TV and lots of comfy couches and bean bags. It would be good to have a night where they could eat loads of unhealthy rubbish and shout at the TV screen.

They'd hardly got in the door when Megan had Chloe by the shoulders. "What on earth is this I hear about you getting engaged?"

"Who told you?" Chloe looked at her mother.

"Don't blame me." Mum walked straight past.

"Cam told me. Why didn't you ring and tell me? I didn't even know you were seeing someone!"

Cam told her? Men. They were worse gossips than the proverbial women's sewing circle.

"I want to know everything. And you need to give me time to organize bridesmaid dresses and all that stuff." Megan ushered Chloe to the couch and waved for her to sit down.

"Slow down," Chloe said. "It's only new."

"I'll say."

"Mum!" Chloe stopped short and looked at her mother. "You were the one who set it up. You should be happy."

"But after only one week?" Mum took off her coat and draped it over the back of the couch, then handed the grocery bag to Megan.

"Wait. What? What am I missing?" Megan took the bag of snacks and began opening packets and tipping lollies and chips into bowls.

"Mum showed my photo to her lawyer and recommended he call me for a date."

"And?" Megan stood, with bowls in hand, eyes darting between Chloe and her mother.

"And he did," Mum said. "But only one week later, they're engaged."

"Wow, Chloe. He must be something special."

"It's too soon." Gee. Mum's passive aggressive was in full force.

Megan gave Chloe a knowing look and they laughed.

"It *is* too soon." Mum was determined. "You can laugh all you want, but I never intended you should meet him one week, get engaged the next, and married the week after that."

"No fear of that, Mother. We're all watching football this week. No time for a wedding."

Chloe laughed at her sister's words. "And anyway," Chloe added, "it will be a long engagement. We don't have wedding plans at this stage."

"Still, how exciting." Megan placed the bowls of snacks on the coffee table. "We can do lots of couple things together, and maybe have children together."

Children! Megan's imagination was worse than Mum's. "Easy turbo. Michael and I need to get to know each other a bit first before we start talking about children."

"I'll say." Mum was not happy.

***

The roar of the crowd was deafening—charged with emotion and energy, but deafening. Russell and Pete were hardcore and often stood up to add their suggestions to the umpire and players. Michael wanted to laugh. They were so passionate about different on-field incidents and there was no logical thought involved. The umpires were not going to change their call just because the crowd demanded it.

Right up until the final siren, there had been no opportunity to chat. The scores were close, and this was a knock-out final. There was no 'next week' for the loser.

There were so many words being flung about by fans in front and behind and there was no airspace for the intelligent analysis of the play, usually discussed by television commentators. And when the siren sounded the end of the game and the home team were two points down, the crowd deflated like a soggy beach ball.

It took a good ten minutes after the game, when the men were walking back towards the station, before someone spoke.

"I can't believe we lost." Pete was walking two paces ahead, with his father. "It was so close."

Russell grunted in reply. He wasn't happy.

"Did you enjoy the game?" Chloe's brother-in-law, Cam, walked next to Michael.

"I did. Except for the ending."

Cam sniffed his amusement. "They'll be depressed for days."

"It does take the edge off the night," Michael said.

"It's a good job we have more in life to hope for than a football team."

Sage words, but Michael doubted Russell and Pete would be comforted by them.

"So, you still up for joining the family now you've seen the depth of their fanaticism?"

Michael grinned. "I hear you got set up by Mrs Brooker."

"I hear *you* got set up by Mrs Brooker," Cam threw back at him. "She's determined."

"She's not so happy with me."

"Fast mover, aren't you?"

"Not really."

"I'd call a week fairly fast."

"Yeah, but—"

"Is Chloe just messing with you?"

"We're sort of using each other."

Even while walking, Cam turned his head and frowned. "I hope you have a good explanation, because that sounds dodgy."

It did sound dodgy. It probably was dodgy.

"Michael?" Cam had his police voice on.

"It's probably not as bad as it sounds … and call me Mike."

Cam had lost his friendly demeanor and maintained his frown.

"I have a demanding boss with exacting standards, and he was under the impression I was engaged."

"So rather than tell him the truth, you seduced Chloe?"

"Hold on! I haven't done anything of the kind, and Chloe is in full possession of the facts, as is your father."

"Father-in-law. My father's dead."

"Sorry, man." Michael felt a stab of sympathy.

"So, Russell knows that you're using his daughter?" Cam apparently wasn't in the mood to reflect on his loss.

"We have a business agreement."

"I can't wait to hear it." Cam's sarcasm was not wasted. Michael felt the weight of his disapproval.

"Chloe needs me to help fight a speeding fine."

"Aaaah. The unjust speeding fine." Cam's tone changed and, Michael noted, his facial expression relaxed.

"You know about that?"

"Yeah. She wanted me to get her out of it."

"But the law is the law." Michael could imagine Chloe haranguing her brother-in-law, and the frustration that would have ensued when Cam wouldn't—couldn't—budge.

"Unless you know a lawyer who can find a loophole."

"There are grounds to contest the fine," Michael said.

"And you think they will hold?" Cam asked.

"The local council did not display any notification that there would be a change in speed limit, and there was no grace period observed by the traffic division. The fine was issued unfairly."

"So, once you've won her case, what then? How long are you going to pretend to be engaged?"

"I'm not quite sure why you're being so judgmental. Isn't this the game you played with Megan?"

"Yeah, but I knew right away she was the one for me. I just had to work through all the complications."

"How do you know that isn't how I feel about Chloe?"

"Is it? Do you love Chloe?"

Michael went quiet. How could he admit to such a thing? Mrs Brooker was right. It was too soon. And even if he did, it couldn't go anywhere.

"Does Louise know about this charade?"

"No. Chloe wants to teach her a lesson."

"And how do you feel about that?"

"Awkward."

Cam relented and smiled. "She is incorrigible."

"But effective, apparently. Are you sorry she set you up?"

Cam smiled again. "It was a bit of a drama getting to the altar, but no, not sorry in the least."

Michael smiled. Cam promised to be a good mate—until the show was over. Michael felt that charge of regret electrify his stomach.

He didn't want it to end—not just the relationship with Chloe, but being part of a family. For his whole life, family had consisted of him and his mother, and for the most part he had assumed the role of responsible adult. This night out with the boys represented brothers and a father, each man responsible in their own right. He didn't want to give this up. He didn't want to give Chloe up, either, but he could not afford to marry, unless Chloe was happy to move into a council flat and share debt repayments with him. It was doubtful she would value her speeding ticket that much.

"You've gone all quiet." Cam used his transport card to get through the turnstile into the station.

"Just thinking about Chloe." Michael tapped his card and followed through onto the platform.

"Do you want to go on a double date with the girls?"

Michael grinned. "Yes. When?"

"You free next weekend? We won't be watching the footy obviously."

"Of course we'll watch the footy." Russell joined their conversation as they boarded the train and were pressed together by the crowd of football fans. "Just because our team lost doesn't mean I'm not going to watch the Grand Final."

"What about Friday night?" Cam suggested.

"What are you doing Friday night?" Pete asked, also forced into close proximity.

"Going on a date with the girls. Do you and Collette want to come?" Cam asked.

"I'll have to get back to you. Collette doesn't like me to arrange things without consulting her first."

Russell mumbled something which sounded remarkably like: "Collette doesn't let you do anything without consulting her first."

Michael wondered what Cam and Pete thought about the comment, but no one said anything. Russell didn't sound enamoured with Pete's fiancée.

"I'll check with Chloe," Michael said. He tried to form some solidarity with Pete. He couldn't leave him hanging out there alone with his father's obvious disapproval.

"Great. Give me your phone number and we'll keep in touch."

It was difficult maneuvering the phone with the train being so packed and the four of them standing, but he managed. Friday night out with the girls sounded like a great plan.

***

"Great plan!" Chloe was enthusiastic about the suggestion. "Collette won't come though."

"How do you know?" Michael was driving her car again and backed out of Megan's driveway.

"She doesn't like us."

"I get the feeling your family don't really like her either."

"We tried. She's not really our sort of person."

"What sort of person is that?"

"A bit crazy, football mad, family orientated, loud and if you throw in an eccentric mother …"

"Right. And what sort of person is Collette?"

"Stuck-up."

"That's a bit harsh."

"You're right. She runs with a refined crowd from the fashion world and is into image."

"So, she'd be my sort of person then."

"What?" Chloe turned and looked at Michael. What did he mean by that?

"You sound worried." He kept his eyes on the road as he drove.

"I thought you enjoyed hanging out with my family."

"I do."

"Well are you into image and fashion?"

"You've seen the work suits I wear and the car I drive when I choose to hire a car."

"Yeah, but I thought that was just to keep your boss happy."

Michael laughed. "It is. I mean, I like the designer suits, they feel great to wear, but I'm just as happy in jeans and a t-shirt."

"And you're driving my hatchback. What if your mates saw you now?"

"You'd be surprised to know I don't have any mates—not like you mean, anyway."

Chloe reached over and put her hand on his knee. He covered it with his hand.

"What do you mean, Michael?"

"I couldn't ask mates from high school to come home. They were all picked up by parents in fancy cars and went home to fancy houses in the top end of town, while I caught two buses to get back to the housing commission area. I had to hide who I was. As I got older, my mother got worse and there was more reason to hide. Then the guys I met at Yale were all American. I didn't make any real connections there. Since being back in Australia, the closest thing I have to mates are colleagues from work, and they're all married with families."

Chloe squeezed his hand. "Have you been lonely?"

"I didn't realize how much until I started hanging out with your family."

"But you're not like Collette."

"How do you know?"

"Because you put on an image to keep a job and win your boss's approval. Collette is like that all the time. I don't even know why she thinks my brother is good enough for her."

"Perhaps she loves him."

"I doubt it."

"That's very judgmental, Chloe."

"I know. You're right. I should try to support Pete in his choice of future partner."

"You should. Your brothers and father are all supporting you."

She squeezed his hand again. "Did you tell Cam the truth?"

Michael nodded. "I think you should tell your mother the truth as well."

"I will."

"When?"

Chloe shrugged. "I'm enjoying the friendship we have at the moment. Do you think that will continue after?"

Michael pulled the car up in front of his house. After he switched off the engine, he turned and took both Chloe's hands in his. "I hope so."

He leaned in and kissed her. It was so warm and Chloe felt passion rise as he lingered. She let go of his hands and put her arms around his neck. What friendship? This was not how it should end. But she didn't want to enter into the usual discussion of how he couldn't afford to marry. The nagging conscience—stop pretending this will go anywhere—was silenced as she leaned into his warm embrace. This was tonight. She would deal with tomorrow another day.

Chapter Nine

"Michael." Mum's whisper dragged him from a deep sleep. "Michael."

Michael rolled over and stretched. "What time is it?"

"Nearly 7.30. Are you going to church this morning?"

Seven-thirty. This was Sunday and he usually didn't bother to hurry out of bed, even if he was going to church.

"Do you want to go?" He didn't bother to sit up. He didn't have to hurry.

"I was hoping to meet your girlfriend. She goes to church, doesn't she?"

"She does, but not our church. She lives on the other side of the city."

"Couldn't we visit? I'd really like to meet her, Michael."

"I'd have to get up now, and then we'd probably be late for the start if all the buses run on time."

"Why don't we take an Uber?"

"Mum!" Now Michael sat up. "An Uber all the way across town will cost us nearly forty bucks. You know that's not in our budget."

"Well, hurry up and get ready. I'm all ready to go."

She was already dressed, and even in the dim light he could see she looked better than she had in weeks. Him having a love life had obviously given her a focus on something other than her failures.

"All right. You go and make me a coffee, and I'll have a quick shower."

"I've already made you breakfast. Hurry up, Michael. I don't want to be late."

Was this wise? Mum was obviously on a high and had stars in her eyes with the idea of romance, but it would only take something small to send her to the depths of depression again—and his breakup with Chloe wasn't going to be small. He should check to see if Chloe was even going to be at the service this morning.

By the time he was dressed, his mother had his coffee in a travel-mug and his toast folded in a paper serviette.

"If you hurry up, we'll make the next bus."

There was no stopping her. He put his phone in his backpack, took the coffee and toast from his mother, and followed her out the front door. In some ways, it felt good having his mother take charge of the expedition to church. She'd checked the bus timetables and got everything ready and was now walking briskly down the street towards the bus stop.

Once they were on board, Michael took out his phone and sent a text.

We're on the bus, coming to visit your church this morning. Are you going? Mum is desperate to meet you.

He finished off the last of his coffee and put the mug in his backpack before his phone pinged.

My shift starts at 3. I'll be at church but won't have much time after. Perhaps we can grab a quick bite of lunch before I have to go? I would like to meet your mum as well.

Grabbing a quick bite of lunch usually meant buying something from a restaurant. Michael hated that he didn't have the budget to just do whatever he wanted, when he wanted. But to ignore the budget would be to do what his mother had done all her life. He couldn't—wouldn't—do that. He sent a one-word reply.

Budget.

She would know what he meant.

Grilled cheese sandwich at my house. Dad can drive you home after.

She always understood. Chloe Brooker was a keeper. If only he could.

***

"*What on earth are you doing, old man?*" *Liam's friend and neighbor, Lord Jamieson, hardly bothered to disguise his words as he drew Liam aside. "You can't make a silk purse out of a sow's ear.*"

"*Would you care to lower your voice?*" *Liam hoped he had infused enough aggression into his tone. Jamieson was entirely too opinionated for his liking and had no sensibility.*

"*Old man Dixon has burned all his bridges. He cannot hope his daughter should be accepted in good society.*"

"*If you plan to continue this tirade, would you take it outside? I have no wish to offend my guests.*"

"*You will be shunned, just like Dixon, if you continue down this path. She is not good enough for you and I don't care if she is offended. Perhaps she has better sense than you and will withdraw quietly.*"

Liam was furious. There was no possible way Evelyn could have missed Jamieson's harsh words. She would be crushed. One glance in her direction and he could see she had already withdrawn. She was looking around the room anxiously, as if plotting her escape.

"*Lady Evelyn.*" *His sister, Anne, must have sensed the tension and come to the rescue. "Come sit with me a while." Anne threaded her arm through Evie's and drew her to the bay window. Liam could hear her talking, because his sister intended he should hear—intended everyone should hear.*

"I want to tell you all about Elizabeth's wedding," Anne said. "You should have seen the fuss Lady Emmaline put up. I would have thought she would have given up trying to catch that man. He never had any intentions no matter how her mother maneuvered to throw her in Lord Remmington's way."

Liam watched as Chambers came into the room and announced dinner.

"Grilled cheese sandwiches are served, my Lord."

Grilled Cheese sandwiches. For heaven's sake. First, she goes and gets engaged after only one week, and then she invites her prospective mother-in-law around to eat grilled cheese sandwiches. It was enough to put a writer off her plotting. But then she shouldn't have been plotting during a sermon anyway.

What was the pastor on about? The least of these. The poor, the hungry, the sick, the stranger. It's all very well knowing about the least of these, but one didn't see them very often when one worked out of a home office.

Surely, they could have come up with something better than grilled cheese sandwiches. This was Michael's mother. Michael who was a lawyer and who drove a fancy car and wore Armani suits. What would his mother think of them?

"As we go from here today," the pastor said, "ask the Lord to show you someone you can minister kindness to. Perhaps they are closer than you think."

The pastor asked the congregation to stand to sing a closing song. Louise was aware of Michael standing at the end of the row, Chloe on his one side and his mother on the other. She didn't look rich and snooty. But one could never tell with these well-to-do families. Perhaps she was eccentric.

"Mum." Chloe came to her straight after the service. "We can't stay for coffee. I have to have lunch straight away, then get ready for work."

"Couldn't we at least take the Sullivan's out to lunch at a café?"

Chloe shook her head. "I'll explain later. For now, I need to get home so we have as much time as possible before I have to leave."

"Are you at least going to introduce me to Mrs Sullivan?"

"Best let Michael do that. Come on." Chloe turned and walked out of the aisle and to the back of the church where Michael was talking to Cam and Megan.

He seemed to fit in to the family. Perhaps it was going to be OK after all. But grilled cheese sandwiches? It was all too hard to bear.

***

Introducing his mother to the Brooker family proved to be a pleasure. Mum was beaming, especially when she met Chloe. Michael watched her reaction and saw joy. And just as quickly as he registered this emotion, he felt a jolt of panic. What was going to happen when this all fell apart? He hadn't seen Mum so happy for as long as he could remember, and he dreaded the thought she would slump into those dark depths of despair that had been too prevalent in recent times. But how was he going to maintain this relationship? No matter how much he might want to, the situation had not changed and was not likely to change.

"I'm so sorry we haven't got anything better to offer to eat," Louise said. "I wasn't expecting anyone home for lunch so I didn't have anything prepared."

"Don't think of it," Mum said. "I'm just so thrilled to meet you all, especially you, Chloe. You don't know how long I've waited for Michael to find someone he loves enough to get past his excuses."

"Excuses?" Louise asked.

"Mum!" There was no stopping her once she got confidence in a conversation, but Michael wasn't sure he wanted to hear her version of the situation blurted out.

"He's been in a state of self-imposed singleness for years. Doesn't think he can afford a wife."

"Mum!" He watched Louise lap up every word. She was probably loving the drama of it.

"But you, my dear ..." Mum took Chloe's hands in hers. "You are the one. All the budgets in the world don't mean anything when it comes to you."

Chloe cast him an anxious glance. What was she supposed to say? What was he supposed to say?

"Well, I'm glad." Whether Louise sensed the awkwardness or not, she jumped in to rescue the situation. "Come into the kitchen and sit down, Alison," Louise said. "Lunch won't make itself. We can talk about wedding plans while we work."

Mum cast a beaming smile in Michael's direction. He hadn't told her he was engaged, but she didn't look offended. Far from it. Louise ushered her into the kitchen. Russell had already sat down in front of the television and had the sports news on.

"What now?" Chloe said.

What now, indeed. Things had escalated far beyond an exchanged favor into permanent, covenant relationship territory.

"I will tell Mum the truth first thing tomorrow, before she books a florist." Chloe said.

Michael shook his head. "What am I going to tell my mother?"

"The truth. The same as me."

"But she is so happy. I haven't seen her this happy in years. I'm afraid she'll—"

"Slump?"

Michael nodded.

"Is she on medication?"

"I'm not sure. I know she was, but I can't keep track of whether she follows the doctor's orders or not. All I know is she's on a high."

"That's typical of bi-polar though, isn't it?"

Michael nodded. "This is a brighter and more enthusiastic high than usual. She's genuinely happy about our engagement."

Chloe rolled her lips together as if in thought.

"The trip away is next week," she said. "We have to prepare her for the breakup slowly. Do you think you should go see her doctor on the next visit?"

"I hate to baby her like that." He hated to do it but it was so often the case.

"How low does she go when she is on a down?"

"Doesn't get out of bed, doesn't eat, looks sad all the time."

"Is she a danger to herself?"

Michael felt a jolt of alarm. This was a question he avoided. "I don't think so—I hope not. The thing that worries me is the likelihood of her going to the pokies to try to cheer herself up."

"Do you think she still does that?"

"I'm almost sure of it. She hasn't had grocery money for a couple of weeks, and she doesn't have any other expenses to cover. I hate doubting her, Chloe. She's my mother. This isn't supposed to be how it works."

Chloe stepped closer and put her arms around his waist. He put his arms around her and received the comfort she offered in the hug.

If only he could hide here in her embrace and pretend there were no challenges in his world.

"Let's just go on this retreat," Chloe said. "When we get back, we'll have to see how your mum is. If necessary, we'll need to go see her doctor with her."

"We?" Michael asked.

"I'm a health professional, Michael. I won't do something that will endanger her. If necessary, I'll come with you to talk about treatment and medication."

She was a brilliant. She really was a keeper. How on earth was he going to let her go?

Chapter Ten

This was such a good deal. Not only was she packed ready for an all-expenses paid trip to the sunny Gold Coast, she was being paid to go.

"Did you tell your mother the truth yet?" Dad put her suitcase in the back of his SUV.

"It's complicated."

"I don't approve of you keeping her in the dark, Chloe. And I think you should consider carefully how this will affect Mrs Sullivan."

"Alison." Michael's mother had never married, there was no Mrs.

"Well, there's still time. I'll get Mum to drive you to the airport."

"Dad."

"Chloe." He stood with his feet apart in that stance that said 'I mean business'.

"All right, fine. I'll tell her, but you're going to have to put up with all the fall out."

"You should have told her from the beginning. It was cruel of you to hide the truth from her."

He was in full lecture mode this morning and taking the shine from her anticipation. And it was complicated. This wasn't just a joke anymore. She felt as if she really was engaged to Michael Sullivan and was pushing the idea of a breakup to the back of her mind. A bridge to cross another day.

Dad closed the back of his SUV and stepped around the car to hug her.

"Have the best time, and mind how you speak to Michael's colleagues."

Chloe pulled back. "What do you mean by that?"

"This whole charade is because Ainsworth and Pembroke are over conscientious about their family values."

"Michael and I are sleeping in separate rooms."

"Come on, Chloe. You can tell that equality is not high on Harold Ainsworth's agenda, and that's one of your pet hates."

"I won't say anything."

Dad hummed, with his lips pursed.

He didn't believe she was capable of self-control, and it rankled. "I won't!"

"We'll see. Just remember that Michael needs his job. Don't do anything to have Ainsworth throw him out on his ear."

"Thanks for your confidence."

Dad leaned in and gave her a peck on the cheek. "Have a good time."

He didn't think she had the ability to play the part of a sweet submissive wife. She could if she wanted to, but it was probably time Michael stood up to his colleagues. No! She wouldn't say anything— well she would try her level best not to say anything.

"Ready?" Mum came out the front door and opened the driver's side door.

"Thanks for taking me." Chloe suddenly felt anxious about telling her mother the truth. Bother Dad and his insistence for openness.

"I don't know what got into your father all of a sudden. He was set to take you, and now he's got some business that can't wait an hour."

Chloe fastened her seatbelt and settled into the passenger seat. She took a deep breath. Here we go.

"Mum?"

"Hmm? Something the matter?"

"Actually yes."

Mum kept her eyes on the road punctuated by a quick glance in Chloe's direction. "What's wrong?"

"Michael and I aren't really engaged."

"What?" This time the glance lasted slightly longer, complete with a troubled frown.

"We're just helping each other out. He's fighting my speeding ticket in court, and I'm posing as his fiancée because his boss is a relic from the 1950s and thinks Michael is getting married."

"I don't understand what you're saying."

"Mum. Keep up. You showed my photograph to Michael just prior to his boss telling him about the staff and wives retreat."

"You mean staff and partners?"

"I mean staff and wives. Ainsworth and Pembroke only employ male lawyers."

"I saw a couple of women in their office."

"Reception and admin. Never lawyers."

"And the admin staff aren't going on the retreat?"

"They will stay back and hold the fort while the men go on a morale building retreat."

"That's …"

"Don't say it. I'm trying to adopt the submissive persona. I don't need revving up."

"So, you're saying Michael's just using you to impress his boss?"

"Yes—no—sort of."

There was a tense moment of silence. Chloe took a quick peek to gauge her mother's reaction. Her lips had disappeared and she wore a fierce look. Uh oh. She'd really upset her this time.

"That's despicable," Mum eventually said. "And I had such high hopes for him too."

"No. Wait. Mum. Michael's not despicable. He's desperate."

"Well he must be if he calls up one of his client's daughters on a mother's say so."

Seriously? "You were the one who showed him my photo."

"He called." She was really steamed about this.

"You were excited that he called." Chloe used a logical tone to point out her mother's hypocrisy.

"But I didn't expect him to use you like this."

"I'm using him as well. He's doing all my legal stuff for free."

Mum went quite for a few more moments while she negotiated a lane change.

"So, you're telling me there's nothing between you?"

Time for full disclosure. "Not exactly nothing."

"So, there is a spark?"

"Mum!"

"Well you brought his mother around for lunch two weeks ago."

"As it turns out the situation is far more complex than I imagined it would be."

"I'll say. He even gave you an engagement ring."

"Nan gave it to me. It was her mother's."

Chloe watched her mother's face. She hadn't known her mother-in-law's mother and obviously had not recognized the ring. But she was beginning to get the picture. There was still so much to tell about Alison Sullivan and Michael's financial situation. It was a good job they had a solid twenty-five minutes' drive ahead of them.

***

Michael had arranged to meet Chloe near the city. It was on their way to the airport, and it was cheaper for him to catch a bus to the city and spare the taxi fare. It wouldn't do for him to turn up to the airport alone and on the public bus. Chloe got out of the car when Louise pulled over in the loading zone. She kissed him on the lips. He loved this open affection.

"I told her." Chloe lifted the tailgate on the back of the SUV so he could load his suitcase.

"What?" He stopped and looked at her, and didn't come to himself until Chloe had taken his suitcase and lifted it into the back of the car. Not Ainsworth and Pembroke style at all. "Who did you tell and what?"

"My mother. I told her the truth about us." Chloe slammed the tailgate down.

Michael felt a lump of anxiety build in his throat. "Really? What did she say?"

"That you're despicable."

Just like an elevator falling from the twentieth floor, Michael's stomach left him behind.

"Relax." She took his arm and led him around to the passenger door. "That was before she realized we were trading off. I'm using you, and you're using me."

"But—" she opened the door and indicated he should get in. But he wanted to clarify the situation. He didn't want Louise to think he was using Chloe.

"So, I hear this engagement thing is a charade for your boss's benefit." Louise was as direct as Chloe usually was.

"Kind of."

"And what about your mother?"

"It's complicated." Complicated on the level of world peace talks.

"So Chloe has informed me. And you don't think there's any future in your relationship?"

Talk about being grilled on the witness stand. "If it weren't for my financial situation, I'd be considering something more for the future."

"Your debts are that bad?"

"Mum!" Chloe sounded cross. "Michael is not irresponsible. It wasn't his fault."

"Well, I haven't heard the whole story, but I would be more sensitive if I had been in the know from the beginning, wouldn't I?"

This was a dig at Chloe for playing the game in the first place.

"I'm sorry," Michael said. "We should have told you from the start."

"Yes, you should have."

"But you enjoyed the idea of having another son-in-law, admit it." Chloe was relentless.

"I was warming to the idea, but I'm disappointed to find that both of you are toying with each other's affections with no intention to follow through."

Follow through. He would like nothing better than to be able to follow through.

Louise was approaching the drop off zone at departures, and there wasn't time to have a full discussion.

"I'm sorry," Michael said. "I should have said something from the start."

"You should talk to your boss about accepting you for who you are. You're a fine young man and a good lawyer. He's lucky to have you."

Was that affirmation or lecture? He couldn't quite tell. Louise's tone made him feel as if he'd been properly told off, but somehow her words made him feel warm.

Louise got out of the car and gave Chloe a hug. "I hope you have a great time. Both of you." She looked at him and gave a smile. Had she forgiven him?

Chloe pulled up the handle of her suitcase and put her hand-luggage over her shoulder. Michael waved as Louise pulled out of the drop-off zone, then got his own luggage in tow.

"I'm sorry about this." He took long strides to catch up to Chloe. "I feel bad that I've come between you and your mum."

"It's not your fault. I was the one who wanted to teach her a lesson."

Michael didn't say anything else as they walked into the terminal and up to the booking kiosks. The reservations had been made by the girls at work, so he just had to type in his name and destination to retrieve the booking.

They moved quietly through the line until they'd passed through the security scanning section, then stopped to check the monitor for the departure gate lounge.

"Do you want a coffee?" Michael asked.

Chloe stopped and looked at him. She hadn't looked at him since getting out of the car and he'd felt the tension. "What about your budget? Airport coffee is outrageously priced you know."

"I have a travel budget allocated from the company."

"In that case…" Chloe headed to the nearest coffee shop. "Can we afford food as well? I'm starving."

Michael lined up with Chloe and paid for her order of coffee and croissant as well as his own.

"Michael?" He looked up as his colleague, Daniel, called to him from a table across the way.

"Daniel is one of the other junior lawyers. Is it OK if we sit with them?"

"This is your trip." Chloe picked up her coffee and croissant order. "I'm here to help you out, remember?"

Michael sensed Chloe was out of sorts this morning, and wished they could be alone so he could talk the issue through. But they were on company time, even though they were about to set out on a retreat.

Daniel stood up and shook Michael's hand as they approached. "Sit with us while you have your coffee."

"Thanks. This is Chloe." He would like to have said fiancée, but the lecture from Louise was still ringing in his ears. It wasn't going to last and he shouldn't let himself get settled with the idea.

"Hi Chloe." Daniel waved to an empty seat. "This is my wife, Esther." Michael couldn't remember having met Esther before, but she looked like a proper respectable Ainsworth and Pembroke wife. Chloe smiled at her and took the empty seat.

"Nice to meet you." Michael sat down next to Chloe.

"Glad you were able to get the time off work." Daniel spoke to Chloe. "Esther is usually home with the kids, so there wasn't a problem for her to come."

"How many children do you have?" Chloe asked Esther.

"Three, with another one on the way." Esther smiled as she rubbed her hand protectively over her baby bump.

Four kids. Perfect. Harold Ainsworth would be happy. And all he had was a fake fiancée. Chloe reached out and took his hand and gave it a squeeze, as if she could read his thoughts. He loved this woman. She was so in tune to his situation. How was he going to sort this situation out? Was there a way to make it real? Could he leave his mother to fend for herself?

***

Four kids! *Excellent*. How many kids was the optimum to keep Harold Ainsworth happy? *Michael, when are you going to come out from behind your image and let these people know who you really are?* Chloe allowed him to weave his fingers with hers for a moment. It wasn't conducive to eating a croissant, but she was reluctant to break the contact.

"Which area of nursing do you specialize in?" Esther asked, beaming a beautiful smile in her direction.

"I work in emergency."

"That must be fascinating."

Not so much—heart attacks, road accidents, children who've swallowed coins, and any number of drug and alcohol related injuries. "It pays the bills," Chloe said.

"You must get so much fulfillment out of helping other people in crisis." Esther took a sip of her hot drink.

Chloe nodded as she took a sip of her coffee. She reclaimed her other hand so she could attack her breakfast with balance. "Sometimes there is so much crisis, I'm just thankful to get through the day. But I guess you're right. That was one of the reasons I went into nursing in the first place."

"I had wanted to do medicine in university, but I ended up meeting Daniel and gave up after the second year."

"You might go back to it later," Chloe said.

"Esther is happy enough looking after the children." Daniel's insertion into their conversation annoyed Chloe. Surely she could speak for herself. Michael touched her leg under the table. Could he sense her hackles were raised and wanted to head her off at the pass? Good job. She was about to launch into a spiel on how both parents should be responsible for the children and she should pursue her education in medicine if she wanted.

101

"I really enjoy being at home." Esther caught her gaze. She was slightly flushed.

"Really?" Chloe asked. "You don't find it restrictive?"

"I don't have free rein to do everything I've ever dreamed of doing, but I know this is a season in my life. I won't have the children at home forever."

"We believe in having a stable home-life for our children." Daniel spoke over his wife again. Chloe wanted to tell him to mind his own business. "Esther doesn't need to work outside the home with the wage I bring in. I guess it will be the same for you when you get married."

This time Michael squeezed her knee. What was he afraid of? That she would blow his cover? That she would blurt out that he had never had a stable home life? That his fake fiancée had no specific plans of giving up her career to stay home with children? Besides, she hadn't settled the question of parenting yet, and wouldn't until she found the man she was going to marry and was satisfied that having children was what they both wanted. Then she would have the discussion to see how they would manage family.

"When are you planning to get married?" Esther asked. Perhaps she wanted to steer the conversation away from children.

"We haven't made firm plans yet," Chloe replied.

"What?" Daniel again. "I thought you'd been engaged for years."

Chloe turned to look at Michael. What had he told them?

"Not exactly," he said.

"Harold told us you were a family man, when you came on board, and that you were engaged to be married."

"He may have misunderstood, or I misunderstood his question. I've always hoped to marry and have a family, but I only met Chloe recently."

"So how long have you been engaged?" Esther asked.

"About six weeks." Chloe watched as Esther cast a look at her husband. That was probably the wrong answer. But it was the truthful answer. Well, as truthful as it was likely to get. Michael had proposed six weeks ago, even if he had no intention of following through to marriage.

"We'd better get to the boarding lounge." Michael stood up from the table. "Are you ready, darling?"

Darling? They needed to have a discussion on preferred terms of endearment. Darling was not in the top five.

She got up and gathered her shoulder-bag. "It was lovely to meet you." She beamed a smile in Esther's direction, hoping it came off as genuine.

"I'm looking forward to getting to know you better." Either Esther's smile was genuine or she was an actor. Chloe felt ashamed of herself.

Michael caught Chloe's hand and urged her to follow.

"This is going to be harder than I thought," he said, once they were out of earshot.

"I'm sorry. I'm trying to keep my thoughts to myself."

"But it's not you. I hate how stilted the conversation is. I know what you're thinking and can almost feel you gritting your teeth."

"Are you sure you know what I'm thinking?" Chloe peered at him as they walked down the long concourse.

"We haven't discussed children, or who will stay home to look after them."

"Because we're not really engaged. It shouldn't be any of their business anyway."

"I can almost guarantee this is what everyone will talk about. Harold is at the stage of talking about grandchildren, but most of the others have families. We're the only ones not married."

"The other girls have interests other than children though, surely."

"I doubt it. They're all church-going, family-focused, never-been-in-trouble, nice girls."

"I'm a church-going nice girl. What are you saying?"

"I'm not."

"I can see you're not a girl."

Michael smiled and tugged her hand.

"My life has been nothing but trouble."

"Rubbish. How long have you been a Christian?"

Michael shrugged. "Since I went to the States."

"I assume you believe in the grace of God. Besides, what trouble did you get into while you were so busy trying to succeed at an elite private college?"

"But my mother—"

"You are not your mother."

"I wasn't perfect you know. I've done stuff."

"Yeah? Like what?"

Michael didn't answer. They were at their gate lounge. Please don't let there be any other colleagues waiting that they had to be nice to. Chloe sat down next to Michael and kissed him on the cheek.

"What was that for?"

"I'm glad you've done some stuff. It makes you more real."

"I'm not sure that's a good way to look at it." He looked troubled, yet again.

"I doubt you have done anything more shocking than what I've done."

"I wouldn't bet on it."

"Go on."

Michael pursed his lips.

Chloe continued; "What are the vices you wish you could forget? Drugs?"

He shook his head.

"Sex?"

He shot her a pained look. Wow. There'd been someone else in his life before, and that knowledge pierced her stomach.

"Did you have a girlfriend?"

"Two." Worse and worse.

"At once?"

"Actually, yes."

"Wait, what?" She was trying to be funny. Two at once? Really?

"I was going out with a girl when I was sixteen. Her parents owned half of the CBD. She didn't want them to know about me."

"Did you tell her about your mother?"

Michael shook his head. "She found out."

"How?"

"She followed me home one day after school."

Chloe hated how Michael's shoulders slumped and he wore a defeated look. "And then what happened?"

"She used it to manipulate me. She knew I didn't want anyone else to know about my home life, and she threatened to tell if I didn't do what she wanted."

"And what did she want?"

"She booked a hotel and wanted me to go with her to stay overnight."

"And?"

"I went."

"And?"

"Chloe, use your imagination. I'm not made of stone, and I had no spiritual or moral guidance in those days."

Something cold and solid had formed in her stomach. Michael had been with someone before. Why did she feel so unhappy about that news?

"What about the other girl?" she asked.

"She was the best friend."

"Let me guess, she found out about you from her friend and decided to use you as well?"

"What makes you say that?"

"You're good looking and kind of mysterious. If you were not a player, that would drive the girls nuts. And if the first girl had no scruples about using you like that, I imagine she hung out with friends with a similar lack of moral fiber. It follows that if you were with two girls at once it would not have been your choice."

"How do you know?"

How did she know? She couldn't bear thinking that Michael had used these young women. "Because that's not who you are. You're a man of integrity."

"And yet, here I am, presenting a fake fiancée to protect my nasty secret."

Chloe put her arms around his neck and kissed him. "Your home life is your home life. It isn't anyone else's business, and your mother would be mortified if she thought she was a nasty secret."

Michael returned her kiss. "Thanks, Chloe."

"Nice to see, Mr Sullivan."

Michael pulled back and stood up. He was flushed and flustered at the interruption.

"Mr Ainsworth. Hello."

He shook hands with a fifty-something gentleman with silver hair. This was the enigmatic head of the company, no doubt about it.

"You must be Michael's fiancée. How do you do?"

Chapter Eleven

"*My basket is full.*"

Evie looked up as Anne Bradshaw held her brimming basket of berries up for inspection. Evie's own basket was less than half full, despite having been rambling through the blackberry thickets looking for fruit for half the morning.

"Don't look so downhearted," Anne said. "It isn't a race, you know."

"I wanted to bring a full basket back for cook as well." With all the behind-the-hand gossip that had been going on, Evie had been determined to win favor somewhere, if only with the kitchen staff.

"I'm not in a hurry to return to the house. The sunshine is divine." Anne closed her eyes and tipped her head back, her face to the sun.

"What about freckles? Are you not terrified you will break out?"

"Evelyn Dixon. Stop fussing." Anne turned her attention to the thick bushes nearby and began to pick berries. "Why should you worry if you have a face full of freckles? My brother has set his heart on you, and I doubt he would notice what shade your skin was."

"That is nonsense, Anne. He is already under disapprobation from his peers because he continues to pay court to me. If I should add freckles to my list of faults and lack of wealth, I should think it would kill his passion stone dead."

Anne laughed and continued to pick the plump, juicy blackberries, letting them tumble from her hand into Evie's basket. "He asked me to invite you to come with us when we go to London next week. He means to ignore convention and follow through."

"*Are you sure it is not just so I can resume role of companion?*"

"*Aunt Ursula is dead. Who would you serve as companion?*"

"*You.*"

"*Me?*" *Anne laughed again. "Good heavens, Evie. I am to be presented at court and anticipate no end of balls, concerts and assemblies. I will be far too busy to need a companion.*"

"*What about as chaperone?*"

"*It is I who will need to chaperone you, my dear. Liam is quite mad about you. It would be better all round if he would quickly propose and marry you, and then there would be no need to fuss.*"

But he won't. He can't. Marriage to me comes with too many difficulties. He may not think my father's disgrace has anything to do with it, but I know very well that it has. Marriage is impossible. No dowry, no land—only the residual effects of father's scandal.

Louise stopped typing. Michael Sullivan was no different to Evelyn Dixon. He lived under the scandal his parents had given him as an inheritance, and he didn't believe he could expect anyone else to join him. Was he worth it? Would Chloe be better off saying goodbye once their bargain was fulfilled? There were plenty of other men she could fall in love with and marry.

"What's going on?" Russell stepped into her office.

"What do you mean?" Louise asked.

"You've stopped typing and are staring blankly at the wall."

"I often stare blankly at the wall when I'm pondering my plot and characters."

"So, what's happening with them?"

"I'm not sure Michael Sullivan is worth the effort."

"Louise Brooker! Michael Sullivan is not one of your characters. And how can you say that in any case?"

"What sort of man asks a girl to pose as a fiancée so his boss doesn't find out about his past?"

"His mother's past."

"Same thing, isn't it? She has a gambling addiction and suffers from depression. He spends his whole time trying to pay off a debt that is killing them both."

Russell frowned and shook his head.

"What?"

"I'm ashamed of you."

"Thank you very much."

"Well I am. Michael Sullivan is one of the kindest, most responsible young men I have ever met. He doesn't have to do what he does for his mother. Another son might leave her in her own mess and use his salary for himself."

Trust Russell to miss the point. "So, you're happy your daughter is engaged to him then?"

"If they ever come to a place where they decide their relationship has real merit and they decide to get married, I will support them one hundred percent."

"So will I. Of course I will." Good heavens. The conversation had moved to marriage. This was her realm to preside over.

"But I'm hoping they do get married," Russell said. "I think he's a good man, and good, responsible men of integrity are not as easy to find as you might think. Chloe is on a winner, if she chooses to go on with the relationship, in my humble opinion."

Louise slumped back into her office chair and expelled a long breath through her nose. "I'm just worried she would be taking on more than just Michael. His mother seems to need a lot of care."

Russell rolled his eyes, shook his head and walked out of the room.

"Well I'm worried," she called after him.

"Life doesn't always come without trials and burdens," he called back. "That's fantasy."

"Shows how much you know," Louise mumbled to herself. "If Liam pushes on with marrying Evie they are going to have a load of trial and burden."

***

The flight to Coolangatta was uneventful until they began their descent in preparation for landing. Chloe gripped Michael's hand with a fierceness born of fear.

"I assume you're not a fan of turbulence?" Michael watched her face. It was stricken with panic. "It's just bumpy air. We'll be all right."

"Shows how much you know, Michael Sullivan. Haven't you ever watched *Air Crash Investigation*?"

Michael laughed.

"It's not funny," Chloe complained.

"Why would you watch a show like that just before you have to fly?"

"I watched it with Mum and Dad a couple of weeks ago."

The plane hit a particularly large bump in the air and the plane moved so violently that all passengers were thrown side to side and there were a number of cries—Chloe's the loudest. Michael put his other hand on the side of her face and forced her to look at him.

"It's going to be all right, Chloe. Look at me." He searched her face until she met his gaze. "Just breathe and relax. It'll be all right."

She examined him, and he could see the panic seeping out of her expression, as her facial muscles slowly relaxed.

"There, you see?" He smiled at her, and she allowed a smile in return. Then the plane hit the ground with a more-dramatic-than-usual thud, and it felt as if they were jerked sideways. More cries of panic.

"We could have died," Chloe said, burying her face in Michael's shoulder.

"I've been on worse flights. Always seem to get where I'm going without mishap."

"But I have an imagination," Chloe argued.

"Like your mother?"

"Worse, I think sometimes. And I watched that stupid TV show."

"Well, we are here now, on the ground, safe and sound. We've got a full six days to relax and enjoy the sunshine and water." He planted a quick kiss on her cheek. Then undid his seat belt, ready to stand up and retrieve their hand luggage from the overhead compartments.

Chloe stood in line outside the women's bathroom while Michael watched the luggage carousel.

"You want to share a taxi to the resort?" Daniel had come to stand next to him.

"Sure. It might be a bit squeezy with the four of us and luggage."

"They have maxi-cabs. We'll grab one of those. I'd really like Esther to get to know Chloe. Esther doesn't get out much and I think they'd get on well together."

"Great." Michael pasted on a smile. They probably would get on well together, but Michael couldn't guarantee Chloe wouldn't have Esther enrolling in medical school with the children booked in at childcare before their retreat was over. But he didn't tell Daniel that. Daniel didn't impress Michael as the sort of man who'd look favorably on his wife choosing education and career over looking after the family.

The resort that had been booked for the staff of Ainsworth and Pembroke was like most of the resorts on the Gold Coast, only a short drive away from the usual fast-paced Surfers Paradise. They had technically crossed the border into New South Wales, and the beaches were less crowded with fewer resort hotels populating the area.

"Nice." Chloe had her sun glasses on and was taking in the sight of the pool areas.

"Let's get checked in," Michael said.

"Are you sure your boss is OK paying for a separate room for me? After all, I'm not even on staff."

"He wants you here."

"Because I'm your soon-to-be wife."

"Doesn't really matter why. It's a blessing. You've got a week's paid leave so just soak it up."

"I feel kind of bad that your admin staff haven't been given the same opportunity."

Michael ignored the comment. They were lined up at the reception desk waiting to check in, and he didn't want to be discussing the inequality that existed among the staff of Ainsworth and Pembroke. He couldn't do anything about it anyway.

"We've given you adjoining rooms, Mr Sullivan." The hotel receptionist handed over two key-card packets.

Michael smiled. What was that look the receptionist was giving him?

"She thinks our situation is highly irregular," Chloe said in a low tone as they walked away.

"Why would she think that?"

"We're obviously a couple. Why shouldn't we sleep together?"

"Chloe." Michael pressed the button to call the lift, then frowned in her direction.

She shrugged. "I'm just saying. If we were normal, we wouldn't be paying for two separate rooms."

"We're not paying for them, for starters, and I thought this was the condition of your coming in any case."

"Oh, yeah. Of course, it is. I'm just making an observation that this is not the usual practice for engaged couples in the Twenty-First Century."

Duh. Michael rolled his eyes, but didn't bother to keep the discussion going.

"Esther seems nice," Chloe said, after several moments of silence. "Though I could cheerfully wallop her husband."

Michael let out a breath. Should he say something, or just let it go?

"It's like she can hardly have an opinion of her own before he jumps in and smothers her attempts to communicate."

"You don't know him, Chloe." Daniel had been unusually overbearing on the ride from the airport to the resort. Michael had hoped Chloe wouldn't notice, but of course she picked it up.

She shrugged. "I don't think I really want to know him too much."

"You did say you would play nice this week. Couldn't you just spend some time with Esther and allow her to be who she is without making judgments?"

"Fine by me. So long as her husband doesn't shadow us everywhere and insist on telling me exactly what he thinks his wife should be saying."

"That is overstating it, Chloe."

But was it an overstatement? Michael would never have minded before, but since Chloe was with him he was suddenly sensitive to this sort of behavior.

The lift doors opened and Michael stepped out of the elevator first.

"This way." Chloe moved past him and headed right, then turned left down a long corridor. "Which room do you want? 412 or 413? Are you superstitious?"

"I'm not superstitious, and I'm happy to take whichever room you don't want."

Chloe stood in front of 412 and held out her hand. "I'll take this one."

"Are you superstitious?" He wouldn't put it past her.

"I like even numbers better."

"Sure." He waited while she opened the door and began to drag her suitcase in.

"Come in and take a look," she said.

"I'm sure my room will look pretty much the same." Would crossing the threshold into her room constitute a breach of family values?

"Are we going to spend the whole week sitting alone in separate rooms?"

"I imagine we will be eating together, walking on the beach together and probably sitting by the pool together. I wouldn't want you to get sick of me."

"Right."

Chloe turned away and the door started to close. Had he just offended her? He held the door open. "Chloe?"

"Don't let me keep you."

She *was* offended. He stepped inside her room pulling his suitcase behind him.

"I didn't mean I didn't want to spend time with you."

"You've been sounding mighty uptight since we got off that plane."

"I'm a bit stressed."

"Why?"

"Because you and I are playing a charade for the benefit of my colleagues and I'm scared you won't fit in, and I'm scared they'll discover we aren't really on the cusp of marriage, and I'm scared of what my boss will think of you—you and me."

"You're afraid I will open my big mouth and let everyone know what I really think?"

Was that a trick question? Michael studied her face to gauge how she would respond.

"It's all right, Michael. I get it. I know how to play the game, as promised."

He let out a sigh. "I'm sorry, Chloe. I shouldn't have asked you to play a part that's so not you."

She raised her eyebrows at him and gave a half smile. "I didn't have to agree. I could have told you to get lost."

"Except for the speeding ticket."

"I can play the part for a week, Michael. I'm sorry to be out of sorts."

"How about you unpack, relax for half an hour, and then we meet downstairs in the bar by the pool? OK?"

She still looked annoyed.

"OK, Chloe?"

She nodded. "I'd feel better if you gave me a hug."

He left his suitcase and let the door close properly before holding out his arms. She stepped into his embrace, resting her head on his shoulder.

"I'm sorry," she said. "I like you, but I'm scared that you might be ashamed of me."

He kissed her forehead. "I'm not ashamed of you."

"But you're afraid your boss will find out about me and he won't approve, will he?"

"Probably not." He hugged her a little tighter. "But let's not borrow trouble. Let's just enjoy the perks of the resort and try to enjoy spending time together, hey?"

"OK." Chloe lifted her head and kissed him on the lips—quickly—thank goodness. Alone, together in a hotel room, and any lingering lip-locking might have sent them in a direction neither of them could, or should, go.

"Now get out of my room, and I'll see you in half an hour," she said.

Chapter Twelve

I'm such a bad person—so totally shallow. Despite her thoughts, Chloe didn't bat an eyelid as she watched Michael climb out of the pool. Talk about a hot body.

"How long did you say until the wedding?"

Chloe was jarred from her ogling by Esther's question. They'd already discussed this. Had she forgotten?

"Better not leave it too long," Esther said, a grin stealing across her expression.

Chloe felt the heat rise in her face. Michael Sullivan looked good in a business suit, but that was nothing to his beach body that was well on display poolside.

"How long were you and Daniel engaged before you got married?" Redirect the conversation—quick, before Esther uncovered the course of her thoughts.

"We met in youth group and followed the trend."

Chloe watched Esther, expecting more information to follow.

"I mean, I love Daniel, but we didn't really know each other before we got married."

"So, you got married quickly?"

Esther nodded. "And we were young—by today's standards, anyway."

"How old were you?"

"I was twenty and Daniel was twenty-two."

"Wow, that is young."

"And our first child was born nine months later."

"Honeymoon baby. Was it planned?"

"I wanted kids, and so I guess we just let nature take its course."

Chloe was ultra-aware of Esther's new baby-bump under her modest beach wrap. Nature seemed to have been having a jolly good time with this one coming in at number four.

"How old are you now?" Chloe asked.

"Twenty-eight."

"Same as me."

"Do you and Michael plan to have kids straight away?"

"Nooo. Nuh-uh. Not likely."

"You feel pretty strongly about it then?" Esther smiled again and took a sip of her mocktail.

That *was* a powerful negative response to an innocent question. Had she offended Esther?

"I mean, I guess I will have kids one day," Chloe hurried on, "but I've paid too high a price to get into the work I do to just throw it away and become a nobody imprisoned at home."

Chloe, shut-up. Too late, the words had not even stopped by her brain to ask permission to come out.

"You don't have a very high opinion of domestic management as a career then?" There was an edge to Esther's tone.

"I'm sorry, Esther. That was thoughtless of me."

"Yes, it was. I mean, it's not that I'm not used to the disrespect. Women who choose to parent at home are not given much credibility in terms of intelligence or contribution to society."

"I don't think that's true. Bringing up kids in a stable and loving environment is proven to be valuable to society."

"I prefer to call it domestic management—and trust me, there are so many different areas of expertise needed to properly care for children and manage households. The title hardly covers it."

"But you did give up a career in medicine?"

"I need medical knowledge in my current role—trust me. Plus, psychology, education, nutrition, coaching techniques, art, music, event management—you name it, I need to know about it."

Chloe took a sip of her fruity punch. She knew this argument verbatim. Her mother had hounded her about it constantly and, annoyingly, her father had laughed at Chloe's responses. It was infuriating.

"Well, I don't mean to let my husband talk for me in a conversation."

Esther actually sat up straight on her sun lounge, put her legs over the side and caught Chloe in a stern gaze. Why did she have to open her big mouth? This was Dad's fault—provoking this argument and mocking her feminist ideals.

"You're very judgmental, Chloe. And since you feel comfortable to speak your mind, I may as well speak mine."

"I'm sorry—"

"No." Esther held up her hand. "It's my turn to speak."

Chloe swallowed the lump in her throat. She'd trodden on delicate ground with elephantine feet. She'd read that phrase in a classic novel once, and it summed up this situation perfectly.

"I chose to marry young and, while Daniel is not perfect, I love him. Yes, he's outspoken and does tend to speak for me too often, but that is part of who he is and an attribute that is used every day of his working life as a lawyer. When I front him on it, he always apologizes. But you don't know that, because you don't know him."

"I'm sorry—"

"I haven't finished."

Esther had the bull by the horns now. Chloe sat tight and braced for the next wave of scolding.

"I chose to have children, and I might not stop at four. I'm enjoying this period of my life and, as Daniel says, we don't have the financial pressure on us that would otherwise force me to work for paid employment. So why should I toss these years away and pay a childcare provider to take away my privilege of this time with my kids? It is not my prison, Chloe, it is my life, and I love it."

Chloe held still, studying Esther's face. Was she finished?

"And you might as well know …"

She hadn't finished. Gulp.

"… I realize that what I have is a privilege. Not all mothers have the opportunity to spend the early years together with their children, what with the cost of living. So, I'd appreciate it if you didn't judge me for my choice of career. I would also appreciate it if you'd come down from your high-horse and engage in getting to know me a bit. My husband admires Michael, and he hopes you and I will be friends."

Chloe watched, opened her mouth to speak, then closed it again. Was that twitch a sign that there was more to come?

"All right. You can speak now."

Chloe let out the breath she'd been holding then sucked in an equally large amount of air.

"Wow. You're a formidable force to be reckoned with."

"I am, Chloe Brooker, and if we're to be friends, you had best prepare yourself for me to speak my mind."

"Then I had best speak mine while I have the opportunity."

Esther waved her hand accompanied by a nod of her head.

"I fight with my parents on this topic constantly," Chloe said. "They're always trying to get me matched with a suitable husband, hoping I'll settle down and have multiple grandbabies."

"And ...?"

"And I resist them on principle."

"Because ...?"

"Because I don't want my father to be right. Feminism was hard fought for, and women's rights are not something I should just throw away."

"Agreed. Do you think I have thrown my rights away by marrying a strong man?"

This was a trick question, surely.

"Noooo." Chloe didn't sound overly confident.

"Don't be ridiculous, Chloe. Daniel is strong and sometimes overbearing, but I match it with him when we talk in private. He knows how I feel about him speaking for me."

"But you don't take him to task in public?"

"No, I don't. He doesn't need to be brought down a peg and humiliated. And you wouldn't believe how many women I see doing that to their husbands."

"But aren't you humiliated when he talks over you?"

"I'm stronger than that. A small tap on his knee under the table and he knows he's on thin ice."

"And yet he still does it to you in public."

"Will you embarrass Michael in public if something crosses your mind?"

"I guess I just have, haven't I?"

"Does that make you a bad person?"

"I hope not."

"We all make clangers at times. I forgive Daniel and I forgive you. Life's too short to be huffing and puffing and emotionally manipulating when we feel offended."

Chloe nodded. She liked that Esther was willing to forgive, and so quickly.

"Are you going to swim?" Esther asked.

"Are you?"

Esther smiled and undid her wrap. Her pregnant belly was round and beautiful in the bathing suit she was wearing. This kind of maternity was wonderful to see. What was the small thud that hit Chloe mid-chest? Did she want to be pregnant too? *Not in a million years.* With Michael? The thud turned into a buzz. How odd. Chloe dropped her brightly-colored, Hawaiian sarong to the plastic deck-chair and dived into the pool.

***

What had Chloe and Esther been talking about poolside? It looked intense whatever it was. But thoughts of what the topic of conversation might have been were soon replaced by an overwhelming brain-fade.

She was a babe.

And she would kill him if he ever used that word.

How can someone so strong, determined and always citing the rights of women be so mind-bogglingly beautiful? He was going to have to talk to her, as he was sure her bathing-suit image didn't fit with her ideals against the sexualization of women.

"Hey." Chloe swam up to him. "You look like you swallowed a bee."

"I was just—I mean—you look—that is to say —"

"Spit it out counsellor."

"You look great in a swimsuit, Chloe. Don't hate me. I've got eyes in my head, and—well, I can't stay underwater forever."

She laughed—thank you, Lord—she laughed.

"You look pretty good yourself," she said.

Michael hoisted himself out of the water and sat on the edge of the pool. "I'm surprised to see your choice of swimwear. I would have thought it went against your ideals."

"What do you mean?" Chloe was still in the pool, moving her arms to help her stay upright.

"As a feminist, I imagined you'd be against fashion that promotes the objectification of women."

"I'm against the objectification of anybody. I was feeling quite guilty myself a little while ago."

"About?"

"You have heard the expression, 'eye-candy'?"

Suddenly Michael felt naked. He was half-naked with only his swimming shorts on. This conversation was in deeper than where Chloe was currently treading water.

"Relax, Michael. So, I'm attracted to you and you to me. I guess that's OK, given we're engaged."

"I was attracted to you before, but this is a whole new level."

"Considering your boss's propensity for conservative family values, I have an overwhelming urge to go find a large hotel robe."

Michael laughed. He had to laugh. What else could he do?

"Well, don't just sit there showing off in the sun. Join me in the water, and we'll swim a few laps. We can write it up as fitness." She reached up her hand, he took it and she pulled him back in. Yes, best to swim laps. Sitting around in this attitude could lead to nowhere good—by the Ainsworth and Pembroke conservative family value's definition of good, anyway.

***

"You sure did a lot of swimming this afternoon." Daniel punched the button to call the elevator.

"Yeah."

"You in training or something?"

"No." Michael did not want to continue this conversation.

"You trying to swim off some steam?"

"Meaning?"

"Meaning you better set a date soon, mate, or you'll self-combust."

He really didn't want to have this conversation—that his colleague was right on the money was not the point. The whole mixing together at the pool had ignited something new between himself and Chloe. He'd liked her before, enjoyed her company, and found her personality strangely attractive—her strength so in contrast to his mother's apathy. But now he'd seen her in a bathing suit, and who was he kidding? He was turned on by her, and there was no going back from that. He might have thought Harold Ainsworth's conservative standards were cold and unbending, but he believed in the sanctity of marriage and had no intention of sleeping with a woman who was not his wife. And she was not going to be his wife—not in the next ten years, anyway.

"You want to talk about it?" Daniel asked as they got into the elevator.

"Maybe later."

"Whenever you need me, mate, just call."

Thankfully they were on different floors, and Michael got out first.

"See you at dinner."

"Don't forget Harold has got that team-building games evening planned," Daniel said. "Hope you haven't tuckered yourself out."

Michael smiled and waved as the elevator doors closed. Team-building games. Daniel had told him about Harold's famous games, including the relationship game. He'd better warn Chloe.

***

Ironically, the definition of a cold shower chased around Chloe's mind as she washed the chlorine from her hair. This was exactly why she was a campaigner against the fashion-industry's careless use of sex to sell image. But it turned out she was a hypocrite, because she liked the bathers she had bought and felt she looked good in them. She did look good—as evidenced by the look on Michael's face. But then he looked good too, and the vibes were all sexual attraction. Sheesh. What a philosophical conundrum. How many times had she posted self-righteous statements about staying true to yourself and how much a woman did not need to dress up for anybody? With all of the image disorders and eating disorders, and girls hating themselves as a result of the highly sexualized, fake-model media that circulated, Chloe had considered herself immune to the charm of magazine-generated beauty. Sheesh. Apparently, she wasn't immune. Not that she hated herself or wanted to indulge in self-harm. But subconsciously she'd known Michael would be attracted to her in swimming attire, and she had been attracted to him, and it was all so shallow. If they had been a normal Twenty-First Century couple, they would have been in bed together right now with no scruples. The worst of it was, she subscribed to the Christian ideal of keeping oneself for one's marriage partner. And yet …

She turned the water off and listened. There it was again. Someone was at the door. Probably Michael. In this frame of mind she should ignore it, however she had the bathrobe on, and had wrapped a towel around her head before she stopped to consider it further.

"Uhh ..." It was Michael, looking like a stunned mullet with his mouth hanging open.

"Do you want to come in?"

"Umm ..."

"I'll take that as a yes."

"Yeah, no. I better not." He stepped back a couple of feet.

"I know what you mean." She offered a grin but he continued in his state of deer-in-the-headlights, swallowing as if his mouth was dry.

"I'll meet you downstairs for dinner?" Chloe asked.

"Yeah." He nodded his head as if he didn't know how to speak English.

"Oookaaay."

Chloe began to close the door when he stepped forward again.

"Wait. Sorry. I came to tell you there would be team-building games tonight."

"All right. Anything I should know?"

"I've heard they do a 'how-well-do-you-know-your-partner' game. I thought I'd best warn you."

"Do you want to go over notes?"

He opened his mouth again as if stumped for words.

"I'll meet you downstairs half an hour early, and you can coach me on anything you think I should know. However, I think I've pretty much got you summed up."

"Yeah."

He really was lost for words. She closed the door and shook her head. They should rush off to Vegas and just get it over with.

Chapter Thirteen

Chloe squirmed in her seat. She was seated in the dining room, having turned her chair to face the small podium at the front of the room. Harold Ainsworth could not be more clueless if he'd tried to be.

"Welcome to you all. I'm grateful that you lovely ladies have been able to join your husbands on this retreat."

This speech was so gender-role orientated.

"I hope you're not missing the kids too much," he continued, "but after all, you deserve some time away from cooking and cleaning."

What year did he think this was—1955, downtown Stepford? Chloe glanced across to Esther, seated next to her. Esther's smile in her direction caused Chloe's thoughts to bump into each other, like the carriages behind a suddenly stopped locomotive. Was Esther a relic from the 1950s housewife collection?

"And I know your husbands appreciate having you with them as we all enjoy a bit of downtime." There was a smattering of applause.

Partners is the PC term. Just as quickly as the mental correction flashed in her mind, Chloe felt a stab of awareness. Esther was still smiling, and a quick glance around the other tables revealed other women also smiling. Were their smiles genuine? Was she the only one who felt patronized by Harold Ainsworth's condescension?

"Sorry." Michael whispered in her ear as he squeezed her hand.

Chloe felt another stab of conscience. Was Michael the only man in the room constantly on tenterhooks, nervous his partner would be offended?

"And I'm so pleased to be able to meet Michael Sullivan's fiancée," Harold continued. "Chloe, welcome. We hope you feel comfortable in our corporate family." Another round of polite applause.

Chloe could feel her face smiling, but how did it look? Her thoughts were in chaos—one part protest, one part chagrin. Could her face portray sweet, charming and submissive wife when five minutes ago all she'd wanted to do was jump up and object to the condescension? And now she wanted to get these women together and find out what was going on in *their* heads.

"Enjoy your dinner, and afterward we will spend some time encouraging and building on our relationships."

"That will be interesting," Chloe said under her breath.

"I really am sorry." Michael looked troubled. He really did care how she felt.

"I'm sorry, Michael. My mind is in a riot of confusion at the moment."

"Are you all right?" His concern was evident.

"Let's call it cognitive dissonance, shall we."

"What …?"

"Don't worry, Michael. I'll be fine." She patted his knee.

"Michael, Chloe." Harold approached them, weaving his way through the tables. "I'd love to have you sit with Bernice and me during dinner."

No, no, no. Please. So many other happy wives you could sit with.

"Thank you, Harold. We'd be honored." Michael squeezed her hand again as he accepted the invitation.

"Splendid. We are sitting at table one." He pointed towards the table at the front of the private dining room.

Despite the urge to whine and beg off accepting, Chloe stiffened her spine and followed Michael as he led them towards the boss's table. It was like she was stuck in a strange dream. Michael pulled out her chair, and without fussing, she graciously accepted his help to be seated. He took her light cardigan from her hand, and hung it over the back of her chair.

"Thank you." The usual objection—that she was not an invalid, and could manage her own chair without assistance—died in her mouth as Michael smiled at her. She could read the tension in his eyes.

"It is so lovely to see that chivalry is not dead." The older woman—must be Bernice Ainsworth—smiled a sickly-sweet smile in their direction. Chloe hated to point out to Bernice that chivalry was a code of conduct from nine hundred years ago, meant for knights and warriors. It hardly had anything to do with assisting a perfectly able woman to sit down.

"My dear," Harold addressed his wife, "this is Michael Sullivan, one of my bright up-and-coming lawyers."

"How do you do?" Bernice smiled in his direction. "And this darling young woman is your wife?"

Was she not paying attention? Her husband had just welcomed her five minutes ago.

"This is Chloe, my fiancée." Michael answered, before Chloe could speak for herself.

"How do you do, Chloe? When is the wedding? I hope we haven't torn you away from wedding preparations."

"No date set, as yet." At last Chloe managed to get a word in.

"Set a date, Michael," Harold said. "Let's get you settled and your mind fully on the job."

Chloe felt her blood rise, and Michael's hand on her knee give a small squeeze.

"I assure you my mind is fully on the job for all that's required. And when I need to focus on my family, I make it a priority to do so."

He wasn't talking about her of course. He was talking about his mother. But Harold obviously didn't know that.

"As it should be, my boy ..."

So condescending.

"...but make sure you don't frustrate yourself. Having your wife in your home will not only make sure your domestic needs are met, but ... well, you know what I mean."

Was he serious?

"Chloe is a busy professional herself. I'm not sure she's quite ready to sit at home and dust bookshelves."

Chloe glanced at Michael. How far would he go in standing up for her?

"Yes, yes. I'm sure that's the case, but once you get married she won't need to work, and she'll enjoy being able to give all her time to the children once they start to arrive. Don't leave it too long. I'd hate to see you lose focus."

Michael's hand had tightened on hers to an almost strangling degree. He wasn't happy.

"Now, my dear," Bernice cut in. "Stop pushing these young people. I'm sure they know their own mind and will make their own plans in good time."

"Just remember, we run a family business, and home stability is the image I want people seeing from my employees." Harold took a sip of water from the tumbler in front of him.

"Yes, we're aware of your values," Michael said. "You may be assured Chloe and I have discussed this at length."

Well that part was true. They had discussed it prior and would certainly discuss it again after this trip. But Harold wouldn't be happy with the direction of their discussion.

The meal was difficult to enjoy. Harold Ainsworth was paternalistic, sexist and horribly condescending. Chloe spent most of the time trying to swallow her words. How could Michael work in such an environment—unless that was who he secretly was?

***

This was awful. Perhaps if he pretended to choke, they'd call an ambulance and call off this monumental display of personal intrusion called the 'marriage game'—supposedly to build team morale.

"Which parent do you take after more?" Bernice Ainsworth asked Michael the question with a lovely smile on her face, oblivious to the internal turmoil she was causing. How on earth could he answer these game questions and still maintain his 'family friendly' façade? And what answers would Chloe give when it was her turn?

"That's a difficult one," Michael hedged. "I'm not sure I should answer on the grounds that I might offend."

Everyone laughed. Michael tried to swallow the large ball of anxiety that had blocked his throat. When they brought the 'wives' back from their sound-proof exclusion zone, what would Chloe say?

"How many children would make up your ideal family?" Bernice seemed to be enjoying herself playing the part of the game host, and the questions kept on rolling. He and Chloe had not discussed children, because they didn't plan to have any.

"Eight or nine."

This ridiculous answer amused those colleagues not in the hot seat. But it was one thing to be sarcastic for the sake of a show, and another when his beloved needed to match answers with him to win the game. *Chloe, please read my mind.*

"How does your wife handle the in-laws?" Bernice asked.

"Remembering, Chloe and I are not yet married …"

"Apologies. How does your fiancée handle the in-laws?"

"I can honestly say, Chloe is caring, kind and thoughtful towards the rest of my family."

"And how do you handle your in-laws?"

"My mother-in-law-to-be set us up, actually. I like her, and Russell, I can honestly say, has been like a father to me."

Whoops. That information was not supposed to come out. *Please don't ask about my own father. Please.*

"What childhood secret would Chloe know, that no one else knows?"

"It wouldn't be a secret if I told you, would it? Chloe knows all my secrets. I haven't hidden anything from her. And she loves me anyway."

Everybody laughed again, and Bernice waggled her eyebrows. "Though I could not imagine you would have any skeletons in the closet—such a fine upstanding young man, like you."

Please let this torture end. Why couldn't he say what he really felt—like—mind your own business?

Finally, Bernice decided to turn her nosey personal questions in Daniel's direction. Daniel gave neat and tidy answers for everything and didn't appear to break a sweat. Could everyone else in the room see the anxiety he felt at having been selected and scrutinised in public? How was this team-building?

"Ian, we've now heard all the answers from our husbands." Michael snapped back to attention at Bernice's announcement. "Could you fetch the ladies back?"

Now was the moment of truth.

Chloe was gorgeous, and outshone all the other wives who walked back into the main room. It struck him as ironic that she was dressed in a pretty, floral-patterned 1950s style dress with a black belt. The dress matched the image they were all trying to portray. She smiled at him. Was that confidence she was beaming in his direction? Could they get through this, and two more days by the pool, and be home without blowing their cover?

***

How impossibly rude! Chloe couldn't believe the questions that were being asked of Esther and Caroline—questions that presumed so much about the relationships of the people being questioned. What if the wife didn't get along with her in-laws? What if they didn't want to have a child once a year for the next decade? Had they asked Michael about who he took after? What would he have said since his mother was a mess, and he didn't know who his father was? Did Bernice Ainsworth really want to know the truth, or should she prepare trite acceptable answers like the rest of them? Chloe could feel her blood rising in temperature. This game was insipid and stupid. Even after having heard Esther tell her she was happy in her current role as housewife and mother—well bully for her. She fit in this group—Michael did not. Michael did not fit the mold of Ainsworth and Pembroke and that did not make him a bad person. She loved who he was and was not ashamed of his situation either. These people needed to hear the truth.

She looked across and saw the panic on Michael's face. She couldn't do it. She couldn't humiliate him in public. It was her turn now for the hot seat, and she would have to make up the appropriate answers and hope they matched what he'd said.

"Well, from what I've observed, I would guess Michael takes after his father."

Question one down. Michael hadn't burst into flames, so she assumed she should press forward.

"Though we have not had a firm conversation on this, I would guess Michael would want a number of children." She watched him and saw him mouth the words 'thank you'.

"The number he stated was eight or nine," Bernice said.

There was raucous laughter around the room. What! Just because half the women in the room were rearing a brood of four or more children, did they think Michael incapable of being a good parent? Just because he only had one parent, and one who was unable to care for him. How dare they make fun of him like that?

"How do you handle Michael's parents?" Bernice asked the question.

"Given Michael only has a mother, who is not very well, and he doesn't even know who his father is, I'd say I handle her with care and kindness. And I might just as well say, he does have secrets, but not any he would trust with the likes of you people. Michael is a man of honor and has had to educate himself to get where he is. And he's had to pretend he's from some stable family just to suit your company image. Well, that's not his background. He doesn't have the nice Christian upbringing that you favor but he's managed anyway."

The words flew out of her mouth unchecked, until she caught sight of Michael's face. He'd gone pale, and the look on his face was devastating. Was he angry? Disappointed? Embarrassed? Humiliated?

She'd done just what Esther had encouraged her not to do. She'd exposed Michael in a way that made him vulnerable. Why, why, why couldn't she keep her mouth shut?

Michael shook his head at her, his mouth a grim line.

"I'm sorry, Michael," she said.

He held up his hand to stop her, got up from his seat and left the room. Chloe got up to follow but was stayed by Esther's hand.

"Leave him for a bit, Chloe. Give him some time to sort through his feelings."

"If it wasn't for the pressure you people put on him, he wouldn't have had to hide who he really was."

"Perhaps it would be best if you went back to your room." Harold Ainsworth had stood to take control of the mess. "We can discuss this later, privately."

Privately. That sounded ominous.

"I'll come with you," Esther offered.

Chloe glanced at Daniel, who was staring daggers in her direction. He didn't want his wife associating with a loose-tongued feminist, but he didn't stop Esther. They walked out of the room into the hotel foyer.

"I shouldn't have done that, should I?"

"That may be stating the obvious." Esther's tone was not harsh.

"But I couldn't stand it any longer. Do you know what lengths Michael goes to just so he can please his boss and keep his job?"

"Like coming up with a fake engagement?"

Chloe stopped and looked closely at Esther.

"What makes you say that?"

"He presented you at the time the memo went out about the retreat. We hadn't heard a word about you before then."

"But I thought it was understood that he was engaged?"

"Harold assumed it, but as there was never any fiancée mentioned or showcased, most of us guessed he wasn't."

"But Michael thinks Mr Ainsworth expects marriage. He thinks his job depends on it." Chloe could feel panic welling up. They paused at the open elevator and waited for it to empty before entering.

"Has Michael spoken to Harold about it?" Esther asked once the elevator began its ascent.

"You know he hasn't, or we wouldn't be having this conversation."

"Harold Ainsworth is conservative, no doubt about it."

"Impossibly so."

"Not impossibly."

"He's so politically incorrect it makes my head spin."

"Does that make him a bad person?"

"He's paternalistic and sexist. The only women in his company are a couple of admin staff. The rest are home with their children, baking scones and volunteering at the church fete."

"Chloe, really? Harold Ainsworth might be unbalanced when it comes to equal opportunities, but you are judgmental and thoughtless when you talk about people like me. I thought we discussed this before."

Chloe felt the blood rise in her face. Esther's calm tone had been replaced by something stronger. *Judgmental and thoughtless? Me?* They had reached her floor and Esther seemed intent on coming with her. They walked down the corridor and entered her room.

"I'm sorry, Esther."

"If you want to work in the emergency room all your life, that's your choice. But don't look down on me because I've chosen the home as my work environment. You've judged all of those women in there, and you've well and truly embarrassed Michael." Esther was on her high horse now.

136

"I know."

There were several beats of strained silence. Chloe could feel Esther's gaze practically reducing her to a pile of ash, right there in her hotel room.

"I didn't know his mum wasn't well," Esther said. Poof. The tension evaporated.

"No. He keeps his home life private."

"But he let you in, didn't he?"

"He trusted me with all his background." A trust she'd just abused.

"So, your relationship isn't really fake, is it?"

"It was to start with. But we've grown really close over the last few weeks."

"Yes, I saw."

"Goodness knows if he'll forgive me for that outburst."

"I'd send him a text and ask if he wants to talk."

"Good idea. Thanks Esther." Chloe threw her arms around the other woman. "I appreciate your support."

***

It was one thing to set out with courage and determination, but another to stop in front of room 413 and have doubt and shame crash into her from behind. Chloe shouldn't have revealed Michael's private business. She'd just accused everyone else of not being worthy of his trust and then turned around and exposed his deepest fears.

The weight in her arm was as heavy as lead, but she forced herself to knock. The original agreement had been they would break up after the retreat. Well she'd provided plenty of credible excuse for a massive fight and she had no doubt a breakup would be the end result. Even as she heard Michael approach to open the door, her heart squeezed with dismay. She didn't want to end her relationship like this. She didn't want to end this relationship—period.

The latch released and the door opened, but only a fraction.

"I don't want to talk about it, Chloe."

"Michael, I'm sorry. I shouldn't have said …"

"No, you shouldn't. I shared the deepest part of me with you, and you treated it like rubbish."

"I didn't mean …"

"Just because you don't like old-fashioned conservative behavior, doesn't make these people bad people."

"Don't tell me their happy-family club doesn't hurt you. How can you sit there and not feel excluded when all they talk about is mothers and fathers and idyllic family barbeques?"

"That's my choice, Chloe. Not yours. I'm the one who has to face my personal loss, not you. I'm the one who has to work to make up for what's missing. Not you."

Chloe opened her mouth to speak but couldn't find the right words.

"Just because you're all equal rights and politically correct doesn't mean you don't hurt me as well. Do you think I like the idea that you don't approve of my workplace, or that you don't think my work colleagues—who happen to be my only friends, by the way—are not up to your high-and-mighty standards? You need to get over yourself, Chloe. Stop being so self-righteous."

The door was closed in her face before she could manufacture a word to say. Esther's accusation had shaken her, but the same sentiment from Michael, and in such a harsh tone, blew her equilibrium out of the water. The muscles in her face started to quiver and a sob emerged from somewhere deep in her soul. This was the worst breakup she could ever have imagined. Michael had taken a mirror and turned it in her direction. She was everything he said—self-righteous, judgmental and insensitive. To think that was how she'd described all the staff at Ainsworth and Pembroke and then to realize she was no different, stung. And Michael was angry with her. Would he ever forgive her, or was this the end?

Her shaking hand fumbled with the key-card as she opened the door to room 412. She dropped her key on the floor, crossed the room and collapsed on the bed. The first sob having been joined by a party of others, all intent on bringing her crashing down until she'd curled into a foetal position.

***

How was he going to last another two days pretending to have a great time on retreat? Booking an early flight was out of the question, given the outrageous prices the airlines charged for short-notice flights. He couldn't afford it anyway, and his return flights for this trip had been paid by the company.

Michael stood under the stream of water in the shower for a good twenty minutes. Bernice and Harold Ainsworth were intrusive and insensitive. He expected that from them. But Chloe—how could she have exposed him like that? He'd never let anyone know about his mother or his fatherless state. Even Abbie and Imogen from high school—they'd found out some of the situation but not all. He'd given into their seductive demands to hide the full extent of his family shame.

But Chloe. He'd felt he could trust her. Why? Because he loved her? Did he? And if it was love, could it survive a betrayal like this?

He turned off the water and just stood staring at the shower screen. He didn't want to face her. He didn't want to face any of his colleagues. He just wanted to go home and hide in his room until he went moldy.

It was after midnight by the time Michael turned off the bedside light. But he couldn't sleep. Other than Chloe, no one had come after him or tried to talk to him. Now they knew his situation—or at least the basic bones of the situation—would they look down on him like they did others who weren't all straight and tidy? Had Chloe gone back to them and told them all the dirty details? No. She wouldn't do that. Would she? This was going to be a long night. Sleep would be a wonderful comfort at the moment, but it seemed impossibly elusive. There was the minibar, but he'd never been a drinker. His mother had enough vices without him joining in and adding to the dysfunction and expense. No, the minibar was safe for the time being.

He sat up in his bed, snapped the light back on and threw the sheet off. Where was his laptop when he needed it? Back in the office of course. This was supposed to be a retreat from work. But there was hotel stationary and the complementary hotel pen. He was going to have to write his thoughts down or they would drive him mad overnight.

Chapter Fourteen

$\mathcal{E}$velyn inched closer to the wall. She was out in public, dressed in a fine ballgown that could not be accounted for in her father's ledger. Anne had sent her maid to primp and preen Evelyn until she looked the same as all the other young ladies who were now engaged in chatter or dancing. But she didn't feel the same. She knew that her dress was as good as a charity handout. She knew that she came with no reputation and no dowry. And despite the finery that was supposed to disguise her poverty and shame, she knew the matrons and mamas in the room were talking about her behind their hands. It was not easy, but she kept her head up and eyes forward, so she saw the looks—some of pity, some of derision—that were cast in her direction.

"Pardon me, madam." A foppish looking gentleman stood in front of her and gave a quick bow. "Have we been introduced?"

Evelyn could feel the color in her cheeks. Even she knew it was the height of impropriety to talk with a young man to whom she had not been properly introduced. But there was no respectable lady or gentleman in the room who would do this service for her. Anne had been swept away to dance almost the moment they'd entered the room, and Liam had been drawn into another room, ostensibly on a matter of business. It was an unsatisfactory state of affairs, but the gentleman persisted, searching her face for an answer, despite her awkward silence.

"I was quite sure I had met you at Bradshaw's last winter."

"I apologize, sir. I do not recall."

Most of her visits to Bradshaw Manor were characterized by her keeping her head down, and hoping not to attract any mention from the outspoken visitors who frequented.

"I am quite sure Lady Anne has introduced us, and as such, I would be vastly pleased if you would honor me with the next dance."

Evelyn fought to keep her eyes politely on the unnamed gentleman—for he obviously didn't think it necessary to re-introduce himself. Where was Anne? Where was Liam? They had promised they would not leave her unattended.

"Were you expecting someone else to come by, perhaps?" Mr Mysterious asked.

"I came this evening with Lord and Lady Bradshaw."

He laughed. Why did he laugh? That was not a comment worthy of amusement.

"My dear lady. Liam Bradshaw is not a man to stand around doting on one woman. Why, at this very moment he is out in the gardens with another young lady—one of large fortune, I believe. But do not be alarmed. You will be perfectly safe with me."

Alarmed! Of a strange man who told horrid stories? Why would she be alarmed?

What alarmed her was the fact that her phone was ringing, and it was past the middle of the night.

"Louise." Russell's gruff voice pulled her from her sleep.

"Mmm. What? Oh bother." Louise threw her hand out in the dark and patted around on the bedside table trying to find the phone that was vibrating. Who was calling in the wee small hours? Who dared break into an excellent dream? She hoped she would remember the plot details in the morning.

"Hello." Was there any use pretending a cheerful tone as if she'd been awake for hours? It might have been her publisher from the states.

"Mum."

Chloe.

"What's wrong? Has something happened? Are you all right?"

There was no answer, but Louise fancied she could hear the sounds of stifled emotions.

"Chloe?"

"What's wrong?" Russell turned over and suddenly sounded alert.

"Chloe, speak to me."

"Give me the phone," Russell demanded.

That wasn't going to happen.

"Are you all right?"

"No." The one word was followed by some strangled noises that sounded like crying.

"What's happened? Are you hurt?"

"No ... yes ...no."

"Are you hurt, or aren't you?" Louise struggled to a sitting position and snapped on the beside light. Russell was already up and looking at her with a demanding expression. She held her hand up to stave him off.

"Michael and I have broken up." The last words were uttered with a lack of starch to support.

"Oh, darling. I'm sorry. But you were always going to break up eventually, weren't you?"

"But I love him."

"See!" Russell could obviously hear Chloe and sounded distressed himself.

"What happened?"

"It was my fault." She seemed to have found some gelatine to support her speech.

"Tell me what happened."

"I sold him out in front of his colleagues—told them about his mother and father."

"Put it on open line," Russell said. "I want to be in on this conversation."

Louise lowered her phone and pressed the sound icon.

"Dad's listening. We're on open line."

"Don't be angry with me, Dad."

"Why would I be angry with you?" Russell asked.

"I just got frustrated with the way his boss and the whole company presumed that Michael had a stable family, and that we would get married and have buckets of kids, and I blabbed out that Michael didn't know who his father was and that his mother was ill."

"Chloe …"

"I know, Dad. You don't have to nag."

"So has Michael talked to you about how he feels?" Louise asked.

"He told me I need to get over myself, and stop being so judgmental and self-righteous."

"Is that how you see it?" Russell asked.

"I guess. I know I shouldn't have betrayed his family secrets."

"Well, what else did he say?" Louise asked.

"Nothing. He just wrote me a letter and put it under my door."

"What did the letter say?"

Louise heard Chloe take a deep breath.

"Chloe? Do you want to tell us?"

There was the sound of paper unfolding.

"Dear Chloe, I think it is best all round if we finish our relationship now. We never intended it would go this far, and so it's better if we just leave it. I will still see to the matter of the speeding ticket. I'll send notice of the court date once all the paperwork has been finalized. In the meantime, if you could not say anything else about my family to the rest of my work-mates, I'd really appreciate it."

"Is that all?" Russell asked.

"No love Michael or anything?" Louise said.

"He just signed it. That's it. We're done."

"Perhaps it's for the best, Chloe. It's not like you ever intended for it to be anything but a week in the sun." Louise could feel Russell's frown as she spoke.

"But I care for him. I love him. I'm so sorry to have hurt him."

"Why don't you come home?" Russell said. "I'll pay for a new ticket."

"Would you, Dad? I don't think I could bear to be here two more days. I feel so awful."

"Go and try to get some sleep. Dad will ring you in the morning with the new flight details."

"I don't think I'll be able to sleep knowing Michael won't forgive me."

"He'll forgive you in time. He's a good man," Russell said.

"Maybe, but I don't think he'll ever trust me again."

"Go to sleep now, Chloe," Louise said. "We'll call you in the morning."

Louise closed her phone and put it back on the bedside table.

"Well, I think that's probably for the best." She lay down and switched the light off, but there was still a glow from the other side of the bed.

"Russell, what on earth are you doing with your phone at 3:42 in the morning?"

"I'm calling Michael."

"What? Why?"

"Because the poor boy needs a father at a time like this."

***

When the phone rang at 3.42am Michael was wide awake. Russell. Should he answer it? Chloe had obviously called him and filled him in, and the phone call now could only mean a lambasting. He watched the lit phone buzz a couple more times. Chloe had hurt him by her careless words, and Russell would no doubt support her. Michael winced at the idea of disappointing Russell. They'd connected like father and son in their few times together, and Michael hated the idea of letting him down. The least he owed was to talk to the man.

"Hello." His tone was tentative.

"Michael. Did I wake you?"

"No." He didn't say anything else. What was Russell's mood like? Was he an enraged father calling to defend his little girl?

"I heard what happened." There was no rage in Russell's voice. Just the usual patient and caring tone. "Do you want to talk about it?"

Did he? This wasn't something he was used to. When things went wrong in his life he usually had to suck it up and deal with it. Who was he going to talk to for encouragement anyway? Would this end in encouragement or reprimand?

"Chloe had no right to say what she did," Russell said. "It's not the first time she's burst out when she gets her dander up."

"I don't think she meant to hurt me," Michael said.

"She didn't. She cares about you, more than is normal for a casual friend."

"I don't know what to do now. My boss now knows a whole lot of stuff I never meant him to know—stuff that will affect the way he views me."

"My advice is you should look for an opportunity to talk to your boss," Russell said. "Not even he could get away with firing you because of your family background."

Despite the care and wisdom offered by Chloe's dad, Michael was still awake as the sun rose. His head was full of cotton wool, and his heart was in pieces. He pulled the sheet over his head in an attempt to pretend the new day was not urging him to get up.

Sleep began to tug at his eyes and he let his mind drift off, only to be jarred awake by knocking on his door. Wow. Sleep deprivation was worse than a hangover—from his limited experience with hangovers. A quick look at the bedside clock—where did three hours go?

"Michael!" It was Daniel shouting through the door. Thank goodness. He didn't want to face Chloe.

"Just a moment." He rolled out of bed, pulled on his board shorts and trudged across to open the door.

"It's nearly nine o'clock. Are you all right?"

"I broke up with Chloe last night. Haven't slept since."

"Oh, man, I'm sorry." Daniel came into the room and put his hand on Michael's shoulder, guiding him back to sit on the bed. "Do you want to talk about it?"

"I suppose I'm going to have to, given Chloe's burst of information last night."

"About your family?"

"Yeah, about my family. Why, what else did she tell you?"

Daniel held up his hand. "Easy, mate. No need to be all defensive."

"Have you talked to Chloe since last night?"

"A bit, when Esther and I dropped her to the airport this morning."

The airport. A block of ice hit the bottom of his stomach. "What? Has she gone?"

"What do you expect? You broke up with her, and she's devastated. Her dad has paid for her to go home early." Daniel sat down on the edge of the unmade bed.

"What else did she tell you?"

"That's real nice of you, Mike, to show so much concern for the woman you were going to marry."

"It was fake. We were never engaged." The engagement may have been fake, but the pain didn't feel fake.

Daniel raised his eyebrows and caught Michael's attention. "Really, Mike? It was all fake? You have no feelings for her whatsoever?"

Michael swallowed. He had feelings all right. They'd been bludgeoned to death when Chloe had broken his trust and let out his most guarded secret.

"I know it was more than some pretend arrangement, Mike. I saw the way you looked at her. I saw the way the two of you got on together. There was some serious chemistry going on. Don't deny it."

Michael shrugged. "She has exposed a part of me I never intended anyone should ever know."

"And yet you told her. Why?"

Michael closed his eyes and flopped back on the bed.

"You need to talk, mate. This situation with your family has obviously controlled you forever. It's time you got it out in the open."

"What about Harold? My situation is as ugly as it gets in terms of family values. I'm not what he thinks he hired."

"Have you talked to Harold about it?"

Michael shook his head.

"Don't you think you should give him a chance before judging him?" Daniel said.

"Me? I'm not the one who's judgmental!" Michael sat back up, his body tense.

"Really? It looks pretty judgmental to me. You might be right about Harold, but you haven't given him a chance to defend himself." This was why Daniel was a good lawyer.

"I can't afford to find out that he'll fire me. I need the job."

"He can't fire you. If he did, you could take him to the Fair Work Tribunal and sue him. He knows that, and you know that as well."

Michael blew out another breath. Of course he knew that, but that wasn't the point.

"What's really going on, Mike? You've got to talk about it."

A thousand different thoughts and emotions chased around in Michael's sleep-fudged brain, pretending to land, and then flying off again.

"So, you don't know who your father is. Could it be you're looking for approval from the boss?"

Michael swallowed. Daniel was too perceptive by half.

"What makes you think Harold will disapprove," Daniel continued, "just because you have a different family background?"

"Because that's what he's always said, right from the first interview. Those are the values he espouses in every staff meeting and on every bit of promotional information. Stable family makes for stable community. Mother, father, three kids and a dog. You know the drill, Daniel. You epitomise the drill."

Daniel closed his eyes and put his hand on his chin.

"I guess you could look at it like that."

"What other way is there to look at it? My family has consisted of my unwed mother, who struggles with mental illness and a gambling addiction, and myself, who was born as the result of an affair with a married man. This is not the sterling foundation required of Ainsworth and Pembroke employees. I'm not like you."

"We're not that different, I don't think."

"Really? Describe your family for me?"

"Come on, Mike. We're both good lawyers, and your social ethics are the same as mine. You're honest …"

"Not really. I engaged Chloe to help hide my dirty family history."

"OK. If that's how you want it. We're not the same." Daniel sounded like he was losing patience.

"And another thing, I don't support Harold Ainsworth's policy of employing only male lawyers. Our work environment does not reflect gender equality, or inclusiveness," Michael blurted. May as well be hung for a sheep as a lamb.

"Well, if it means so much to you, why haven't you talked to him about it?"

Michael stalled. He was back to square one.

"If you're honest—you're looking for his approval."

"Well, I guess that's blown now, isn't it? I'm sure he won't approve of this last stunt, even if he might have overlooked my history."

"Once again, mate, I think you're pre-judging, and you should give the man a chance to speak for himself."

"I wish I had your confidence." Michael's shoulders slumped again.

"I'll come with you, when you're ready to talk to him."

Michael looked at Daniel—the man who had a wife and three plus kids.

"I don't like the way you control your wife either." Did he just say that? Michael waited for Daniel's reaction.

"Are you practising your confrontation technique?"

"You always talk over her and treat her as if she's the little woman at home."

"Don't you worry about Esther. She's got her own mind, and we work as a team."

"I don't see any evidence of that."

"That's because you don't know us. In all the time we've worked together, you've yet to respond to an invitation of friendship. Is that because you don't approve of us? Don't we meet up to your standards?"

"What?" How had Daniel turned the responsibility back on him?

"Do you not trust us because we come from a different background to you?"

"Well, let's face it. You have no idea what it's like to live on social security in a council flat, scaping every last cent to just make ends meet."

"True. But we've tried to understand. Twice a month I go with that charity shower-bus that serves the homeless."

"What?"

"They need volunteers to cook a barbeque for the clients who use the shower-bus, then I sit with them and chat while they eat. I've tried to understand who they are and what their needs are."

"I didn't know that."

"You don't know me, Michael. I wish you'd pull your guard down and get to know me. I still think we'd get on really well together, and Esther has connected with Chloe."

"Yeah, well, it's too late for that now. Chloe and I are not going to happen. It never was going to happen. I can't afford a wife. If you only knew how bad things were at my house, you'd understand."

"You get some more sleep, and we'll talk about this some more later. I mean to understand you, Michael Sullivan. And I hope you'll allow us in your life. You never know what might happen from there."

***

Michael jolted awake at 2:59 pm exactly. Most of the day had gone and no one else had come knocking on his door. Were they ignoring him? Or was his situation too hard to deal with? Well, fine. He didn't need their prying.

Chloe wouldn't have pried. She would have hugged him and held on until their breathing came into unison. Chloe understood him. And yet she'd broken his trust by blabbing.

Why would she do that?

He loved her and her actions had hurt. Still, he missed her.

He rolled over and retrieved his phone from the bedside table, opened his favorite contacts and hovered his thumb over Chloe's number.

He was desperate to talk to her and have her tell him it would be all right. But he'd broken it off with her, and she'd gone home. It was best. That's what they'd always planned would happen, but he'd had no idea this heartache would be part of it.

A low gurgling in his stomach forced his attention to the fact he'd not eaten since last night. Room service was an option so he sat on the edge of the bed and opened the hotel directory to read the menu. If Chloe had still been here, he would have got her to join him and they could have talked. She'd said she was sorry last night. He would have forgiven her. But she wasn't here. He'd told her they were finished. He'd signed the letter as if it were a legal document and callously left it for her to find under her door.

Would she forgive him?

He banged the hotel guide down on the bed. It was finished. They had only done what they'd originally planned. Their relationship had no future. He could not afford a wife, and that situation was not going to change.

His phone buzzed and he picked it up. Daniel.

Come on down for a bite to eat when you're ready.

That man was like a dog at a bone. Could he go down and face everyone? *Should* he go down and face everyone? Chloe would say 'yes'. She would tell him the longer he left it, the harder it would get.

Why had she left?

Because he'd told her he was finished with her. *I'm such an idiot.* But it would have happened sooner or later. He couldn't take the relationship to the next level. That was his status. It had always been his status—nothing had changed.

Except he loved Chloe.

The phone buzzed again.

I'm ordering you a burger with the lot. Hope you're not allergic to beetroot.

Chapter Fifteen

The ride home from the airport was awkward. Chloe didn't know if she wanted to talk about it, but she could tell her mother was dying to know details.

"Do you want me to pick you up something to eat?" Mum asked.

"I don't feel like eating."

"That's typical of a broken heart."

"Mum! You said you thought it was for the best. You haven't been happy with Michael since we announced our engagement."

"Your fake engagement."

"OK. Listen, I'm sorry. I just wanted to teach you a lesson. You can't go around showing my photograph to random strangers."

"And yet …"

"Don't quote Cam and Megan at me. I'm not in the mood."

"I was talking about you. You're heartbroken over Michael—and this from a fake relationship."

"The relationship wasn't fake—in the end—only the engagement."

"But you would have liked for it to have been real?"

"Mum. Please. I fell for him so bad. This breakup has torn my heart out."

"But you knew it was going to happen."

"I'd hoped he would change his mind. I don't care if he hasn't got any money. He's so worried about his mother—thinking that I couldn't handle her with her problems—but honestly, with the proper care and with a family to love her, I'm sure she would improve."

"That's not always how it works out, darling."

"But it might have worked out—mightn't it?"

"Michael has been dealing with his mother's issues all his life. From what you've told me, her case seems to be chronic."

"So, is that a reason to abandon a good man? I thought you were the one who said that life wasn't always rosy and plain sailing. Sometimes people deal with issues that last a lifetime. For better or worse, right?"

"Are you prepared to understand how serious his mother's condition is? And are you prepared to stick with him—and her—for the rest of your life?"

Chloe took in a deep breath. To be honest, she could only think about Michael and how she felt when they were together. It wasn't a pleasant thought to consider they might be on call constantly for a person who struggled with life.

She let go the breath. "Well it doesn't matter anyway, because Michael has ended it."

Mum let go of one hand on the steering wheel and reached across to squeeze her forearm.

"Give him time, Chloe. If what you felt was real for you, it was probably real for him as well. This is the first time in his life he's had to let his work-world get a glimpse of his home life, and it's obvious that's something he'd hoped would never happen."

"Do you think he'll forgive me?"

"What do you think? You know him better than me."

"I hope so. I miss him something fierce."

***

This was awkward. Were they all talking about him behind their hands?

"Relax," Daniel plonked the loaded plate in front him. An Aussie burger with egg, beetroot, onions—the lot. Plus, a huge pile of golden fried chips. "Get that in you, and then we'll talk about step two."

Michael was too hungry to stop and consider what step two might be. Eat first, panic later.

"You mind sharing the chips?" Daniel asked.

"You bought them. Help yourself."

"Ainsworth and Pembroke bought them, to be precise. Just wasn't sure how hungry you were." Daniel reached across and swiped a couple of chips.

"I'll order something else after if this isn't enough." Michael ignored the knife and fork and lifted the loaded burger, dripping with beetroot juice and mayonnaise.

"You always eat when you're anxious?"

"How do you know I'm anxious?" Michael ignored manners and talked around the food in his mouth.

"It's written all over your face, and I've become an expert in body language. It always helps when I'm trying to discern the truth from witnesses."

Michael grunted as he shoved two chips in his mouth.

"Speaking of discerning the truth …"

"Don't—please."

"You love Chloe, don't you?"

Michael picked up the massive burger again and bit into it, hoping it would serve as a barrier between him and the question he didn't want to answer.

"I'll take that as a yes."

Michael took another bite, but the food was becoming more difficult to swallow. Daniel's superpower was unnerving.

"So, I've arranged for you and me to play a round of golf with the boss in the morning."

"What?" This came out over a mouthful of half masticated beef burger and bread.

"Nice, Sullivan. I see that private school education did wonders for your table etiquette."

Michael chewed the half-processed chunks of food. "I'm not going to talk to Harold Ainsworth," he said after swallowing what was in his mouth.

"Actually, he asked me to set it up. He's the boss. You're on his time—so—we're playing golf in the morning."

Michael stared at Daniel. If he maintained the eye contact, would his colleague fold?

"You're going. End of story." Daniel swiped another chip.

Apparently not.

"You've taken a high-handed approach here," Michael said.

"Mate, I'm concerned for you, and this whole business—you and Chloe, your mother, Harold Ainsworth—it's all a horrible mess, and it has to be brought out into the open."

"So, you don't think Chloe should have kept her mouth shut?"

"If you'd treated her properly in the first place and weren't so intent on hiding things, she wouldn't have needed to keep her mouth shut. You were the one who put her in that impossible situation. Fancy letting her be subjected to a relationships game, where you knew they were going to ask personal questions. What did you expect her to do?"

Daniel raised a valid point. He should argue in a court of law.

"Do you want to stay in and watch a movie tonight?" Daniel kept talking as if he hadn't just made a huge accusation.

"Yeah. I think I'd prefer to be alone."

"I didn't mean on your own. I meant with me and Esther."

"What? No! I don't want to sit and watch your domestic bliss."

"OK, then I'll just come on my own."

"You're just going to ditch your wife to come and mope with me in my misery?"

"Esther is worried about you."

"Just me?"

"She's worried about you and Chloe. She thinks you're made for each other, and she can't stand the fact that you've broken up."

Michael thinned his lips and hummed.

"So, I'll drop by your room around seven?"

"Nothing corporate planned for this evening?"

"Nothing we need be worried about. I'll come and keep you company."

They say misery loves company, but did misery love a pushy, meddling friend? That remained to be seen.

***

Michael hated golf. It was so stereotypical for lawyers to walk around the green with white cardigans draped over their shoulders. He opted to wear his basketball shorts and sneakers with a blue t-shirt. He felt out of place—he may as well look out of place.

"I've been looking forward to spending time with you, Michael," Harold said, as they walked out of the club room onto the course.

"Thank you for inviting me."

Michael waited for Daniel to fill in the awkward gaps but he didn't say anything. *Now he chooses to keep his mouth shut.*

"What's your handicap?" Harold asked.

"I'm a little over par," Daniel answered throwing Michael a quick frown. Talk about body language.

"And you, Michael?"

"I'm just handicapped when it comes to golf. I've only ever played a couple of times when they forced us to for sport."

Harold laughed.

Michael hadn't meant it to be funny.

"Not to worry," Harold said. "My main purpose this morning is fresh air, exercise and getting to know you a bit better."

They were at the first tee and Harold had already pulled a ball and plastic tee from his pocket. "I'll go first, if you like."

Michael was just as happy for him to go first, second and third. He would count himself lucky if he hit the ball at all.

After a few seconds watching a beautiful swing and follow through, the ball sailed in a gorgeous arc towards the first hole. Then Daniel had his shot. It wasn't quite as beautiful to watch, but at least he hit the ball in the right direction.

"Your shot," Daniel said.

Thank you, Captain Obvious.

Michael tried to copy the movement and style of his two companions and ended up digging a divot out of the tee, with his ball stumbling and falling to a dead halt ten meters along and in the rough. This was going to be a long morning.

"You really haven't played much golf, have you?" Harold said, as he sheathed his driving iron and began to pull the golf cart along the green.

"I haven't had time to focus on anything but study and work, if I'm entirely honest."

"Your CV indicated you'd gone to an exclusive college and international university. How did your mother manage, if she was on her own?"

"I won scholarships, and I worked jobs on the side to help make ends meet."

"Even in high school?"

Michael shrugged. What did it matter now? He was going to hear the whole ugly truth. This is what Daniel and Russell had advised.

"And your father? Did he pay child support?"

"I don't know who my father is. I was the result of an affair with a married man."

The words slipped out easily now. Since Chloe's explosive revelation, all of Michael's defenses had been blown away.

"I'm very sorry to hear that."

Michael dropped his head. Now it would come. Perhaps he couldn't fire him, but he could certainly shun him and push him to the back office under paperwork."

"Michael has had to work very hard to get where he is, and he still supports his mother." Daniel offered this information. Michael hardly remembered telling him. Perhaps Chloe had told him.

"That is an admirable quality, Michael."

Michael looked up. Did he just hear affirmation from Harold Ainsworth?

"My mother has a mental illness, and she has a gambling problem. With all of my student loans and the gambling debts she ran up while I was overseas, I am on the brink of bankruptcy."

"You could declare bankruptcy, if it's that bad," Harold said. "You could start again. They'll let you keep your car, but you'd have to sell your house."

"We've never owned a house. We live in a council rental, and I don't own a car."

"I've seen you drive a car many times. An expensive car, if memory serves."

"I hire a car if the situation requires. Other than that, it's pushbike and public transport."

Harold sighed. What was that look on his face? Pity? Compassion?

"You could still file for bankruptcy."

"I'm trying to be honorable and pay my debts."

"I'm sorry, Michael. I had no idea you were doing it so tough."

Michael shrugged his shoulders again. "It is what it is."

They were at his ball and Harold drew out a driver and handed it to Michael. "I think this is the best one to get you out of this mess."

If only he could hand him something to get him out of his financial and relational mess just as easily.

Chapter Sixteen

Chloe checked her phone so often it drew comment from her work colleagues.

"Chloe, keep your mind on the job," Nicki said.

"Sorry."

"Are you expecting a call from someone?"

"Hoping, not expecting."

"Your fiancé?" Nicki snapped the file shut and handed it to Chloe to put away.

"We had a fight while we were away. I haven't heard from him since."

"Why don't you call him on your next break and find out what's going on?"

"He told me we should call it off."

"But you haven't accepted that."

"It's hard, Nicki. I still love him."

"Part of life, darl. I bet you're not the only one in this crazy department who's nursing a broken heart."

"Maybe not, but I'm the only one pretending it doesn't hurt."

Nicki shook her head, picked up her tray of instruments and walked out of the room. OK, so that comment was totally self-focussed. There were people waiting to be seen all round the emergency department, and it was obvious a heap of them had more troubles than you could poke a stick at.

But it hurt. Chloe wanted to call Michael and beg him to see her. She hated how much not seeing him hurt.

By the time the shift was over she was still dwelling on the pain in her heart, having attended to her nursing duties on autopilot. She plugged her phone into her car and was toying with the idea of sending a text to Michael when she was taken aback by an incoming text flashing across her screen—Michael was texting her.

Heart beating faster than usual, and anxiety twisting her intestines into a knot, she slid her finger across the text to open it.

Hey Chloe. Can I catch up with you for half an hour after you finish work?

Was this a good thing? Too bad if not, because she had to see him. She quickly fired back an answer.

I just finished. Where do you want to meet?

Several tense seconds while she waited for a reply to ping.

At my office.

He'd included the address. Her heart plummeted. Was this just business? She opened her maps app and punched in the address. Too bad if it was just business, she was desperate to see him. She would take what she could get.

"I'm here to see Michael Sullivan." Chloe leaned on the sleek wooden reception counter and smiled as sweetly as she could at the receptionist.

"Are you Ms Brooker?"

"Yes. He's expecting me."

"Just take a seat for a few moments. He's just finishing with another client."

Another client? Was that how it was—her being the next client waiting? Please God, let him forgive her.

A few moments turned into ten minutes, and the waiting was torture. Eventually she heard his voice in the hallway leading to the offices. Should she stand up? Chloe, the fiancée, would stand up ready to throw herself into his arms. Chloe, the client, should sit and wait demurely until called. She didn't want to be a client, but she'd embarrassed him enough their last time together, so she forced herself to sit tight and wait patiently.

A young couple walked out into the reception area and went to finalize their bill. Chloe watched. Watched and waited. Watched and waited and wrestled with the urge to run in search of him.

"You may go through now, Ms Brooker." Finally, the receptionist spoke. "Third door on the left."

Taking a deep breath and trying to rein in her turbulent emotions, Chloe took her bag and walked down the hall to the third door on the left. His name—Michael Sullivan—was inscribed on the gold nameplate. Mouth dry and heart hammering, she knocked on the slightly ajar door with her knuckles.

"Come in." His voice, so professional—and aloof.

"Come in, Chloe. Have a seat."

No welcoming hug, or smile, or kiss, or profession of undying love. This was killing her. Still she sat.

"Thanks for coming."

"Michael, I'm so sorry for what happened."

His face tightened, but there was no softness there.

"If I could take it back I would. I've missed you so much."

"Chloe …"

"I don't care about your background, or your family, or your debt. I just want to be with you."

"Chloe, please."

She shut her mouth. His tone said it all. He had not called her here to reopen the relationship.

"I just need to let you know about the court case for your speeding fine. I can go and represent you in court, unless you'd like to come as well. I believe it will be a straightforward affair."

"I should go, shouldn't I?"

"It would be better if you were there, but given … our … you know … situation."

"I'll be there."

"Chloe …"

She looked up when she heard the softness in his tone. He was looking at her with a sad expression.

"Won't you forgive me?" Chloe asked, her throat tightening and eyes stinging with tears.

"I forgive you, Chloe, it's just that nothing has changed."

"Everything has changed. We love each other, don't we?"

"Love is not going to pay the bills, and the love you feel now would dim fairly quickly if you were forced to live in a small council flat with my mother."

"But I can afford to pay for a better house for us."

"That's just it, Chloe. At this point, I can't leave my mother alone. In many ways, she's a danger to herself. I need to look after her, and I can't ask you to take that on."

His words dampened her argument. Mum had advised her to consider what it would be like to take on someone as vulnerable as Alison Sullivan, for better or for worse. It was difficult.

"I always said we would break up after the retreat. That's how it has to be. I'm sorry."

Her traitorous chin began to quiver again, and her eyes began to leak. Was there any use begging him to change his mind—to take her in his arms—to kiss her hurt away?

"Here are the papers for you to sign." He spoke softly as he pushed a folder to the other side of his desk. "I'll take care of this for you. Perhaps it's better if you don't worry to come."

Biting her bottom lip and swiping at a couple of stray tears, Chloe stepped over and picked up the pen. His beautiful hand held the papers firm while she signed. This was too hard. Why couldn't they make this work?

"I'll let you know once it's all sorted."

She heard 'goodbye' in his tone. This was goodbye. He wanted her to let him go.

She swallowed the lump in her throat, picked up her bag and forced a smile.

"Thank you, Michael."

So many other things she wanted to say, but couldn't. She turned and walked out of his office—and his life.

***

Michael stood up and closed the door after Chloe. He leaned his head against it, eyes closed, emotion threatening to choke him. Why did this have to be so hard? If he left his mother to her own devices, to manage her own financial burdens and illness, he could chase after a future with a woman whom he'd definitely come to adore.

But he couldn't. Mum had already slumped when she'd heard about the breakup, and he had to take her back to the psych to see if they needed to change meds. He knew he shouldn't have introduced Chloe to her.

A rapping on the door caught Michael by surprise, and he drew back, ran his hand through his hair and checked to see if his tie was straight.

"Michael." It was Daniel. It didn't matter if he saw him in a state.

"Come in." Michael opened the door and waved his colleague—friend would describe him better since their time away—into the office.

"I just saw Chloe in the hall. She seemed upset."

"Yeah."

"Mate. Why can't you fix things with her?"

"Because I can't. I don't have the means to fix everybody."

"You mean your mother."

"You know I can't just leave her to her to fend for herself. I have a plan to get us back in the black, and a plan to try and manage her mental state."

"Have you asked your mother if she's happy with the plan?"

"She trusts me to take care of everything."

"So, she doesn't know about Chloe?"

"That's the only thing she's not happy about."

"She doesn't like Chloe?"

"The opposite. She wants me to marry her and get busy having grandbabies for her."

"But...?"

"We've been over this. I don't want to have to keep defending my decisions."

Daniel shrugged.

"It's your call, mate, but Chloe looked pretty cut up as she was leaving."

"I can't help it."

"Do you want to come around for a barbeque on the weekend?"

Michael sighed. "I don't think I would be much company."

"Bring your mum with you. Perhaps we can cheer you both up."

"I'll see. Not promising anything."

"Good enough. Oh, and by the way, Harold wants you to do some research on a child support situation."

"That's not really my area."

"Yeah, I know, but he's doing a favor for someone and they need to find out if they can sue for damages."

"Damages? Doesn't he mean to make the father—I assume the parent at fault is the father—pay what he owes?"

"I'm not sure. Could you just do the research and find out the rough numbers and get back to him?" Daniel put the file on Michael's desk. "Let me know about Saturday night. Esther wants you to come."

"Mmm." No way was he committing to a social outing. If they thought Chloe was upset and miserable, it was nothing to what he felt. He just wanted to do his work, go home and sleep.

Chapter Seventeen

Harold Ainsworth had made an appointment to see him. That was ominous. Nothing bad had come of the disastrous revelation so far. Daniel had been nothing but supportive, and his other co-workers had gone about their business as usual, as if they didn't know that his home life was a mess.

How would Harold Ainsworth act? The horrible golf day had yielded only concern. But who wouldn't feel sorry for him—his golf swing was useless. It was unlikely Harold would do anything drastic like end Michael's employment. There had been no sign of that. But what did he want to talk about? Hopefully it was just about this research he'd been doing into this outstanding child support case. He had some figures ready, but wasn't sure of the particulars of the case. Had some effort already been made to recover the money through the tax department, as was usual practice, automatic deductions taken out of pay along with tax?

Eleven o'clock ticked past and Michael picked up his research folder to take to Harold's office. Just as he turned the handle on his office door, there was a knock, and he opened it straight away.

"Harold. I was just on my way."

"I thought I'd come to you this time."

How odd. Harold Ainsworth had never met him in his office before.

"Is that all right?" Harold asked.

"Right. Yes. Of course. Come in."

The awe-inspiring boss came into Michael's office, and he was suddenly aware of how impersonal his space was. The other lawyers had ornaments, framed family photos, and personal items like inscribed paper weights that reflected personality. Michael had nothing but the company furniture and fixtures and the lone photograph of him and his mother.

Harold walked straight over to it and picked it up.

"This is your mother, I assume."

"Yes. That was taken when I was four."

Harold returned the photograph to the shelf but didn't say anything. What was he thinking? Mum didn't look like a nicely-dressed wife of anybody significant. She looked like Mum, when she had been less mentally fragile. The big-hair style with teased fringe, dressed in a lime-green t-shirt and navy skirt with floral patterns—all reminiscent of the 1980s. It was the best photograph he had of the two of them.

"I just wanted to follow up on that child support case I asked you to research," Harold said. "What have you found out?"

"There are still a lot of unknowns about the case, and so everything is ballpark and probables."

"I'm encouraging you to chase up the unknowns, Michael."

"I don't know the client."

"You're the client." Harold looked at him with a no-nonsense expression.

A jolt of something sharp hit Michael mid-chest.

"What? I didn't ask you to look into my past. I didn't want you to even know about it."

"Nonetheless, I'm encouraging you—asking you—to investigate."

There was an authority to Harold. Michael had seen it before, of course, but he'd always been amenable to whatever job needed doing. But this …?

"No. I couldn't chase something like this up."

"Why?"

"For a start, I have no idea who my father is."

"Have you asked your mother?"

"I used to ask when I was younger, but she said it was better I didn't know."

"Why?"

"Because he'd been married at the time of the affair. There was no way he was going to acknowledge a child, given he already had a wife."

"That isn't an excuse for him to leave you and your mother to fend for yourselves all these years. You know that isn't an excuse, Michael."

"I just don't see how I can do anything about it. It's probably too late now."

"I'm not so sure it is."

"Regardless, I doubt Mum would tell me who he is. She's not been well—mental illness—for years. She's not emotionally strong."

"Michael, I would like to meet your mother."

That sharp pang again. Why was Harold pushing this?

"Why?"

"Perhaps if I explain to her the importance of knowing who your father is and how much that might mean if we were to pursue this case."

"What if he's a derelict, down-on-his-luck no-hoper?"

"What if he's the CEO of a national bank?"

"Unlikely."

"Do you take after your mother in terms of your academic ability?"

"She was at university when she became pregnant with me, so she obviously had some academic intelligence."

"If she met your father at university, don't you think it possible he went on to a successful and well-paying career?"

"I guess it's possible."

"I would like to meet your mother and ask her blessing to represent you in this case."

"Really?" Suddenly tears stung Michael's eyes. Far from judging him for his dysfunctional background, Harold Ainsworth was proposing to act as his champion against the poverty and neglect that had been his inheritance from his father. "I don't know what to say."

"Make a telephone call and see when is a convenient time to call on your mother."

How would she react to meeting his boss? Would she be pleased? Would she hide in her room? Would she even have the energy to get up and be polite?

"I'm not really sure she'll cope."

"It's all right, Michael. I'm not going to judge you, or her, just because she's been struggling with life. Make the appointment for later this afternoon, and I'll drive you home. Save you catching public transport."

***

Mum had been cagey when he called.

"What do you want to bring *him* here for?"

"He's my boss and he's wanting to help recover money owed to us."

172

"Is he just? We'll see how long that lasts."

Michael hung up from the call but was confused. He knew he'd not sung Harold Ainsworth's praises, but he hadn't realized he'd conveyed so much negative feeling to his mother. He felt somewhat ashamed of the way he'd presumed Harold was a self-righteous snob, particularly when Harold continued to show care and determination to fight for Michael's rights.

"I hope this isn't a mistake," Michael said as they pulled up outside the front of his small duplex council house.

"I only want to help," Harold said.

"I apologize ahead of time if she's aggressive or indifferent. Her moods swing around a lot."

"I'm sure she will understand once I've explained it all to her."

Michael didn't have the same confidence but opened the small gate that led onto the garden path. The lawn needed mowing again. It wasn't as high as the grass on some houses in the street, but it was shabby nonetheless. But it was no use wishing that either his mother would take on the extra responsibility, or that a genie would appear and see to it that the front yard was kept clipped and neat.

Michael inserted his key into the lock and opened the front door.

"Come in." He led Harold into the small sitting room. "Mum. We have a visitor."

There was no answer and Michael's heart sank. Was she curled up in bed with the covers over her head again?

"Mum?" He stepped toward the bedroom door that came off the sitting room. "I'm sorry, Harold. I won't be a moment."

He pushed the bedroom door open, but she wasn't there. "Mum?" This scene was ludicrous—evidence of dysfunction marked every aspect of his home, and yet his boss stood confidently just inside the door with a look on his face that said … what was that? Sadness? He didn't want pity.

Michael stepped through to the small kitchen at the back of the house. She wasn't there either. Where was she? He opened the back door and called. "Mum?"

"What? Are you home already?" His mother walked out of the laundry door with a basket of washing under her arm. This was strange. She looked tidy—focused—and as if she had energy and purpose.

"We have a visitor. Can you come inside for a few minutes?"

"Go and put the kettle on. I'll just hang these on the line."

There was no use arguing with her. Michael couldn't tell where she was in her mood cycle. He would guess on a high—given the energy to do laundry. He stepped inside and went back to the sitting room. "She won't be a few minutes, Harold. I'll put the kettle on. Do you want tea? Sorry, I don't have proper coffee."

"Just a glass of water, if that's all right," Harold replied.

"Please have a seat. I'll just be a moment."

This was so awkward. Why did his mother have to take to domestic diligence just when he needed her to come inside and listen to Harold's proposal?

He took a glass of water back to the sitting room and handed it to Harold.

"How long have you lived here?" Harold asked.

"As long as I can remember. Apparently, my grandparents kicked Mum out when she came home pregnant. She's never had any other family support."

"I'm so sorry, Michael."

"Not your fault."

The back door banged and Michael looked up to see his mother come into the sitting room.

"Hello, Harry." Mum said.

"Alison."

What. Was. That? Michael looked from one to the other, his head beginning to spin.

"Have you met before?"

Harold ignored him as he stood up, face to face with his mother. "Tell me the truth, Alison. Is Michael my son?"

***

Michael wanted to run and hide—on second thought, he wanted to punch someone. No that wouldn't do. This was a crazy nightmare.

"I thought you knew," Mum said. "I thought that was why you gave him the job."

"Knew what? Mum, what are you saying?"

"I didn't know," Harold persisted.

"What? Didn't you remember my last name was Sullivan?"

Michael's eyes swung to watch Harold's response.

"How many Sullivan's are there in this state? I had no idea. I thought you'd—"

"Got rid of him?" Mum gave a bitter smile. "Turns out I couldn't do it."

This conversation was a nightmare, and Michael could hardly keep up.

"Why didn't you tell me?" Harold asked.

"What would your wife have said?"

"Stop!" Michael broke into the dialog. "Just stop!"

They both ceased talking and looked at him.

"What ... I don't ... I'm confused."

"I thought you knew Harry was your father."

Michael looked at his mother as if she'd lost her mind. "How would I know?"

"I thought he would have told you."

"I didn't know," Harold defended. "Why didn't you say something?"

"Because you wanted it kept quiet before, and if you'd wanted to say something I figured you would."

"But I didn't know." Harold sounded angry.

"Just look at him. Can't you see your family resemblance in him?" Mum asked.

Both eyes turned to scrutinise him and Michael felt like a bug under a magnifying glass.

"When I saw your picture in his office, it was the first time I knew for sure he must be mine."

Michael swallowed the tension in his throat. They were standing there talking about him as if he wasn't in the room. Harold Ainsworth—the man so insistent on family values—was standing in his house admitting to an adulterous affair and a plot to end his illegitimate son's existence by aborting him. Anger began to boil deep within. For months Michael had tiptoed around his workplace, hiding his family heritage, when all the time, his boss was the one who'd caused their misfortune.

"Michael?" Mum looked at him. "Don't tell me you didn't know."

Michael shook his head.

"I can't believe you—either of you. Mum, you knew I was working for the man who got us into this mess, and you never said anything."

"I didn't ..."

He held up his hand to stave her off.

"And you, Harold, right from the start kept impressing on me how important it was that your firm represented honesty, integrity and family moral values ... and all the time ... you're a bloody hypocrite."

"I'm sorry ..."

"I don't want to hear it."

Michael turned and left the house by the front door. How useless was this? He felt like getting in a fast car and spinning the wheels as he roared out of the street. But as it was, he didn't even have his bicycle. He had left it at work so he could ride home with Harold the hypocrite. All he had was his two good walking legs, and he put on some speed to put distance between himself and this hideous revelation.

Chapter Eighteen

Why did everything have to boil down to money? Liam knew he'd allowed Evelyn to believe he could overlook her social and financial situation—he wanted to. Society, however, was not as forgiving, and quite suddenly obsessed with calling in debts and favors. The Bradshaw estate could support the family as it was, and perhaps if he took on a destitute wife, but that was only if no calamity befell them. Liam knew there were no funds put aside as insurance against disaster. Without such insurance, Liam was putting his whole staff and the tenants in a precarious position. Could he turn aside a plea for help should a flood destroy the year's crops? He knew he couldn't. And his neighbor, wealthy merchant, Rufus Havecock, knew that he knew that he couldn't.

"My terms are simple, Bradshaw," Havecock said. "You take on my Henrietta, and I will see that a dowry comes with her worth your estate and more."

Liam didn't want to seem ungrateful, or proud, but he wasn't in love with Lady Henrietta Havecock. The woman he loved was alone inside, unprotected and unwanted by any gentleman of means—except him. He wanted her. He loved Evelyn Dixon, but he was coming to the conclusion that love may not be enough. It was his duty as Lord of Bradshaw Manor, to see to the interests of all who depended on him. Lady Henrietta could help him with this. Evelyn could not.

Stupid situation. How am I going to get them out of this one? Louise hated painting herself into a corner and not having already plotted a suitable way out. She should have taken more time to get the story sorted out—not just the obligatory happily-ever-after ending but all the points leading up to it.

She was pulled from her frustration by her phone. A convenient distraction, until she saw the caller ID. Michael. He was as bad as Liam with his indecision.

"Hello, Michael. How can I help?" She sounded laissez-faire. This relationship was going nowhere and she was reluctant to become more emotionally invested.

"Hi, Louise. How are you?"

"I'm good, Michael. If you're calling to speak to Chloe, she's at work."

"Actually, I was wondering if Russell was home?"

Louise scrambled to mentally adjust. What was going on? Why Russell?

"Sorry if it's a bother," Michael continued. "I don't want to interrupt your dinner."

That's a thought. I probably should have dinner on by now.

"Russell isn't home yet," Louise said. "Is there anything I can help you with?"

"Would it be OK if you sent me his phone number? I have something I'd like to talk to him about."

Was he going to renew the courtship? What could Russell help him with that she couldn't. She hated to be left out of the loop.

"I'll text his contact details to you. Is everything all right?"

"Yes. Fine. I just need some advice."

That was her department—love advice particularly. This not-knowing was killing her.

"Is there anything I can help you with—advice wise, I mean?"

"Not at the moment, but thanks for asking."

She was losing her grip. How infuriating.

"I'm sending it through now, Michael. I hope everything is all right."

She was casting more bait than Captain Ahab and catching nothing. Michael didn't even bite on that last comment.

She heard a ping on his end and knew the information was transferred.

"Thanks, Louise. I appreciate your help."

Help? What help? All she'd done was send him her husband's number. This mystery was going to drive her nuts until she had all the details. How was she supposed to put her best foot forward if she didn't know what direction they were heading in?

***

This was absolutely ridiculous. Without a moment's hesitation Russell had said he'd come and pick him up—a good half hour's drive out of his way. Michael sat in a café in the city and toyed with the coffee he'd bought just so he had an excuse to sit somewhere.

He had a father. A man he knew well, but didn't know at all. Harold Ainsworth was a phoney. He'd lied to his wife and he'd lied to his employees—continually spouting about how a strong and stable family was a good foundation for society, and therefore their number one priority.

Michael's phone pinged. Russell was parked outside and waiting. Michael took a long swig of the tepid coffee and left the café. He recognized the SUV parked several doors down and approached, but when he opened the passenger door, he was suddenly overwhelmed with emotion.

"Hey, Mike. Get in." Russell's tone was kind and caring, and that made it worse. Standing on the street was not an option, so he had to bank the tears stinging his eyes and force himself to breathe over the lump in his throat.

"You OK?"

Simple innocuous words, but they were the catalyst that caused the explosion. No macho-mask to put into place, just open vulnerability which had found a safe landing place.

"You OK, mate?" Russell was looking at him, and the concern was evident in his tone. "What happened?"

Michael's vocal apparatus refused to work. He had a job to keep his facial muscles in any semblance of order. He could only shake his head in response.

"Chloe?"

If only. Just thinking of her was the last straw, and his whole demeanor completely collapsed. He covered his face with his hands and began to sob. Poor Russell. Bet this wasn't his usual method of operation when talking to the boys.

But Russell didn't say anything. He just put his hand on Michael's shoulder and let him cry. It took about two minutes to rein the runaway emotions in.

"Tell me what happened."

"My father has made an appearance at last."

"Go on."

"Harold Ainsworth."

There was an awkward silence while Russell was obviously trying to process.

"Your boss?"

Michael nodded.

"Your boss is your father?"

181

This was sounding very *Star Wars*, but what else could he say?

"How did you find out?"

"That business where Chloe let everyone know my family background must have got him thinking. I'm not sure how he put two and two together, but this afternoon he fronted my mother and asked her straight out."

"Did you know he was going to do that?"

"I had no idea. Mum knew all along but didn't tell me because she thought he would tell me. I feel like such an idiot."

"So, it wasn't a joyful reunion?"

"He makes me sick. I can't believe he would come forward now after pushing to have me aborted, and then ignoring me all these years, while Mum and I struggled to get food on the table."

"To be fair, did he know your Mum had carried the pregnancy and not terminated?"

"He says not."

Russell shrugged.

"Why on earth did he turn into a conservative crusader, looking down on anyone who didn't fit the straight and moral image he pretended to have?"

"Did you ask him why?"

Michael shook his head. "I couldn't stomach listening to any more from either of them."

Russell didn't say anything. Michael's thoughts were still tumultuous and burning with bitterness but Russell's quiet, accepting strength soon drew his attention.

"How do you think I should have responded?" Michael eventually asked.

"I guess you have every right to be hurt and angry."

"But?"

"But we all make mistakes. Somewhere along the line, we have to try to get our lives back into order and hope others forgive us."

"I don't even want to think about forgiving him at the moment."

"Fair enough. Do you want to stay over at our house for the night? Give yourself a chance to process what's just happened?"

Michael looked at his hands. He couldn't face going home. He could hardly go and sleep at the office. And he still couldn't afford to spring for a hotel room.

"I'm not sure Chloe would want to see me."

"She's on night shift tonight. It's doubtful you'd see her."

"I hate to impose."

"I know. But sometimes, you have to find a place to rest."

And that was the truth. Russell was a safe haven. His wife and daughter were quite feisty, but he could live with that—given the alternative.

***

Thank goodness the shift was over. There seemed to be a never-ending supply of emergencies, most people desperate for help, some too high to care whether they hurt themselves or anybody else who tried to assist. Chloe loved that she was able to make a difference in situations where people were in crisis, but sometimes it was so exhausting that one idiot out of their mind on ICE was enough to make her wish she never had to go back into the emergency room again.

It was nearing midnight when she pulled her car into the driveway. She didn't expect Mum and Dad would still be awake, but there was a light on—in the spare bedroom. What was Mum doing there in the middle of the night?

The front door opened into a dark hallway and Chloe toed her shoes off. It was her usual practice to try not to disturb her parents after they'd gone to sleep. Tiptoeing along the wooden floorboards, she listened carefully. Light was shining underneath the door but there was no sound coming from within the room. And no other sound in the house either, except for the usual hum of the refrigerator. Perhaps one of them had been in the room and forgotten to turn the light off.

Chloe put her hand on the door handle and opened the door, intending to flick off the light switch just inside the door, but it wasn't the main light that was on—the bedside lamp—bother. She pushed the door open and stepped into the room.

"Chloe!"

She gave a yelp and stepped back. Heart rate accelerated by fight-or-flight, she took a moment to gather her words.

"What are you doing in my parent's spare room?"

Michael Sullivan was propped up in the spare bed, reading a book, and he was not wearing a shirt of any description.

"Your dad said you were working night shift."

"Late shift."

Typical Dad. He always gets things mixed up. Not that that had anything to do with answering the question.

"So why are you here?"

Michael had tugged at the sheet, but it didn't hide his beautifully carved torso and shoulders.

"I'm sorry. I just needed somewhere to stay for the night, but I can go."

Chloe didn't move from her position by the door. Neither did she avert her gaze.

"Why did you need somewhere to stay? Is your mum OK?"

"I can go, Chloe. You don't need to worry about me."

"Of course I worry about you. Tell me what's happened."

She pulled the spare chair in the corner over to sit near the bed.

"I'm naked here, Chloe. Do you mind?"

"Really?" She grinned at him. He was uncomfortable. "I can't see anything."

"I can't talk to you like this."

"Where's your shirt?"

He looked over at the dressing chest where his suit and dress shirt were draped.

"I've only got my work clothes."

Chloe got up and opened the wardrobe. She knew Pete had left a few bits and pieces for emergencies in his old room. Pete was a bigger man than Michael, but his old t-shirt would do for now. She threw it at Michael.

"This belongs to my brother."

He put it on but still didn't look comfortable.

"Talk to me," Chloe said.

"You know I'd like to talk to you more than anybody else."

"I'm listening."

"But we already discussed this ..." he waved his hand between them.

"Can't we be friends, Michael?"

"No. We can't."

That stung.

"We get on well together, I enjoy your company, and I trust you to share my problems with," she said.

"I know, Chloe, but friendship isn't going to work."

"Come on, Michael. Are you ever going to forgive me?"

"It's got nothing to do with whether I'll forgive you or not."

"What's your problem then?"

"I don't want to be your friend, Chloe."

"You're ridiculous …"

Michael held up his hand.

"If I can't be your husband and lover, I can't just pretend that friendship is going to be enough."

Was that a proposal? Should Chloe feel glad?

"It's not enough, Chloe. I'm sorry."

"I told you before, I don't care about your background or—"

"I found out who my father is today."

"What?"

"My biological father."

"Michael, that's …" she wanted to say 'great', 'brilliant', 'fantastic news', but the look on his face slowed her down. "That's news. How do you feel about it?"

"It's Harold Ainsworth."

It was late and Chloe was tired, but she thought he said …

"Harold Ainsworth? Are you joking?"

"I wish I was."

"I don't get it."

"Believe me, neither do I. And my mother knew I'd been working for him from the beginning."

"She didn't tell you?"

Michael shrugged.

"You're upset about it?"

"Understatement."

"Michael, I don't know what to say."

"There's nothing to say. I just couldn't go home tonight. I feel like Mum has betrayed me."

"So you called my dad."

"When I met your father, it was the first time I've ever felt like I had a dad. You don't know what you've got, Chloe. You should be grateful."

Was he lecturing her on how she should get along with her father?

"Anyway, I don't want to make this awkward for you. Your dad didn't think you'd get home before I left in the morning."

"Yeah, well, I'm here now. Like it or not, I'm your friend, and I don't care if you're staying in the spare room. And I don't care if you want to talk to me about it—or anything you want to talk about."

Chloe didn't move, and Michael just looked at her.

"Are you going to go to bed now?" Michael asked.

"I guess so. Are you sure you don't want to talk about anything else?"

"I doubt I will sleep. There are too many thoughts going around and round in my mind."

"Do you want me to stay with you and keep you company?"

The look on his face said 'yes' even as his lips said 'no'.

"Scared of my dad, are you?"

"Not scared of your dad. I'm scared of myself. I'll be fine, Chloe. Go to bed."

"On one condition."

"Chloe."

"You have to promise to call me and talk if you need to. I'm your friend, even if you want to pretend we mean nothing to each other."

Michael didn't say anything but shuffled down into the bed coverings.

"Promise?" Chloe persisted.

"I'm going to sleep now. Unless you want to sit all night in that chair, I'm going to turn the light out."

What she wanted was to crawl into bed with him and hold him tight. It was completely innocent, but that would not be how her parents would see it if she was still there in the morning. When was Michael going to see that she was ready—for better or worse; for richer or poorer; in sickness and in health?

***

Michael switched the light off as Chloe closed the bedroom door. If he wasn't agitated enough about the day's revelation, having Chloe in such close proximity was sure to provoke his imagination until he went into a flat spin. He should get up and leave, but where would he go at this time of night, even if the buses were running?

He turned over, intent on at least trying to close his eyes when the door opened again.

"Michael?"

Why was she whispering? He rolled over to face the direction her voice was coming through the darkness.

"Yes?"

"I realize you're the sort of person who has to have all his ducks in a row before you can make a decision on anything, but I advise you consider that you might not be able to control everything in your life."

"What do you mean by that?"

"If you're waiting for all the conditions to be exactly right, I might have got old and joined a convent by the time you're ready."

He wanted to laugh at the ridiculous idea.

"You can't fix everything. Sometimes the time is right, even if your ducks aren't in a row."

"The day I met you, was when all my ducks got blown out of the water."

There was an awkward silence. Had he offended her? Not the Chloe he knew, who was ready to speak her mind at any opportunity.

"Well, I'm just saying …" No. She wasn't offended.

"OK. I'll consider your advice."

"And just so you know, I will drive you to work in the morning so you don't have to get up with the birds."

What's with all the bird metaphors? And could he even go to work in the morning? But he was too emotionally exhausted to argue now.

"OK. Thank you, Chloe."

"Good."

"Goodnight, Chloe."

"Goodnight, Michael."

Michael smiled as he buried himself deeper into the bedding. Ducks in a row, huh? If it were possible she would be the only duck he needed to get lined up. Right at this moment, the rest of the world could look after themselves. He was glad she'd forced her way in and let him talk. Hopefully he would be able to sleep.

An hour later, it became apparent that, even though he was comfortable, his mind would not rest. That moment between his mother and boss—Hello, Harry. Hello Alison—it was like an earthquake that kept delivering aftershocks. He closed his eyes but sleep was nowhere to be found, only agitation and confusion. And Chloe's words kept intruding into the emotional re-runs. *You can't fix everything.* Was she insinuating he was a control freak? A quick mental inventory and he decided his whole life was carefully compartmentalised, measured and considered, and he really did believe everything would fall apart if he let go. His mother couldn't cope if he wasn't there to watch over her—could she? Chloe would never be happy sharing his debts and burdens—would she? Harold Ainsworth would never accept him in his state of dysfunction—would he? Now that he knew who Harold really was, did he even want to be accepted by him?

These thoughts rolled around and round, agitated by anger at his mother and boss, and longing for his ex-fake-fiancée.

Chapter Nineteen

$\mathcal{M}$ichael was jolted awake by a knocking on the door.

"It's past seven thirty." It was Louise Brooker calling at the door. "Do you want breakfast?"

"No, thanks, Louise. I better get going."

Get going where? He wasn't ready to go back to work. And he was hungry. He should have accepted the offer.

His head spun with sleep deprivation like a bike in a velodrome. After having put his slightly creased shirt and suit on, he adjusted the tie while looking in the dresser-mirror. No shave this morning. He looked like a bushranger, not a trusted legal professional. There was no way he could go into the office today.

"Do you want to borrow a razor?" Russell asked when he emerged into the kitchen.

Did he? Should he go through the motions of pretending to get ready for work? Would he actually end up going?

"I'll get one for you. You can take a shower too, if you want."

Michael cast his eyes down over his clothes. Did he look like a wreck? He felt like a wreck. He followed Russell to the bathroom and took the towel, razor and soap offered.

"I'll put some toast on for you," Russell said as he left Michael to it.

Michael was tempted to stand under the steady stream and let the hot water work some tension from his neck and shoulders, but it looked like the expectation was he would go to work. He'd better at least try to be on time.

With hair still damp and his creased shirt still open at the neck, Michael opened the door and walked straight into Chloe.

"Good morning, my love." She reached up and kissed him on the cheek. "You smell nice and fresh."

"Chloe, please." The circling bicycle in his head crashed into a barrier and his emotions splatted on the floor.

"Eat your breakfast and I'll be ready in a jiffy to drive you to work, as promised."

She stepped past him into the bathroom and effectively pushed him out the door.

For someone who was so obsessively controlling, he'd lost control of his life this morning. The Brookers seemed to have him sorted out and were batting him around the house from one chore to the next.

Breakfasted, brushed and clothed, Michael followed Chloe out of the house and to her car. He didn't say anything as they fastened their seatbelts, and she pulled out of the driveway.

"Chloe."

"Yes, Michael?"

"I can't go to work."

Chloe didn't respond but kept driving. They passed the turnoff that would have led them to the freeway into the city and kept driving until Chloe pulled her car up next to a local park.

"Do you want me to call in and tell them you're not coming?"

Did he? Could he summon the emotional energy to make this call?

"Here." Chloe took his phone from him. "What's your password?"

He held out his hand and used a fingerprint to open the phone.

Chloe went to his contacts list and found Harold Ainsworth's number. She put it on open line and waited while the ring tone rattled the atmosphere. Could he let her do this?

The call connected. "Michael? Are you OK?" Michael's heart clenched.

Chloe raised her eyebrows in Michael's direction as a question. He shook his head.

"Hi Mr Ainsworth, this is Chloe."

"Chloe." Was that relief he heard in his boss's voice? "Is Michael all right?"

"He's not real flash, to be honest. I'm just calling to let you know he won't be in for work today."

"Did he tell you?" Harold asked.

"That you're his father?"

Michael felt his heart rate quicken. Chloe had no fear when it came to confrontation.

"How much did he tell you?" Harold asked.

"Not a great deal. He's quite upset though. Perhaps he just needs time."

Michael heard his boss take a deep breath.

"Why do you put on such a righteous front when you have skeletons in your own closet?"

Michael wondered if he could—should—snatch his phone away and hang up. Never in a million years would he have blurted out this question—the question that was the one burning brightest in his mind—but Chloe …

"I don't know what to say, Chloe," Harold replied. "I was young—"

"That's not an excuse."

She was ruthless. She should take the bar exam.

"Since my son is not prepared to speak with me, and I want to talk about this, would you humor me and let me get this off my chest? It's been nearly thirty years."

Michael watched Chloe's expression. She was as angry as he was, if the fire coming from her eyes was any indication. Would she let Harold talk? He wanted to hear what the man had to say. She tipped her chin in his direction as if to ask what he thought. He nodded in reply.

"All right, Mr Ainsworth. Tell me what happened."

"Bernice and I married young—too young really. She was just out of high school and I was still midway through my uni course. At the time, she was demanding and I was immature. I couldn't cope with her neediness, and my attention started to drift towards a girl at uni."

"Mrs Sullivan?"

"We were assigned in the same work group for a history assignment, and she made me laugh. Then I discovered she worked at the library part-time, so I started to study at the library rather than go home."

"Go on."

"One thing led to another. Bernice was insecure and controlling, and we were at war. I regretted having married her. Alison was a good listener, and, well—"

"Yes, I get the picture."

"Then Alison told me she was pregnant and I panicked. Bernice had recently told me *she* was pregnant, and all of a sudden the responsibilities of fatherhood were bearing down on me from two directions—one I could not possibly justify."

"So you paid Alison to get an abortion?"

Michael clenched his teeth. His jaw ached from keeping his emotion in, listening to this story. Chloe put her hand on his arm.

He shook his head at her. His eyes were stinging. Did he want to hear any more?

"Do your children know they have a half-brother?"

Michael hadn't even considered he must have siblings. Harold was always talking about his grandchildren.

"I don't have any other children."

What!? Michael frowned and mouthed the word 'liar'. Chloe squeezed his hand again.

"Bernice lost the first baby, and four others. The fifth pregnancy she lost at twenty-eight weeks, and they called it a stillbirth. We gave up after that."

Chloe looked to Michael. Could she tell how agitated he was? He wanted to ask a question but didn't want Harold to know he was there.

"I thought you had grandchildren?" Chloe was so in tune. She'd discerned the question he wanted to ask.

"Bernice's sister asked us to be god-parents to her three children. Bernice, as their aunt, has treated them almost like her own, but they are no blood relation to Michael. He is my only son. And I can't tell you, Chloe, how that discovery has both brought me such joy, and blown my world apart, all in the same moment."

Michael couldn't listen to any more. He mimed the 'kill it' sign with his hand across his throat. He had to stop and process. This revelation had not brought him joy. Only anger.

"I'm sorry to have to cut you off," Chloe said, "but Michael is trying to contact me. I better see how he is."

"Can I just tell you how grateful I am that you broke protocol and blurted out what Michael never wanted any of us to know. If you hadn't, I would never have started to consider who he really was."

"So it was my blabbing?" She cast an 'I told you so' look in Michael's direction.

"When you said he didn't know who his father was, I remembered Alison and the child I'd sentenced to death. And I began to wonder what he would have been like. Later, I calculated the dates against Michael's record, and of course his name was Sullivan, and then I began to see what had been in front of me all the time."

"Which was?"

"He's the dead spit of my father. I have a son, Chloe. Alison didn't kill him. You don't know how much weight has been lifted from me just knowing that."

"But Bernice?"

"That's a whole other story. But you better speak to Michael. I'm worried about him and so glad that you're back together. He needs someone like you."

"OK. Thanks Mr Ainsworth."

She disconnected the call.

"He knows I was listening," Michael said.

"How would he know?"

"You called on my phone. If he hadn't thought of it while you were talking, he'll realize shortly."

Chloe shrugged. "So, what do you think?" she asked.

"He still didn't answer the question about his moralistic crusader role."

"My guess, he was trying to make up for what he did to his marriage. And I think he's felt guilty about aborting you."

"I don't think that's good enough for absolution."

"Yeah, well, I guess that's the process you're going to have to go through, isn't it?"

"What process?"

"Towards forgiveness for having abandoned you."
Not likely. No way. Not even maybe.
Forgiveness? That was out of the question.

Chapter Twenty

Love was not enough. She had always known that—she had told Anne so, many times. Besides, Liam had never actually declared his affections or intentions. It had always been Anne's enthusiasm, invitations, and encouragements that had swept Evelyn along a path that had just ended in an abrupt hole. Liam was engaged—to someone else.

"He doesn't love her," Anne said for the hundredth time. "He's not thinking straight."

"Perhaps he is thinking straight. How on earth could we have ever considered that I would make a suitable wife for a man such as your brother?"

"But he loves you, Evie. I know he does."

"Has he ever said that to you, in so many words?"

Anne went quiet, her face a mask of panic.

"He has never spoken of love for me, has he?" Evelyn challenged her friend with a pointed look.

Anne swallowed and shook her head. "He may never have said the words, but his every kind action, every wistful look, and warm smile shouted it. Why, he went to your father's house in search of you."

"Kindness to a former staff member. That is all."

"It's more than that. Why won't you see it?"

"Because your brother has announced his engagement to another woman."

"A woman with money." Anne spat the words out with distaste.

"Exactly. I am not the woman for your brother. I have nothing, ever since my father lost his land and fortune. I must share in his poverty."

"You are ridiculous, Evelyn Dixon. And Liam is ridiculous."

"Ridiculous, huh?"

Louise was startled from her thoughts as Chloe spoke over her shoulder.

"Why are Evelyn and Liam ridiculous?" Chloe asked.

"They're like you and Michael."

"What do you mean?"

"They love each other, yet they can't seem to overcome the barrier between them. She is destitute and his peers believe he would be foolish to marry a woman with nothing."

"Mmm. That does sound like Michael and me—a bit." Chloe pulled the spare office chair closer.

"A bit! You love him, don't you?"

"Not that I have made a huge display of affection in front of you, but yes. I believe I do."

"So why can't you just work together to make up for his difficult financial situation?"

"I think there's more to it than that, Mum."

"Really? What else is going on? Nobody is telling me anything."

"Didn't Dad tell you?" Chloe sat up straighter. What was that look on her face?

"Tell me about what?"

"Michael's father—biological father."

"What? That he doesn't know who his father is?" A strange feeling crept over her. Something had been going on. She knew it.

"I can't believe Dad actually kept this secret from you."

"Well if it's a secret, you've just let the cat out of the bag."

199

"I didn't say a word."

"What's going on Chloe? Even I can see that your relationship, if it did start out as a farce, has turned into love."

"Perhaps. But in this situation, love doesn't appear to be enough."

Louise sniffed. "You see, you are just like Liam. Making all sorts of ridiculous decisions when love is right in front of him."

"Mum, you know you're in control of your characters, right?"

Louise's lips thinned and she shook her head. "Maybe I'm in control of them, but I still haven't figured out how to stop him from marrying the wrong woman."

"Well, take heart. Neither Michael nor I are planning to marry anyone else. Perhaps, when you figure out how to sort out your character's problem, you can share your insights."

***

Michael stood out the front of his house. He'd been delaying going inside for over an hour, having walked a few kilometers to the supermarket just so he didn't have to face his mother. But he was dressed in his business suit—he hadn't taken anything else with him when he'd stormed out yesterday.

He took a deep breath. He had nowhere else to go, so he inserted his key in the lock and opened the front door.

"Michael. Thank goodness you're home."

Michael tightened his lips, inhaled deeply and exhaled leaving a sound that could not be mistaken for anything other than exasperation.

"I was worried all night." His mother was standing directly in front of him, as if she had actually been standing there ever since he'd walked out fifteen hours ago.

"Were you?" He chanced a glance at her expression, which negated the need for an answer. She looked haggard and disheveled. She hadn't slept. Good. Neither had he.

"I really thought Harry would have told you who he was."

"Don't you think I would have mentioned that I'd discovered my father if he had?"

"Well, I don't know. You never share anything deep with me."

"Mum."

"It's like you think I'm an idiot."

"Mum."

"Just because I have a mental illness doesn't mean I don't understand what's going on."

"Can you tell *me* what's going on? Because I don't think I can figure it out."

"For a start with, you've dumped the one good thing that has happened to us in years."

"This isn't about Chloe."

"No, but she should be part of it. She is a wonderful girl, Michael. Why did you have to break it off with her?"

"You know why. I'm in debt up to my eyeballs, and it's your fault."

Mum's face went pale and tears began to shine in her eyes.

"I'm sorry, I shouldn't have said that."

Mum took a deep breath that was like a shudder. "I know it's my fault, Michael. I haven't coped since—well, you know—since I was left pregnant and then my family threw me out."

"I'm well acquainted with your situation, Mum. I've lived with it all my life."

"But Chloe was your chance to find a new life—love, and family of your own."

"And who's going to look after you? Who's going to pay these debts?"

Mum's face crumpled and she hid behind her hands, crying. Michael felt like he was being cruel.

"Look, I'm sorry. I shouldn't have said all those things."

Was this confrontation going to end in another emotional crash, where his mother took to her bed and refused to eat for days? Michael had bigger concerns to deal with today, and the idea of mollycoddling his mother was not in the top ten.

"I'm going to put the kettle on and get changed." He walked past her into the kitchen, filled the jug and put it on the charging stand, flicking the switch as he left.

He went back into the family room and crossed to where his bedroom door opened. This house was small and depressing.

"Aren't you going to work today?" Mum asked as he came by the second time.

"I'm not up to facing him yet."

Michael went into the bedroom and shut the door. Without pausing, he tore off his suit, threw it on the bed, and found a t-shirt and jeans to wear. Could he be bothered going through this emotional rollercoaster again? He wished he was still back at the Brookers. There was a possibility they would leave him alone while he moped.

"Kettle's boiled. Do you want tea or coffee?"

Michael wanted to ignore her but he knew he was being childish. "Tea, please," he called back through the door. Throwing himself backward on the bed he stared at the ceiling with his arms stretched behind his head. He couldn't sit at home forever. Chloe was right. He had to find a way to face Harold but he couldn't—wouldn't—call him Dad. The man was his boss—his dishonest, hypocritical boss—

and until he could find another well paying position, he had to keep turning up to work.

Mum knocked on the bedroom door.

"Can I come in?"

"If you want."

The door cracked open and Mum slid into the room with two mugs of tea in her hand. Michael sat up and took the one she held out to him.

"I put two sugars in."

"I should be cutting back."

"Not today. Can I sit down?" She looked at the bed and Michael shuffled across to give her space to sit next to him.

Silence descended for several minutes while they sipped their tea. Michael didn't know what to feel with his mother sitting beside him like a companion—a caring, concerned companion. It was almost as if she was ... a real mother.

"I'm sorry, Michael. I know your life has been hard because of me."

"It's all right Mum. I shouldn't have said those things before."

"The Harry I remember was a funny, caring person."

"If he'd cared, he wouldn't have messed with you when he was married to someone else."

"He was looking for a friend. His wife was demanding and critical."

"It's not an excuse, Mum."

She dropped her head and examined the dregs in her tea cup.

"You're right. It wasn't an excuse. But that was a long time ago. And he's your father. I always regretted you never had him in your life."

"Why didn't you tell me years ago? Perhaps I might have approached him before going to work for him."

"When he gave me the money to get rid of you, he told me not to tell anyone because it would destroy his marriage."

"That was nice and considerate of him."

"I knew he was married when I got involved with him."

Michael turned a frown on his mother.

"It was as much my fault as his."

"Really? Do you think this is helping?"

"I'm just saying, he is your father despite the circumstances wherein you were conceived. We were both young and silly, and you're right, we should not have got involved, but we did, and you were the blessing that resulted."

"You think I was a blessing?"

"I would never have managed if I hadn't had your love and support."

"You wouldn't have been in these straights if I'd never been born."

She closed her mouth and looked down again.

"Are my grandparents—your parents—still alive?"

"I believe so. I haven't heard from them in years."

"There you are, you see. If I'd never been born, you would still have had your parent's support."

"They tried to contact me when you were about six or seven."

"What?"

"I didn't want to see them. I wasn't ready to forgive them for throwing me out when I needed them most."

"Do you mean to tell me I could have had family support through high school and university?"

"Michael. It is as it is. I can't change it."

How convenient, being able to confess to these huge transgressions at a time when he didn't believe he could do anything about it—and he was too scared to go hard on her, since she was always on the brink of relapse.

"Well, if it makes any difference to you, I will talk to Harold tomorrow. Lord knows what I'll say." Michael swallowed the last mouthful of tea.

"Be patient with him, Michael. Please."

"I'm not feeling particularly generous, as it happens. The way he's treated his staff—as if he is the paragon of moral integrity for us all to emulate—is the height of duplicity, given what we know is the story behind the man."

"We all do stupid things, Michael …"

"Not as stupid as this."

"I don't know. Who was it who found a fake fiancée to go on a business trip so he could pretend he was good enough?"

"Who told you she was fake?"

"I'm not entirely stupid, Michael."

He held her in his glare.

"All right—Harry told me."

"Well it wasn't entirely fake, either."

"I knew it. Will you go back to her?"

"I don't know. Not while things are so restricted financially."

"You have a good job, and she has a good job. You can make something of it. I know you can."

Michael pursed his lips. Not while Mum was still a loose cannon when it came to financial responsibility. But he couldn't say that to her. He'd said enough unkind things for the day.

***

Yesterday's confrontation, last night's emotional breakdown, and this morning's heart-to-heart with his mother had taken a toll. After Mum had taken the teacups back to the kitchen, Michael had found his pillow, punched it into shape and gone to sleep. When his phone rang, it took a while for him to reorientate—what time was it? What day was it?

He opened the phone cover and saw Russell's number as a missed call. He also saw that it was four-thirty in the afternoon. He'd not only missed lunch, he'd missed the entire day lost in the comforting arms of sleep.

What did Russell want? One thing was certain, he trusted Russell, and so he pressed return on the number.

"Hi Russell. Sorry I missed your call."

"You up for a boy's night out?"

Where was this man's head? Last night Michael had been crying on his shoulder, and tonight he was suggesting a boy's night out.

"What did you have in mind?"

"Cam and Pete want to go to the T-20 cricket. Do you like cricket?"

He was as good a couch competitor as anybody. And it was un-Australian not to like cricket. Was he up for a night out?

"If you're too busy, that's OK. I just thought you probably could use some company."

What were his other options? Go back to sleep. That seemed unlikely now he'd slept for over four hours. Did he really want to sit with Mum and chit chat about her affair with Harold?

"Where will I meet you?"

"We're catching the train in. Our tickets are for the East Gate."

"Will I be able to get a ticket this late in the day?"

"Pete bought four. We have yours already."

His ticket. They bought the ticket for him just in case? It was like they were family.

Michael didn't take long to put some gear into a backpack. He didn't want to have an invitation to stay over at the Brookers and not be prepared.

"Are you going out?" Mum looked up from watching her game show as Michael walked into the family room.

"Yep. I might not come home tonight. I'll see."

"Where are you going?"

"Boy's night out."

"Oh?" Mum's eyes lit up. She was curious. Should he tell her? "Which boys?"

Given he had never brought mates around, and didn't usually go out, she had a right to be curious.

"My father-in-law and brothers-in-law."

The look of confusion was pasted all over Mum's face.

"Chloe's dad and brothers."

"So …"

"So, nothing. I get on well with Russell and his sons. They invited me to the cricket, and I want to go."

"Does this mean …?"

"It doesn't mean anything. I guess I'm old enough to have mates of my own and to go out now and again."

Crestfallen was the best word to describe the look that came over Mum's face.

"I'm sorry I'm being so snarky. I just have a lot to deal with emotionally."

"OK." She sounded resigned.

"I'll see you later, maybe tomorrow."

***

Like the time Michael had gone with the Brooker men to the football, the cricket was another night where the crowd roared, and Michael was amused to watch the fans go crazy over big hitting and spectacular catches. One ball hit for six flew up into the stands near where they were sitting, and for a few heart-stopping micro-seconds, Michael thought he would catch it. A man three rows back took the catch, and the top of Michael's head enjoyed ten seconds of fame on screen with all the appropriate fanfare that accompanied the crowd catch.

The enjoyment of the night only added to Michael's craving for family and friends. Was it legitimate—insinuating himself into Chloe's family—when he had no intention of marrying her? Was it honest to be lapping up the parental attention from a man who might never rightfully be his father-in-law, especially when he now knew he had a father of his own?

"What a game!" Cam's euphoria over the narrow-margin win was evident in his whole expression. "I didn't think they would pull it off with only one ball to go and down four runs."

"That's why T-20 cricket is becoming so popular. The crowd love those nail-biting finishes." Russell's grin, fifteen minutes after leaving the stadium, was also evidence that his adrenaline had not yet subdued. "Did you enjoy the game, Michael?"

"Yeah." That answer sounded quite flat against the enthusiasm buzzing around him. Russell obviously noticed and dropped back to walk next to him allowing Pete and Cam to walk ahead.

"You OK?" Russell asked. "It's been a rough couple of days."

Michael opened his mouth, but didn't have the words. Instead he inhaled deeply and then blew out a breath through loose lips.

"How is your mum?"

Once again, Michael struggled to find words. 'Annoying' was not really a satisfactory response, so he just shook his head.

"Have you talked to your boss yet?"

Michael's respect for Russell ratcheted up another couple of notches. He could tell it was too early to refer to Harold Ainsworth as his father.

"I didn't go into work today."

"Will you go tomorrow?"

Michael shrugged. "Everybody seems to think I should go and talk to Harold."

"Everybody?"

"Chloe and my mother."

"What do you think?"

"I'm angry. Disillusioned. Angry. Mad. Flipping furious."

"It was a shock."

"It was an eleven on the Richter Scale. I can't believe Harold's self-righteous, judgmental, insensitive, moralistic standards he imposed on everybody were just a cover-up because he'd …"

Russell didn't say anything. He just kept in step as they walked to the train and boarded.

"Do you think I'm being too harsh?" Michael asked.

"I've never been in your place," Russell answered. "You've done it tough, and if I'm entirely honest, my heart broke for you before you found out about Harold."

Pressed close in a packed train of cricket fans probably wasn't the best place to have this sort of emotional heart-to-heart, but Russell was in tune and he was available.

"Since you're coming back to our stop, why don't you come home again for the night? We'll have a proper talk about it and pray together for some wisdom and grace."

Michael had already decided he would accept this invitation if it came up. He nodded his head. Cam and Pete didn't need to see him in the middle of another emotional meltdown.

***

Chloe arrived home from her late shift ready to fall into bed. The emergency room had been hectic tonight. When she opened the front door, not only were the lights still on in the lounge room, but she could hear voices. It was unlike her parents to sit up so late. Who was there?

Michael.

Her heart tripped over and went splat. Having him pop in and out of her house was nice—but sweet torture at the same time. Dropping her bag in her bedroom, she took a quick look in the mirror to see what damage the day had done to her appearance. Nothing eight hours of sleep wouldn't cure. She couldn't ignore the meeting that was going on two rooms down. Time to pull her dizzy self together and pretend she was full of vim and vigor.

"Hi." She put her head inside the door. "Can I come in?"

Dad looked to Michael for approval, and he nodded.

"Sure. Come in. Do you want to make us a cup of tea?"

"Dad! I'm not the tea lady."

"I know, darl, but Michael could probably use something to fortify him at the moment. Would you mind, this once?"

Speaking of fortification at midnight, she probably should drink chamomile and honey, and go to bed. It wasn't the smartest move to get involved with deep and meaningful conversations at this time of night. But she couldn't resist. She had to know how Michael was.

A small tray with three steaming cups in hand, Chloe returned to the lounge room and handed the drinks around.

"Did you have a good shift?" Russell asked.

"Crazy, but that's usual."

"Thanks, Chloe." Michael gave her a tired smile as he took the tea from her hand.

"So, I thought you guys were going to the cricket tonight. Who won?"

"We did," Russell replied. "Then I thought I'd ask Michael to stay over again. We've had a good chance to talk some stuff through."

What were the chances the stuff was about her and Michael? Pretty low, going by the look on Michael's face. His head was in another place entirely.

"How are you holding up, Michael?" Chloe asked.

"I'd be lying if I said, 'OK.'"

"Did you have a chance to talk to your … Mr Ainsworth?"

"Couldn't face him, but I'm going to try tomorrow."

Dad stood up from his seat and stretched his shoulders out, even while still balancing his cup.

"I might turn in," he said.

Convenient. Dad must have been taking lessons from Mum. Still, this was a good opportunity.

"Thanks, Russell," Michael said. "I really appreciate you taking the time to help me process."

"No worries. I'll see you in the morning."

Dad left the room and things became awkward.

"I think I better go to bed too," Michael said.

Chloe swallowed. Was he avoiding her?

"OK. Do you want a lift home in the morning?"

"Maybe."

He went quiet, but Chloe could see he was thinking about something.

"Listen, Chloe. I'm really sorry. This whole business has knocked me over emotionally. I'm not ready for ..." He stopped and shrugged his shoulder in her direction. That hurt. She was not helping him. He didn't need her. He didn't want her.

"It's OK. I get it."

She got up from her seat and took her cup back to the kitchen, splashing the remaining tea down the sink. Why did this hurt so much? By the time she got back to the lounge room, he'd left his cup on the coffee table and gone. That was best. They couldn't really talk with him in this state. The horrible question lurking in the back of her mind was: would they ever be able to talk, or was their chance at a relationship gone?

Chapter Twenty-one

Liam didn't want to see Evelyn. How could he face her now that he'd pledged his troth to another woman? How could he bear to watch her beauty and grace and know that she was now forever out of his reach— and it was all his own doing?

"*I have invited her to tea, brother, so I suggest you find the courage to speak to her face-to-face.*"

"*I will not see her, Anne. What you ask is unthinkable.*"

"*What I'm asking is that you have the decency to tell the woman you love that you no longer care for her.*"

"*Anne, you have lost your sense of reason—I blame those blasted novels you insist on borrowing. Marriage is not about love; it is about responsibility. I need to make decisions that will serve best my family and the estate. Evelyn Dixon, no matter how much I may care for her, is in no position to assist me in my responsibilities.*"

"*You have used her abominably. I should never have taken you for a cad.*"

"*Anne, I beg you would not use such language.*"

"*I beg you would reconsider. Who is to rescue Evelyn from the poverty thrust upon her by her father's selfish incompetence?*"

"*That is her father's responsibility, not mine.*"

"*What happens when a father has relinquished his responsibility, and has left his child to wallow in the misery of his foolish decisions?*"

For just a split second, Liam allowed the memory of seeing Evelyn answer the door to her broken-down hovel—the beauty and the misery in one image. She did not belong in a place like that. He had the power to lift her from that place of disgrace. A dagger of regret pierced his heart.

"All right, sister. I will see her."

"Truly, Liam?" *The passioned excitement in Anne's voice warned him he was on a perilous path.*

"I will see her, and I will tell her that she may return to my employ."

"What? Employ? Liam, what are you proposing?"

"You will need a companion until you are wed. You will love your friend and will keep her safe. This is all I can do for her, Anne. Don't push me for more."

"Did you hear me, Mum? All he wants is friendship. He won't be pushed for more."

"What?"

"Are you even listening to me, or have you drifted off to the 1800s to visit with your characters?"

"Of course not." Did that denial sound like the lie it was?

"Michael has conceded—reluctantly, I might add—to friendship. That's it."

"How do you feel about that?"

"I don't think I can take it. Every time I see him, I just want to go into his arms and hug him."

"Friends can hug."

"What dream world do you live in? Oh, that's right, you write fiction."

"There's no need to be snarky."

"If this isn't going anywhere, I think I'm going to have to end it permanently. The emotional pull is too strong."

"I'm sorry, Chloe. I feel as if it's all my fault."

"Mmm. If I was in a blaming mood, I suppose I could trace the disaster back to you showing my photograph to him in the first place …"

"But you're not in a blaming mood?"

"I really like him, Mum. Probably love him. If we could work things out, you could probably take the credit."

"But …"

"I don't think it's going to happen."

"So you're what … going to stop seeing him all together?"

"I think that's best for both of us."

"You might be right."

Did those words just come out of her mouth? It was as right as allowing Liam to marry that Henrietta woman. This was a crisis, and she would have to do something to stop it.

Chloe kissed her cheek. "Thanks for your support, Mum. At least I know I can depend on you."

Louise watched as Chloe took out her phone. Should she tell her the truth, or just leave it alone?

"You're texting him now?"

"It's best. I need to pick up my heart before I waste months hoping and then find it's completely shattered."

***

Michael's mobile phone buzzed in his pocket. Given the amount of emotional energy it was taking to get himself in the door at work, he decided to ignore it. His focus needed to stay on the one problem—facing Harold Ainsworth.

"Hi, Michael," Rosanne greeted him as he came into the reception area. "I'm glad to see you back. Are you feeling better?"

What had Harold told them?

"Still working through some things."

Rosanne gave him a quizzical look. Was he supposed to have been ill? Too bad. He was tired of lies. She could think what she wanted. Or he could tell her what a two-faced hypocrite the boss was?

No. Not yet. He needed to face Harold first.

"I don't have anyone booked in for you today," Rosanne continued. "I didn't know you'd be back so soon."

"That's all right. I have some things I need to catch up on."

"Will you have appointments available for tomorrow?"

Michael paused for a moment. Would he even work here tomorrow? He didn't want to lie to the receptionist. He would have to give notice if he was going to leave. And then he could … what? Where would he go? How would he make the payments he was committed to?

"I should be able to manage appointments by then. Thanks, Rosanne."

Michael picked up the stack of messages in his pigeon hole and then went through to his office. He hadn't got hand on the door knob before Daniel appeared in the hallway.

"Man, how are you? I heard you were under the weather."

"I've had better days."

"Are you on the mend?"

"Depends. A lot of stuff going on at the moment."

"Have you and Chloe broken up for good?"

Chloe. She was that breath of fresh air that sometimes breezed into his thoughts. But at the moment, he couldn't deal with a relationship—even a friendship that would never go anywhere.

"I don't think it's going to work out."

"I'm really sorry, mate. Anything I can do to help?"

Michael shrugged. "Not really. There's a whole lot of other stuff going on that I'm going to have to deal with at the moment."

"Has Harold given you a hard time about your background?"

"You could say that."

Daniel frowned and shook his head. "I thought better of him than that."

"Did you?" Michael knew he sounded angry. He couldn't pretend he wasn't.

"I didn't think he would judge you so harshly for something outside your control."

"Well, perhaps you don't know him as well as you thought." His tone was definitely bitter now. Too bad.

"All right, mate. I'll pray you can sort something out. We can hope he'll do the right thing."

Michael gave a tight smile. Do the right thing? What exactly would the right thing be at this juncture?

It was probably rude, but Michael opened his office door and went in without bothering to alleviate Daniel's concerns.

He put his bag on the desk, took out his computer, and sat down ready to ... ready to what? Mope was the best he could come up with at the moment. There was a manila folder on the side of his desk which was not odd, except this one had his name printed on the label. It was a legal file on him. He pushed his computer to the other side and brought the file to front and center.

Opening the file, he recognized the top paper. It was a will. Harold Ainsworth's will. He read it to confirm what he suspected. He—Michael Sullivan—was the main beneficiary. Provisions were made for Beatrice Ainsworth, but the rest of the estate—business, investment houses and other assets went to his 'son', Michael Edward Sullivan.

Michael wanted to spit. Was this supposed to make up for the attempt on his life? For the years of neglect? For the years of hypocrisy? He wouldn't be bought. He slammed the file closed, and powered by jet fuel, he rocketed out of his seat, out the door and towards his boss's office.

Jeanette sat at her usual desk—the gatekeeper to Harold's office.

"Hello, Michael. I'm glad you're here. Mr Ainsworth has asked to see you as soon as is convenient for you."

"How about right now?"

Jeanette's eyes widened with surprise. Was there steam coming out of his nostrils and ears? He wouldn't have been surprised.

"He has a client right at this moment, but if you give him fifteen minutes there's a space for you, if you like."

Don't do me any favors. Wait! Easy turbo. Better not shoot the messenger.

"Thank you, Jeanette. Please mark me in for 9:45."

He turned, the offensive file still in hand, and headed to the bathroom. He had fifteen minutes to cool his heals and try to get perspective.

Having washed his hands and studied his face in the bathroom mirror, he decided he should try to apply something of faith to his situation. He was out of control emotionally, and a quick inventory revealed he'd possibly shocked a number of people already this morning. Verses of scripture kept inserting themselves into his thoughts. "A quick-tempered person does foolish things"; "A soft answer turns away wrath"; "In your anger, do not sin". *I get the message, Lord.* Best to rein it in. He could speak civilly.

With still another ten minutes to wait, he returned to his office and took out his phone. The message that had come in earlier was waiting.

Hi Michael.

In light of how things have turned out between us, I am making the tough call. Friendship is not something I am willing to consider, and so I think it's best if we cease to see each other in the future. I'd appreciate it if you didn't keep popping up at my house, as that only makes this decision all the harder. I regret how things have turned out, but I think this is the wisest course of action.

I wish you all the best in the future.

Chloe

A sudden knife to the gut let out the head of steam that had been driving him since he arrived at the office. Never see Chloe again? He'd been kidding himself that she would always be there in the background. But it had been a selfish decision to keep her on a line in case he wanted to reel her in. Friendship was not enough. Well that was true. He'd known that all along. But never see her again?

His desk intercom buzzed.

"Mr Ainsworth is ready to see you now, Michael."

The file with his name on it had been explosive fifteen minutes ago. Now the prospect of a future with no Chloe in it had dramatically shifted his heart's focus.

His approach to Harold's office was much more subdued than earlier.

"How are you, Michael?" Harold's tone was full of uncertainty. Ten minutes ago, Michael would have ignored the pleading that shone in the man's eyes and unloaded his built-up anger. But the threat of losing Chloe for good had undermined his quest for satisfaction where Ainsworth was concerned.

"I've been better."

"I don't know what to say, son ..."

"Don't you dare …" the presumption lit a small pocket of fuel that remained.

"I'm sorry. What can I do to make this better?"

"Perhaps if you'd acknowledged me twenty-nine years ago, instead of paying to have me destroyed—"

"I know it was wrong. Don't you think I've tortured myself over it all these years?"

"Oh, you're breaking my heart." Chloe or no Chloe, the hurt was an open wound, bleeding infected words all over the place.

"I can see you're angry—"

"Very astute, counsellor."

"I guess I don't blame you."

"Is that supposed to make me feel better?"

"Michael, you believe in God—"

"Don't start with your trite religious claptrap."

"You said you were a Christian."

"I am, but that doesn't mean I have to put up with …" he waved his hand around the office, "…with this hypocrisy."

"I have to deal with that, Michael. That is my mess to clean up."

"Yes, it is."

"Yours is to bring your pain to God and allow him to bring healing."

Michael's jaw tensed and his eyes narrowed. How convenient to bring God in as a buffer. "So, you think I should just let you off the hook?"

"That's your call. If you don't want to, you go and wallow in your self-pity. But you may as well know that the will in that folder stands, and so does the money that's coming to you as compensation for the mental and emotional distress you and Alison have suffered over the years as a result of my actions."

"I don't want your money."

"You don't have any choice. I've calculated it and arranged it, and it will be in your bank in the next couple of days."

"I said I don't want it."

"Fine. Give it to your mother. I'm sure she will find a use for it."

"You ..." Several terms questioning Harold's legitimacy came to his mouth, but he couldn't speak it aloud. "How dare you talk about my mother like that!"

"Like what?"

"You just intimated she would take the money and gamble it away."

"I said no such thing. That's what you said. That's what *you* believe of her."

He was caught there. That *was* what he believed of her.

"I am humbly asking for your forgiveness, Michael. As your boss, and as your father."

Michael was stumped. Harold held him with a glare and Michael was still trying to recover from the stumble of assuming his mother would gamble the money.

"I have another appointment now, but I want to continue this conversation."

Still Michael didn't say anything. So many nasty words were pushing to find a place in the sentences beginning to form, but he began to feel as if suddenly he might have been in the wrong. It was an uncomfortable feeling, on top of everything else.

"Have Jeanette book in lunch for us on Monday."

Harold was using the boss's voice and somehow, Michael responded. He let out a loud sniff through his nostrils. It was the only way he had left to express his disgust. But as he went out the door, he had a feeling the disgust was slowly turning around to take aim at him.

With no appointments scheduled, and a massive headache brewing, Michael decided to go home. His bicycle was still at the office from the afternoon when Harold had offered to drive him home. He'd left it behind and ridden in Harold's silver Mercedes, feeling as if perhaps things were finally turning around in his favor. But that was until his mother greeted her long-lost lover as if it had been a week, not twenty-nine years. Damn and blast.

Michael pulled his helmet on and cycled to the train station. Chloe had uncovered his secrets and exposed him, Harold had picked up the clues and his mother had not batted an eyelid over the revelation. And as a result, his life was a mess. Ironic. He now had a father, an inheritance, and apparently a sum of money that would almost pay the entire debt that had held him captive the last seven years. But at what price? He valued his own integrity. He'd resisted filing for bankruptcy as he wanted to prove to himself and the world he could make things right if he worked hard enough and stayed focused.

And then Chloe had stolen his focus clean away. Damn and blast.

Michael validated his public transport ticket and wheeled his bike on board the train.

Now a man—a rich man—was swooping in and coming to his rescue. He didn't like how that felt. It undermined his sense of being in charge of his own life—of taking responsibility and beating the odds.

He wouldn't take the money just so Harold Ainsworth could salve his conscience.

But he didn't have a choice, did he?

What if he did take the money? His debt would be reduced to a size that was easily managed. He could probably buy a house, maybe with a granny flat for his mother. He could afford a wife—Chloe.

But how would that make him feel? And besides, Chloe had just made the tough call to end things completely. She might have moved on already. Damn and blast.

By the time the train reached his station, his head was ready to burst with a tight band squeezing mercilessly. It was all too hard, and his mother wasn't going to magically get well. Nothing much had changed—not for the immediate present at least.

Chapter Twenty-two

"*I* will most certainly not take his offer. I have never been so insulted in my life!"

Evie stood up and tended to the kettle boiling over the fire, turning her back on her visitor.

"I don't know what else to say," Anne said. "I told him it was an insult, but he would not listen."

Evie lifted the boiling kettle from the hook, holding the iron handle with a thick folded cloth. She poured the water into the chipped teapot, and then re-hung the kettle. Anne did not say anything else, but Evie could feel her friend's tension. It was too hard to talk about Liam and his offer to rescue her from poverty. Did he think she was made of stone—that she could sit in his house, eat at his table, and bow and curtsy to another woman—his wife?

"I'm sorry we do not have sugar or milk," Evie said.

"I'll take my tea plain, if you please."

Evie felt the disgrace of handing Anne a mismatched cup and saucer—the only pieces in the house that were not chipped. She didn't have enough flour and sugar to bake a cake or even a biscuit. Anne took the tea cup with grace, but it did not prevent Evie from feeling embarrassed.

"You know I cannot see him every day, knowing he is another woman's husband?"

"I know," Anne said, taking a small sip of tea.

"*It is not that I would not be delighted to have you as my daily companion. But …*"

"*I understand, Evie. Really, I do.*"

Evie sipped her own cup of black tea, trying to imagine what it would be like to have the luxury of cream and sugar. They were lucky to have tea.

"*I fear Liam will be most unhappy having made this decision,*" *Anne said.*

Should she feel sorry for Liam? He was a man in charge of his own destiny. He did not need to ask a stranger to be his wife. She would have done her best to be all that he needed, if only he had asked her.

"*I will relay your decision to him, Evie. May I say anything else on your behalf?*"

Yes. Tell him to marry me. But of course, she would not say that.

"*I will not be able to see you anymore. I fear it would be too difficult.*"

"*Nonsense. I shall visit here as often as I choose.*"

"*Until you find a husband who will forbid such an association.*"

Anne cast her eyes to her lap. "*I will not marry such a man if he forbids my friendship with you.*"

"*I fear you will never find a man who would approve, and you will be left a spinster.*"

"*This situation is unsatisfactory …*"

That hardly described the state of affairs. The situation sucked, but that word didn't fit in the Regency vocabulary. What Evelyn needed was a rich uncle in the West Indies, leaving her as rich as Croesus, then she could march up to the Bradford manor and give Liam a piece of her mind. But knowing her, she would be too proud to do it.

"What's got you fuming?" Russell poked his head in the door.

"I'm frustrated. Why do these young people have to be so proud? When money comes their way, why do they have to make such a fuss about backing down and confessing they loved each other all along?"

"Who told you?"

"Who told me what?"

"About Michael's father offering to pay his debts."

"Michael's father? What are you talking about? I thought he didn't know who his father was?"

"Who were you talking about—proud young people who refused to accept help when it came?"

"Liam and Evelyn."

"From your book?"

"You were talking about Michael. What's this about a father? And he wants to get Michael out of debt?"

"I wasn't supposed to say anything yet."

"Now, who can't keep a secret?" Louise felt a jolt of vindication for all her previous meddling.

"Honestly, I thought you knew, the way you were talking."

"Well, now you've gone this far, you'd better fill me in on the whole story. It sounds unbelievable."

"It is, almost. Only it's not. And then there's the business that Michael is talking about refusing to take the money."

Louise got up from her desk, took Russell by the shoulders and turned him around, gently pushing him out the door and toward the kitchen.

"This sounds like it needs a cup of tea and a little Luella Linley magic."

"He's going to kill me—that I let the cat out of the bag."

"Too late now."

***

Chloe was home for dinner, for a change, after several days of afternoon shift. She preferred getting up before the birds and being able to come home in the mid-afternoon with plenty of time to reset before dinner.

"How was your day?"

What was with Mum? She was using a smug tone. What was she hiding?

"Why do you ask?" Chloe pulled out a chair and sat down at the dinner table.

"Don't I always ask how your day was?"

"Not with that tone of voice."

"What tone of voice?"

"You sound as if you're plotting something and just waiting to trick me into going along with it."

"Funny you should say that."

"Mum, stop!"

"I was just thinking about the young man your father and I met this morning."

"Don't drag me into your schemes, woman." Dad wasn't even in the room but still yelled his objection through the house.

"Mum, please. I thought you'd learned your lesson with trying to matchmake."

"He is very nice, Chloe, and has loads of money."

"What has money got to do with it? You know that I'm not over Michael Sullivan, whether he has money or not."

"I thought you'd called it off with Michael."

"Not because I don't love him—I can't stand to see him when I know nothing is going to come of our relationship."

"So, you love Michael Sullivan?"

"I would have thought that was obvious."

"And the only reason you don't pursue him …?"

"He does not want to take the relationship beyond friendship. I can't stand it."

"So if he changed his mind …?"

"The only way he would change his mind would be if he'd suddenly come into a ton of money—wait a minute. What do you know that I don't?"

"I believe Michael Sullivan is the sole heir to the Ainsworth estate, and his father is planning to help settle his debts."

"Louise Brooker!" Dad stomped into the room. "That was supposed to be privileged information."

Chloe's eyes shifted between her father and mother.

"If the woman who loves him is not privileged, then I don't know who is."

"Are you saying Michael will soon have the money to afford a wife?" Chloe felt a glow of warmth inside. What an intriguing thought.

"That's exactly what I'm saying. Isn't that good news?"

"No! It's terrible news. I can't go running back to him now. It will look as if I'm a money-hungry mercenary."

Mum's face blanched. She hadn't thought of that, obviously.

"See." Dad looked cross. "You can't always fix things, Louise."

"Surely, if the two of you love each other, you can sort out these small problems."

"I'd say living in poverty one day, and suddenly being the heir to a large estate the next can hardly be considered a small thing."

"It's just money, Chloe. You said yourself you don't care about the money."

"I don't, but I will not go chasing after Michael Sullivan in the hopes he will give me a second chance. If I was not good enough for him when he was poor, I don't suppose I will be good enough for him now when there is money to complicate the issue."

Mum looked defeated. "You're as bad as Evelyn."

"Haven't you sorted them out yet?"

"No."

"Well, for goodness sake, leave me alone and go sort out the people who are under your control."

"Can you help me brainstorm for a bit?"

"I thought you had the plot all sorted in your head before you started."

"That's how I used to write, but lately, with the publisher demanding more books in less time, I've had to write on the fly."

"How exasperating. At that rate your characters could form a mutiny and take hold of your story."

"Tell me about it."

Dad laughed.

"Russell Brooker. Don't you be scoffing at things you don't understand."

"That's like saying my plans might up and move the bathroom in a building in the middle of the night, if the notion takes them."

"You don't understand how these characters work."

Mum sounded annoyed. Time to intervene.

"OK. Let's talk plot, if it will help you get your story finished. Where are they at?"

"Liam has accepted an offer from Rufus Havecock to marry his daughter, Henrietta."

"Who's Rufus Havecock?"

"A rich merchant."

"So, we're talking a man who has money but not breeding?"

Mum nodded. Dad sniffed, as he eavesdropped while sipping his tea.

"Russell. This is serious business."

"But Liam doesn't love Henrietta?" Keep Mum focused on the plot. Do not get distracted.

"He loves Evie, but won't confess it."

"And he won't marry Evie because …?"

"Her father has gambled their wealth and left them destitute."

"What a despicable man!"

"Who?" Dad asked. "The father or Liam?"

"Liam. Fancy turning his back on the woman he loves because of money!"

Dad raised his eyebrows at Chloe.

"Don't start, Dad. Let's stick to this story and get this pair sorted out."

"Liam accepted Havecock's offer because he needs the money to support his tenants and staff. Their livelihood depends on his income."

"So, Liam has sacrificed true love, accepted Henrietta, and Evie is sitting in her broken-down hovel refusing to beg him to reconsider?" Dad smirked as he gave the summary.

"She shouldn't have to beg." Chloe got up from the kitchen table and filled herself a glass of water.

"I'm not quite sure how to end this impasse?" Mum said.

Chloe frowned at her mother. Didn't she have the power to make them do whatever she wanted?

"Why does Evie have to marry Liam anyway? Can't she marry someone else, or live as an independent woman? She doesn't need a man, surely."

"Chloe! This is Regency England. Mary Wollostoncraft might have written *The Vindication of the Rights of Women*, but it was not accepted by decent people. Evie does need a man. She has no means of support without one."

"Well that's stupid."

"I think I'll leave this discussion while I'm still ahead." Dad put his teacup on the sink and left the kitchen.

"The thing is, with no money, Evie will live in poverty until she dies of old age or sickness. No decent gentleman will look twice at her."

"That is stupid. Doesn't Liam love her? He has money, doesn't he? He should ditch Henrietta and just get over it."

"But Liam has entered a betrothal agreement with the father. It's a legal and binding agreement. He can't get out of it now, even if he was overcome with longing for Evie."

"Give Henrietta some sort of fever and kill her off."

"Chloe! That is so convenient. I can't just kill characters off when I don't know what else to do with them."

"Have a mystery uncle die and leave a bucket of money for Evie, then Liam can marry her."

"I had already considered that, but it's also convenient—a bit too easy."

"What? So, you have to make sure you have an impossible challenge to overcome or it's not good writing? How does that work?"

Mum shrugged her shoulders. "It might be romance, but it has to have some grit to it."

"Yeah, well I think she should come into some money."

Mum pursed her lips. Chloe could see the cogs turning.

"Are you going to let her inherit?"

"Yes, I think that might be the best idea."

"What are you going to do with this Henrietta woman to get her out of the way, since you won't kill her?"

More cranking and clicking of cogs.

"I know!" Chloe sat up straight. "Henrietta can't be happy being sold into an arranged marriage. Make her run off with someone else."

A light of satisfaction came into Mum's eyes and she smiled.

"Perfect."

"Really?"

"Henrietta's real love can be an officer of the militia with average pay. She can elope with him and run off to his new posting in New South Wales."

"Leaving Liam heartbroken—"

"No, Liam doesn't love Henrietta."

"Leaving him free to pursue Evie, now that she's rolling in it."

"But he doesn't know she has money."

"Well send him a telegram and tell him."

"Telegrams were not invented yet."

"A letter with a lovely wax seal?"

"And how do you think he will respond, knowing the woman he loves has come into money, and now he comes knocking on her door with an offer of marriage?"

Chloe paused. Was she being shanghaied here? This question seemed awfully familiar. Her answer to this question was the answer to the argument about her pursuing Michael.

"Well played, Mother."

There it was. Smugness written all over her face.

"Was this discussion really about Liam and Evie, or were you backing me into this corner the whole time?"

There was a long pause—a standoff—neither saying anything.

"All right. I admit, Liam and Evie seem to be following your narrative, but I honestly didn't know how to work it out."

"For a start with, you don't have to work us out. All Liam has to do is get on his horse, go to Evie's house and tell her he's been a blockhead, and apologize."

"How will Evie respond?"

"If she loves him, they will get over the money thing and live happily ever after."

Mum's lips tightened.

"What?" Chloe asked.

"Why can't you and Michael stop being so reluctant and just get together?"

"Because."

"Because why? How is it different?"

"Your story is fiction for a start with."

"And? Your point?"

"Why doesn't he call me if he's suddenly in a position to go forward?"

"Perhaps he feels bad."

"Well, shouldn't he get over it? He needs to face the reality of his situation and decide if he wants a wife or not."

"Meaning you."

"Well, yeah. I suppose."

"You've decided you want to be a wife after all."

What was that satisfied smile that had lit Mum's face? Honestly.

"I want Michael—but only if he wants me."

Dad's head poked back in the door.

"You two talk so much nonsense it makes my head hurt."

"Dad! Have you been listening all along?"

"What can I say? The plot is intriguing. I can't wait to see how it turns out."

Chapter Twenty-three

"*I* want to go to church."

Michael didn't bother to open his eyes and hoped his mother would think him still asleep.

"Michael. I mean it. You need to go to church too."

"Mum." He groaned as he rolled over to face her, standing in his bedroom doorway.

"I can't stand seeing you like this." She had her hands on her hips. When did she get so full of authority?

"I'm just tired."

"No, you're not. You're wallowing in self-pity and not dealing with the situation."

Ironic. From a woman who had made an art of crumbling under the pressure of life.

"I will make you breakfast, you get in the shower and get dressed."

"Mum."

"I mean it, Michael. It's time you pulled yourself together."

Really? She was going to talk like that to him, after the years and years of him trying to encourage her out of emotional slumps.

"We've got twenty minutes until the bus comes, so get a wriggle on."

Michael glanced at his bedside clock. Only seven-thirty.

"Mum, the church is only twenty minutes' walk down the road."

"No. We're going back to the Brooker's church. I liked their service."

"Mum!"

No use pursuing this argument. She'd walked out of the room and closed the door behind her. He dragged himself to a sitting position, studied the wall for a few seconds of mind-numbing contemplation. No. Nothing. No sudden spark of revelation or inspiration to give him the motivation to even stand up.

"Hurry up!"

These thin walls were about as sound proof as a chook cage. Summoning sheer willpower, he pulled himself upright, dragged his hand through his disheveled hair, and put one foot in front of the other. Apparently, he was going to church—to Chloe's church. Would she be angry with him, since she'd asked him not to pop up at her house? Did popping up at her church count?

With Vegemite toast in hand and a coffee in the other, Michael followed his mother towards the front door.

"Finish your breakfast before you leave." She stopped short and rounded on him. "Your breath will smell awful with coffee and Vegemite on it."

"Does it matter? I can chew a mint."

"Hurry up and eat. I don't want to miss the bus."

This role reversal was weird. His whole life he'd been his own motivation and spent a load of extra energy trying to encourage her towards positive activities. Michael took three bites of the toast but his mother standing over him, hurrying him along, was not conducive to good digestion. He decided to throw half the toast in the bin.

"I'll drink the coffee on the way," he said.

"No. You need to brush your teeth."

Michael frowned at her. If he didn't know any better, he'd swear she was arranging for him to get up close and personal with someone—and given she'd chosen the Brooker's church to attend, he suspected she had Chloe in mind. Not an unhappy thought. He threw back the now tepid coffee in several gulps, left the cup on the sink and headed to the bathroom.

"We've got five minutes to get to the bus stop."

So, this was what it was like to be nagged into action. He must have driven his mother up the wall all those times she had crashed and didn't have the motivation to get out of the house.

The bus ride into the city center and the second trip out to the southern suburb where Chloe lived, was uneventful. Thankfully, Mum was happy to just sit and stare out the window. That suited him. He wasn't in the mood to chat about life. On the second bus, he leaned his head back against the window and closed his eyes.

"This is our stop." Mum's tugging on his sleeve accompanied these words and jolted him awake. Talk about lack of energy. The only thing that sparked a small amount of anticipation was the likelihood of seeing Chloe—and those feelings were all anxiety. What if she was angry with him for coming? What if she completely ignored him?

Once they'd walked the half a kilometer to the church, Michael was more uptight than he remembered ever having been before. Was it Chloe or was it facing the gospel of forgiveness? He didn't have the confidence to face either, truth be known, but his mother marched through the entrance with an uncharacteristic confidence, shaking hands with the welcome ushers.

"Mike."

Michael turned to see if it was someone he knew. Cam Fletcher stood with Chloe's sister.

"Hey, Cam." Michael responded to Cam's offer of a handshake.

"What brings you out our side of town?"

"Church." Obviously. "My mother enjoyed our visit here a few weeks back and was insistent we should come."

"Well, it's good to see you. How've you been keeping?"

"Had a few challenges at work, but …" He shrugged his shoulders. He didn't want to talk about it.

"Do you and your Mum want to sit with us?" Megan asked.

"That would be lovely." Mum had returned to his side at just the right moment. "I'm Alison, Michael's mother."

"Megan. I'm Chloe's sister." The two women clasped hands and exchanged a kiss on the cheek. Wow! That was familiar.

"Where is Chloe?" Mum's eyes scanned the foyer. Michael had already searched to see if Chloe was about. She wasn't.

"She's on an early shift this morning."

Mum's demeanor dropped. So, she was hoping to affect a meeting.

"She finishes around three, should be home by four. Do you want to come around for lunch, and catch her when she gets home?"

"Yes!"

"No!"

In unison, but not harmony.

"We haven't got anything important on this afternoon." Mum looked at Michael as if seeking his approval.

"I need to get home and do a few things." Please don't ask me what. Please.

"What things?"

Cam and Megan were watching. They weren't stupid. They could tell he was making an excuse.

"I need to get the lawns mowed."

"Not on a Sunday. It's a day of rest."

Why did Mum have to become so logical and insistent today?

"I'll leave it up to you," Cam said. "You'd be welcome if you think you have the time. Otherwise, maybe next week."

Would he come again next week? He doubted it. Too hard to catch two buses, and too much risk of seeing Chloe again when she'd specifically asked him not to come.

As anticipated, the pastor seemed to have read Michael's mail and delivered a sermon specifically directed at him. The Scripture in Matthew couldn't be clearer. If we forgive others, God forgives us. It was like no one else was in the church building and each point was honed to pierce the barrier of bitterness he'd constructed against Harold Ainsworth. The best he could do was hold himself in a pose he hoped looked neutral and not as if he was squirming like a worm on a hook.

"I'd really like to go to lunch with those nice young people," Mum said to him the moment the service was over.

"Mum, you hardly know them."

"But if they're going to be family, I'd like to get to know them."

"Whoa! Look, Mum. Chloe and I broke up. We were never really together…"

"That's nonsense. I saw you together. You've never looked so happy."

He couldn't deny that. But that was not the terms of their arrangement. Besides, too much water had passed under the bridge following that stupid couple's game.

"I don't think we should. I'm not in a great place at the moment, and landing in on the Brookers is making things difficult for both of us."

"Are you talking about this business with your father?"

"Could we talk about this when we get home?" They were still in the crowded foyer and though he couldn't see anyone he knew in the immediate vicinity, he still felt awkward discussing this subject.

"You heard the pastor …" Mum obviously didn't have the same reluctance to discuss personal issues in a crowd of strangers. "If you hold on to this bitterness, it's only going to destroy you. I forgave Harry years ago. I think you should too."

Michael narrowed his eyes. Had she really forgiven the man? Her fragile mental health had made it seem that she carried the emotional baggage of the world. Surely some of that was Harold Ainsworth's fault.

"I think it's best you give me some time to process. I'd like to go home today, please."

Mum wasn't happy as she put her bag over her shoulder and headed towards the exit. He couldn't help it. He wasn't ready to deal with all this stuff going on. Pursuing Chloe was only complicating the issue.

"Michael."

He'd nearly made it to the door to freedom when he heard Russell's voice. He couldn't ignore the one man who'd been there for him in the last few months.

"Hey, Russell. Nice to see you."

"It's great to see you. Did you come on your own?"

"No." He pointed towards his mother who'd already gained the carpark.

"Did you catch the bus?"

Michael nodded. He really had to get going.

"Would you like to have lunch with us, and I'll drive you home?"

Michael let out a sigh. He couldn't say no to this man.

"Chloe asked that I not pop up at your place. She wants to make a clean break of it."

"What day did you hear that piece of news?"

What did the day have to do with it? Still, he counted back in his mind.

"Sometime last week, I think."

"Yes, well that's not what she said yesterday, when she was talking to her mother."

Did he really want to know what Chloe and her mother had been talking about?

"I think it's safe to say she doesn't hate you."

"I didn't think she did."

"Well, what's stopping you from reconnecting?"

"My emotional life is a mess."

"Fair enough. Want to talk about it?"

Yes, he did want to talk about it, and Russell was the very guy to talk about it with. What did it matter if he accepted a lunch invitation? Mum would be happy, he'd be fed, and they'd have a comfortable ride home—and there was always a small chance he might yet see Chloe and not explode.

***

Trust Russell to come straight to the point.

"From your point of view, you can't accept the money Harold Ainsworth is wanting to award to you because …?"

"You know how I feel about it."

"I do. The question is, how long are you going to hold this bitterness?"

"As long as it takes."

"Takes for what?"

A perceptive question. What was he waiting for? What did he expect? Sack-cloth and ashes? Penance in the style of the flagellants of the medieval times?

"I don't really know."

"And you have a lunch appointment with him tomorrow?"

That was what Jeannette had sent to his digital calendar, but would he go?

"You're thinking of bailing?" Russell could read him like a book.

"What's he going to say that could possibly change the way things have turned out?"

"He might say sorry." Russell's eyes were round and intense as he stared Michael down.

What good would saying 'sorry' do? How would that change the situation?

"I can see you don't think it's enough," Russell said. "What would make it better?"

Michael sucked in a deep breath. Nothing would make it better. He was angry, and he wanted to be angry, except the pastor had kindly pointed out that holding a grudge was not a luxury the Bible allowed. He needed to let it go. He needed to forgive.

"I know what you're thinking," Michael said.

"What am I thinking?"

"I should forgive him, and let my anger go."

"And ..."

"What else?"

"Michael, it appears you believe you can control the whole world. You've got your mother organized into a strict routine and on a tight budget. You have everything logged and recorded, and it's as if you believe you can be the savior of your household."

Harsh.

"When Chloe came into the picture she upset your balance, opened up new and unchartered possibilities, threw new variables into your equation, and you lost control."

"It wasn't that—"

"What was it then?"

"I couldn't afford to get married."

"Because you have to be in control of everything, including your finances. Chloe has a good job. She could have pooled her resources with yours and made a permanent relationship possible."

Michael's lips tightened as thoughts ran through his head. Was that it? He wanted to be in control of saving his mother and if he had a family, be in control of feeding and clothing everyone?

Russell was still looking at him with that intense questioning look.

"Well, now I have a 'father'..." he used air quotes, "... who wants to give me financial security."

"And your problem?"

"I feel bad taking it."

"Why? Because you don't deserve it? You've always been the poor kid who's had to scrape for everything. You were the kid who had to work after school to pay for your uniforms. You were the kid who had to work two jobs while studying at college. You were the kid who didn't have a father who would take care of you, or a mother who was able. Does that mean you don't deserve your inheritance?"

Michael fidgeted in his seat. He'd never been happy taking charity, though his mother had relied on it plenty of times. But to actually be an heir—to be a part owner of a healthy, prosperous practice—was difficult to get his head around—difficult to get his heart around. He wasn't that kid who had things easy. He was the kid who had to fight against all odds. Was that the kid who Harold Ainsworth wanted to acknowledge as his son and heir? A poor boy from the wrong side of town, living from hand to mouth, fighting to keep his mother well?

Russell leaned forward and patted Michael's shoulder. "When you go to lunch tomorrow, consider letting Harold open his heart to you. Let him apologize, if he wants to. Give him a chance to build trust between you."

What could he say? Russell was right, and he knew it, despite the fact his advice was the most difficult thing in the world to follow. He opened his mouth to thank his mentor, but held his tongue when he heard the front door open.

"I'm home."

Chloe's voice called down the hallway. He was in trouble now. He should have insisted on leaving earlier.

***

Mum and Dad had visitors. She could hear voices coming from both the lounge room and the kitchen. Kitchen first. She was starved.

"Hello, Chloe."

"Mrs Sullivan!"

"Alison, please." Michael's mother stood up from the kitchen table and stepped close enough to give her a kiss on the cheek. This was awkward.

"I wasn't expecting … is Michael with you?"

Even before she answered, Chloe knew the voice she'd heard talking with her father was the one man she desperately wanted to see—and didn't want to see.

"Have you eaten?" Mum ignored her state of discombobulation. "Sit down. I'll make you a sandwich."

Mum was being all … domesticated. That was odd.

"Michael is in talking with your father," Alison said. "He really values Russell's advice."

Yes, she had noticed that.

"Shall I tell him you're here?"

This all-fire enthusiasm to match-make must be a middle-age mother thing. Alison had beaten her mother to the punch.

"Let me eat something first. I'm sure he and Dad have important things to talk about."

Mum's ham and salad sandwich was produced in record time along with a cup of tea. The trouble was, Chloe's appetite had wandered off in search of Michael. Of course she wanted to see him. And then she wanted to give him a stern talking to. She'd told him not to keep popping up at home. It was all too hard for her to cope with.

Alison and Mum kept chatting about something, shooting a question in her direction every now and then, though Chloe could not catch the thread of conversation. She was knocked off balance. Should she go in and take him to task, or should she just ignore him, or should she run in and kiss him passionately on the lips? The third option appealed to her best.

Having only taken several bites out of one half of the sandwich, Chloe gave up trying to eat. It was like sawdust in her mouth.

"Are you all right?" Mum asked. She knew. She wasn't stupid. The queen of Regency romance knew exactly what was going on and was doing a lousy job of pretending she didn't.

"If you'll excuse me," she directed her apology to Alison, "I have someone I need to speak to quite urgently."

Chloe didn't wait to hear Alison's polite answer, or her mother's oh-so-fake look of surprise. Honestly, later they would be having words.

"Hello, darl." Dad stood up when she came into the room. He was as phoney as her mother. He never stood up to welcome her home. "Just in time. I need to make a phone call, and you can keep Michael company."

Fine. If they were going to play innocent conspirators, she would play along.

"I would be happy to, Father dear." She watched him leave the room, but was acutely aware that Michael had not yet turned to face her.

The door closed and Chloe focused her gaze on the man she had fallen in love with, who she currently wanted to slap silly. She didn't know what to say, so she didn't say anything. Just waited for him to initiate the conversation.

"I'm sorry, Chloe." She was still staring at the back of his head. Fine. She would be the grown up and go stand in front of him.

"Michael Sullivan. If you're going to keep coming to this house, you are going to have to do better than that."

He stood up but the look on his face was one of mild panic.

"What do you mean?"

"The rules were: if this was going to be a clean break, you would not come around anymore."

"Yes, I know. I'm so—"

"Since you're here, I can only assume you've decided against a clean break."

He looked nervously at his feet for a moment, but didn't speak.

"I, personally, am in favor of that decision."

"What?" He looked back at her face.

"You're here, alone with me, and there is this horrid two feet of distance between us. I vote we get rid of it."

"Rid of…?"

"The two feet of distance between us." She took a bold step towards him so that she was standing intimately close.

"What's your vote going to be?" He could step back, turn around and bolt out the door. That was an option. But he didn't. He placed his warm hands on her shoulders and looked deep into her eyes.

"I vote we get back together."

"All in favor?" Chloe barely whispered the words.

"Carried." His lips covered hers with the softest warmth possible, sending rockets of joy exploding through her whole being.

"There's no backing out now, Counselor," she said, as he drew back a half inch.

"You talk too much," he said and moved in to finish what they'd started.

Chapter Twenty-four

He shouldn't have been surprised, but by the time he and Chloe had reconnected, and stayed warmly ensconced in each other's arms for a while, they emerged to find the kitchen—in fact the whole house—empty.

"Mum and Dad have driven your mother home." Chloe picked up a note from the kitchen table.

"They're not very subtle, are they?" Michael said.

"Do you mind? I don't. I get to spend some more time with you alone."

Michael accepted Chloe's hug as she wrapped her arms around his waist. Not since their time at the staff retreat had he been so close to her, and he relished the comfort it brought. That's not all it brought, and he reluctantly loosened his hold and stepped away. Chloe frowned.

"Is something wrong?"

"Not 'wrong'. I feel great, actually, it's just that … well, you know …"

"What?"

"Chloe, don't make me spell it out."

She just grinned at him.

"Are you saying you want more than just kissing and hugging?"

"Don't you?"

"Well, yeah. Of course."

"When we get together, we'll do it properly after a beautiful wedding."

"Is that a proposal?"

"Let's just say, I'm opening a cold case and pursuing it to the end."

Chloe tugged him back into a close embrace, keeping her lips open and available. This could get dangerous. He gave her a quick peck and then untangled himself.

"You better take me home, Chloe. The situation here is not conducive to good behavior."

She laughed. "Let me get changed first."

"Why? I like your scrubs."

"As if." She left the kitchen and Michael helped himself to a glass of cold water. He was tempted to pour it over his head. He must keep within the boundaries of good moral conduct.

Then it hit him. Was that boundary something *he* wished to preserve, or was he merely measuring up to Harold Ainsworth's expectations? The bitterness washed over him again. Harold Ainsworth had not kept his own rigid rules, why should he?

"Ready." Chloe stepped back into the kitchen, her handbag and keys in hand. He was aware of the wall that had gone up during those few minutes it took for her to get changed.

"What's wrong?" she asked.

"It doesn't matter. Let's go. I need to get home."

Why did the thought of Harold Ainsworth always sour his mood?

Chloe had the car on the road before she spoke again. "What's wrong, Michael? And don't say it doesn't matter, because the animosity is radiating off you like a bad sunburn."

"I'm really struggling with my boss."

"Your father."

"I can't … not yet."

"What brought this sad mood on?"

"I was thinking about how we should stay safe within the boundaries of Christian moral behavior and then wondered if that was my own conviction, or Harold's hypocritical demands that I was still living under."

"And what did you decide?"

Michael turned his head and frowned at her. What did she mean?

"Do you hold to your convictions because you believe it's the right thing to do? Because you respect my father? You respect me? Or is it a latent fear of falling short of Harold Ainsworth's expectations?"

"Why don't you say what you really think?"

Chloe smiled.

They drove in silence for a while. He respected Russell—that was certain. He wouldn't want to betray his trust. And he loved Chloe. But was his staying morally safe with her because he loved her? He was aware of the current standard in the 21st Century. Morality had more to do with inclusiveness and care for the environment than it had to do with sexual guidelines. What did he truly believe in his own heart?

He was aware of Chloe, attracted to her, and tempted to go further than just kiss. But he couldn't—wouldn't. He wanted to have and hold her for the rest of their lives, not in a few moments of unguarded passion. But if they were committed to each other, what did it matter if it was before the wedding or after?

"Well, have you made up your mind yet?" Chloe's question broke into his troubled thoughts.

"I respect your father, I love you, and I want to wait until we are married before we come together sexually."

"OK then. Was that so hard?"

"I'd just like to think I was doing it because I believed it, and not because my boss expected it."

"I'll let you sort that out in your own head. But just so you know, I'd like to wait. Mind you, I don't want to wait too long so I hope you have a wedding in mind for the near future." She placed her hand on his knee and he covered it with his own hand.

"I'll let you know."

"And I hope your lunch with your—boss—goes well tomorrow."

Michael pursed his lips. Everyone wanted to say 'your dad' but they were waiting for him to go first. Would it ever come? Would he ever be sure of his own convictions, or was he really a slave to Harold Ainsworth's expectations?

***

This was going to take some doing. Russell had advised he open his heart and listen to Harold, but that was easier said than done.

"Thanks for coming, Michael." Harold stood up as Michael approached the café table overlooking the ocean on the marina. *Open your heart. Hear what he has to say.* Michael had to repeat it like a mantra to keep from turning away.

"Sit down. Would you like a drink?"

Drink? Did he mean alcohol? Not according to the Ainsworth company rules. Not that it mattered, he wasn't a great wine drinker at the best of times, but it poked his irritation yet again.

"I'll just have water thanks." Even to his own ears he sounded belligerent.

Harold ordered table water and a lemon, lime and bitters for himself.

"How are you feeling?" Harold eventually asked.

"I'm struggling."

"That's understandable."

"I still want to know why you've insisted upon such strict moral behavior from your staff when right from the beginning, you were anything but."

"I know."

"That's not an answer."

"I was trying to make up for my fall."

"Does your wife know? About my mother? About me?"

"She suspected all those years ago and threatened to leave me. She was pregnant at the time, and that's what shook me to my core."

"What? That your wife would leave you, or that you would be seen as a philanderer with a broken marriage?"

"Both. My father—your grandfather—was a tough man. He expected the highest moral code from me."

"And yet …?"

"You don't have to lecture me, Michael. I'm aware of the hypocrisy."

"Then why did you impose it on all your staff, to the point you didn't allow women as part of your legal team?"

"Bernice."

"Really? You're going to blame your wife?"

"She was an insecure person. She didn't trust me."

"With good reason, as it turns out."

Harold dropped his head.

"So, what has Bernice said about the surprise return of your son?"

"She has matured over the years and overcome a lot of her insecurities."

"Is that so?"

"The revelation has opened old wounds, and she's struggling with it—same as you."

Michael couldn't help feeling a sense of satisfaction knowing the man was getting it from all quarters. He didn't deserve to feel settled as if nothing had happened.

"Michael, I want to get to know you as my son."

"You already know me."

"As an employee. But the man I thought I knew doesn't exist."

"What do you mean by that?"

"I thought you were engaged. I thought you'd had a stable upbringing with your family intact. I thought you were an easy-going, well-adjusted young man."

"Are you saying I'm not?"

"I don't know who you are, especially considering the fact you're taking great delight in trying to make me pay for my mistakes."

"Don't you think you should pay?"

"Other than making it so that you have financial security now, and in the future, and that my marriage is under some serious strain, and that I am desperately trying to connect with a child I never thought I would have—a child who apparently hates me—I don't know what else I have to do to pay for my sin."

Michael inhaled deeply through his nose and blew out the same way. He *was* being belligerent. There wasn't much else the man could do.

"If you were the Christian you pretended to be, you would know that Jesus has paid for your sin on the cross."

"Michael, you're being difficult. I know that. And I am a Christian. Maybe I'm not a very good one. Maybe I've made mistakes—"

"Understatement."

"But you've made mistakes too. You lied to all of us at work. You toyed with the affections of a young woman so you could appear to be someone you're not."

"Because I wanted to impress you!"

"Does that make it right?"

Silence fell between them. The waitress brought their drinks and a menu. Perhaps she'd been waiting for a lull in the intense conversation before coming to take their orders.

"Would you like to order now?" She looked anxious. Michael suddenly became aware of what his body language must look like to someone who didn't know what was going on—aggressive. He didn't feel hungry and was about to say so, but Harold spoke first.

"Could you give us five more minutes, please?"

The waitress scampered away as if she'd been the one to draw the short straw and enter the chamber of the man-eating ogre, and had barely escaped with her life.

"I want to get to know you, Michael. The real you. The one who's been brought up in council housing. The one who's had to support himself through school. The one who's had to struggle to help his mother stay well. That's the Michael I want to know."

Michael heard the words, but they were so incongruent with the Harold he knew. Or the Harold he thought he knew.

"I've worked hard to make sure you didn't know any of that information."

"I know. Your mother told me."

"I thought you'd make my life at work difficult if you found out my background was dysfunctional."

"Can I be honest, Michael?"

"I thought that's what you were doing—being honest."

"You were probably right. If I had found out about your background, and hadn't figured out who you really were, I might have subconsciously treated you differently."

"Like how?"

"I couldn't have fired you—we both know you would have legal recourse if I'd tried—but I could have made life difficult for you and deliberately stunted your growth in the company."

"See? That is the hypocrisy I'm so angry about."

"And you have every right to be angry. Now I'm seeing it, I'm disgusted with myself."

Michael frowned.

"But that's just because you've been found out."

"No, Michael. I wasn't found out. I didn't have to investigate the hunch when Chloe revealed your circumstances. I could have snubbed her and you, and gone on as I had been."

"Why did you investigate?"

"Michael, I've mourned the loss of you."

Michael expelled a sniffed scoff.

"You're right. Not at first. When I first paid your mother off, I was relieved I'd got away with the affair and that I was able to keep my marriage intact. But when we lost our first child, I began to understand that I'd deliberately ended the life of another child."

"You didn't think to check in with my mother?"

"I had put an end to our relationship—a relationship that should never have started. Of course I didn't check in with her. My wife was grieving, and she was still suspicious. By the time we had lost five pregnancies, the guilt of having murdered Alison's child was overwhelming."

"So ...?"

"So I battened down the hatches, and shored up my entire existence with a set of fundamentalist rules that I imposed on anyone who was under my influence."

Michael sat tight-lipped. He wasn't feeling sorry for Harold, but he began to understand.

"The moment I saw your mother's picture in your office I knew who you were, and you cannot begin to understand the bolt of joy that flooded my heart. You were alive. Alison had ignored me and given you life. Even though revealing who you were came with a whole set of uncomfortable and difficult challenges, there was no way I was going to let you go a second time. You were right in front of me. It was my reputation or you. I chose you, because the reputation I'd built was a lie."

"And it was insufferable—the expectations you'd put on your staff."

"Yes. You're right."

"Are you going to tell them, face to face?"

"When the time is right. I'm going to sit with you and the other senior staff, and we're going to go through our policies and—"

"What do you mean 'me'?"

"You're part owner of the business now. I need your input."

Part owner! This was a whole new level of craziness.

"You can't just make me part owner."

"You're my son. I'm buying Pembroke out, since he retired five years ago and is only a silent partner. The company name will be changed to Ainsworth and Sullivan."

Chapter Twenty-five

"The staff are whispering behind their hands." Evie clasped Liam's arm firmly. "They will never respect me."

"My darling. Let them whisper. You have brought security to their positions. Without you, some of them may have found themselves without employ."

Evie felt her heart sink.

"What is it, Evie?"

Liam was so perceptive.

"It's not just the staff. What about your friends? They were all against me."

"They were. But your mother's inheritance from the West Indies plantation has made a difference to the way they see you."

"And the way they see you. Doesn't it bother you?"

"It does bother me, Evie. I was going to marry Henrietta solely for her money. Thank the Lord she had the sense to follow her heart and elope. I might have been trapped with a woman I cared nothing for and never been able to be with the woman I love."

"But doesn't it bother you that you could only offer for me once I had money?"

"Does it bother you?"

"I love you, Liam. I could have refused your offer on the grounds it was mercenary and a huge insult."

"I love you too. I could have withheld the offer not wanting to appear so in your eyes, or anyone else's."

"That would have left me with money, you with your reputation, and both of us alone and unhappy."

"I'm prepared to endure the whispers of those who have judged me as a mercenary, because it means I have you. Can you bear it?"

"My choice, once I inherited, was to accept one of the many proposals from other men who had never so much as looked in my direction, and were now suddenly at my door like bees around honey."

"I was one of those men."

"But you have always regarded me, even when I was without means."

"I only want to know that you are happy, Evie."

"I am happy, Liam."

"Are you happy, Chloe? Does the ending meet with your approval?"

Chloe twisted her lips in a thoughtful expression.

"Well?"

"Well, they are happily ever after. He didn't jilt anyone. She told the other losers to push off. I think it's OK."

"Just OK?"

"I know how they feel. Accepting Michael as a man struggling to make ends meet seems more noble than as the partner of a prosperous law firm."

"But you wouldn't throw him over because he's suddenly got money."

"No. I want him—money or no money."

"Speaking of which—are you really engaged now, or are we still running on the bogus arrangement you started with?"

"His first proposal was quite romantic ..."

"But not for real."

"That was the lie we were telling ourselves at the time."

"So, no new proposal expected?"

"I don't think so." Was there? They hadn't really talked about that. Just that they wanted to marry and soon.

"Do we have a wedding date? You know there are things to plan?"

"Michael needs some time to settle things with his father and mother first. The situation is weird, and he's trying to get his head around it."

"I imagine."

"Anyway, you've got Pete and Collette's wedding to fuss about."

"Mmm."

"What's that supposed to mean?"

"Nothing."

"Mum. I thought you'd accepted that Pete was going to marry Collette."

"I don't like her."

"I don't think any of us like her very much, but Pete loves her, so we're going to have to be supportive."

"Not much chance of that either."

"You could try …"

"Not after the talking to I got last time Pete was around."

"What do you mean?"

"He's told us to mind our own business."

"That doesn't sound like Pete."

"Collette is not interested in any of our ideas or help for the wedding."

The revelation still hurt, even though she'd tried to tell herself this was the way of young couples today. Parental input was not required.

"Mum, don't take it personally."

"I'm trying not to, but it's a disappointment."

"Why is it a disappointment?"

"I don't know about other mothers, but since you were babies I imagined what it would be like to have my children marry—all the romance and fun choosing themes and decorations."

"That's your problem."

Louise's heart dropped again. It must have shown on her face.

"Your imagination gets the better of you, Mum. Brides today don't want their mothers-in-law to be organizing their life."

Wasn't that the truth. But it still hurt.

"Anyway, if it's of any consolation, I'm happy to team up with you to organize my wedding—when it's the right time."

"Really?"

Chloe laughed.

"Really. I'm useless at planning big events and I'm going to need a team."

"We should try to include Alison as well."

"I know. Michael is her only son, and she's found this new lease of life watching him find love. It would be cruel to hedge her out of the planning."

Louise threw her arms around Chloe.

"Thanks for understanding. You're a good girl."

Chloe hugged her tightly in return, then pulled away.

"Only if you promise to not get carried away." Chloe caught her in a no-nonsense glare. "Mum?"

"I promise."

Maybe. Unless something inspirational turns up.

***

This would be the moment of truth. Having Chloe with him definitely gave him that layer of courage he needed to have this meeting.

"It's going to be all right." Chloe squeezed his hand as they stood at the bottom of the sloping driveway.

"I wish I could skip this part."

"Like it or not, if you're going to accept Harold as your father, you have to face Bernice as your step-mother."

"I wish I knew how she was going to react."

"Harold wouldn't have invited you around if he thought it would go badly."

Michael wasn't so sure. Still, despite his reluctance, he had agreed he would try to build a personal relationship with his boss—his father. It was all too weird.

"Come on." Chloe tugged on his hand and began to ascend the stone steps set amongst plants and solar-powered lights. At the top was the door to a new future. One he still struggled to accept.

"This place is a mansion." Chloe didn't need to state the obvious. It added to his sense of unworthiness. How could he be related to this?

Before they made the porch, the large front door opened and Harold stepped outside. His face was beaming, and Michael's stomach did a funny flip. Harold looked overjoyed to see them, and yet Michael still couldn't grasp why he would.

"Welcome." Harold caught Chloe in a hug first, then set her aside and waited. Michael fought with the desire to run. Was he ready to become so familiar?

"I'm so glad you've come," Harold said. He held his hand out. This was not so threatening, so Michael shook it. He'd shaken hands with Harold before. But this was different.

"Come inside." Harold stood back and allowed them to pass into the front hallway. The entire living area of his council house could have fit in this tiled entryway. This was ridiculous. Michael heard the door close behind him and Chloe put her arm around his waist. There was no running away from this. The only way was forward.

"Is your wife home?" Chloe asked. Bless her. At least she had some presence of mind.

"She is," Harold said. "She's just putting some icing on a cake."

Was it an excuse? Was Bernice as anxious as Michael was?

Harold ushered them through the house and out onto the back patio. His back garden was beautifully landscaped with bushes, flowerbeds, manicured lawn and a fountain in the middle.

"Do you keep this garden up yourself?" Chloe asked.

"Bernice likes to tend the veggies and fruit at the back, but we have a gardener in once a week to keep it all tidy."

Michael shook his head. It was so far removed from where he'd lived his whole life. He could not imagine having someone else come to mow his lawns or weed the few garden beds that were out the back of his place. That had always been his job—one he'd struggled to keep on top of.

"Bernice is bringing some afternoon tea out. Would you like tea, coffee or a cold drink?"

"I'd kill for a coffee," Chloe replied. Michael had to speak. He was like a stunned mullet, having not said a word since coming inside. Chloe squeezed his hand to encourage him.

"Could I just have water?" At last. He'd said something.

"I'll be two minutes."

Harold disappeared and Chloe turned concerned eyes in his direction.

"Are you OK?"

"It's a lot to process. This is so different to Mum's place."

"I get it. You're doing well, though. Just remember to smile once in a while."

Smile. Right. Good plan.

"And be kind to Bernice. She's probably all flustered, the same as you."

Before Chloe had finished speaking, Harold came outside again, this time with his wife following behind. She carried a plate with a delicious-looking cake on it, and Harold had a tray with glasses and a bottle of water.

"You remember Bernice?" Harold stood aside and allowed his wife to step forward. Michael remembered Bernice, the boss's wife. But this was Bernice his step-mother. Would he be able to accept her? Would she be able to accept him?

"Michael, Chloe. Thank you for coming." Bernice set her cake on the outdoor table. She came across and kissed Chloe on the cheek. Then she stood in front of Michael and studied him as if she'd never seen him before.

"Hello." Michael forced the word out, but it sounded stiff and unfriendly.

"Hello, Michael. I'm glad to meet you at last."

Michael frowned. They'd met on a number of occasions before.

"I mean, I'm glad … that is … we never expected … you really do look like Harold's father."

"I'm sorry to have forced myself upon you like this," Michael said.

"You haven't forced yourself," Harold said. "We want—" He stopped as Bernice put her hand up.

"The truth is, Michael, I'm sure you're as shocked about this as I am. You've had a couple of weeks to process it and so have I. When it comes down to it, Harold and I have always wanted a child but it wasn't possible." Tears began to pool in her eyes as she spoke. "When I learned about you—yes, it opened old wounds—but Harold has always sung your praises, even before he knew who you were. When I met you, I had thought you might have been the son we never had. And now it turns out, you are the son—at least, Harold's son..." Bernice swallowed emotion that threatened. "Will you accept me as your step-mother?"

The brimming tears broke their bounds and spilled down Bernice's cheeks. Michael felt her pain. She'd lost so many opportunities to have a child of her own. He would not deny her. She was not his mother, but that did not mean he could not include her in his world. If she would have him.

"Thank you, Bernice. Thanks for being so forgiving."

She held out her arms and it was not hard to embrace her. She was a mother without a child—and now he was that child she had prayed for so many years.

***

Michael was quiet on the ride home. Chloe was bursting to talk about the visit but sensed it would be wise to wait for him to speak. The energy it took to employ self-control was enormous, and she nearly burst open as they pulled up out the front of his mother's small house. If only someone was observing her mammoth effort in sensitivity and self-control. It was hard that she would not earn any applause for it.

"Do you want me to come in for a while?" Surely that wasn't too much.

Michael took a deep breath as if he was going to speak and then let it out again without a word.

"That's OK. Let's catch up tomorrow, all right?" Chloe said.

She watched him closely. He dropped his gaze and simply nodded. Chloe reached over and squeezed his hand.

"I'm proud of you, Michael. That could not have been easy today."

He opened his mouth to speak, but again retreated without a word.

"You go inside and think it over. We'll talk about it later." She leaned closer and kissed his cheek. "I love you."

"I love you too." Finally, he spoke. It was enough.

Chapter Twenty-six

*T*oday was the first day of the rest of his life. Sure, that was an overused cliché, but the rest of Michael's life was not going to be anything like the first twenty-eight years. This was going to take time to get used to.

"Harold wants to see you in his office," Jeannette said as Michael came by the personal assistant's office.

"Now?"

"He said it was urgent."

It was funny how the old bitterness had lost its edge since the visit with Harold and Bernice at their home. Chloe and Russell had been praying for him to be able to forgive and develop a relationship with his father. It felt like it might have been working.

"Michael." Harold stood up from his desk. He was beaming—and he was coming around and bearing down upon him like a Mack truck.

Michael prepared himself to shake hands, though that was not an ordinary thing to do in the office. But Harold wasn't looking for a handshake. He took him by the shoulders. Would he pull him in for a man-hug? Was he ready for something like that?

"I'm so glad you're here," Harold said. Did he think Michael would bail on work? "I'm so proud of you, I could burst, but I won't be telling the staff anything until you're ready." Harold let go of the half-shoulder hug and drew back. Michael felt a twinge of disappointment.

"Until I'm ready?"

"You and I can work on all the paperwork quietly, but sooner or later I'm going to have to announce who you are to me and how

265

things are going to change around here. I just need you to let me know when."

Michael felt his eyes sting with water coming to cloud his vision. That, and a stupid lump in his throat. He wanted to be ready now. Suddenly, he wanted Harold to take him in a proper man-hug— father and son—like he had longed for all his life. Great! Now his chin and lips betrayed him as they quivered with emotion.

"Michael?" Harold looked concerned.

"I'm ..." he swallowed back the lump. "I've always wanted ..." The emotion overwhelmed him, and he began to cry like a baby.

Several snotty handkerchiefs later, Michael realized the wall was down. Harold had taken him in that proper father hug and held him, and sobbed with him. How on earth were the pair of them going to face the rest of the staff now?

"I'm going to ask Jeannette if she will make us a coffee," Harold said. "And then we can talk about things."

"We have work to do for clients."

"This first. I want to make sure you and I are all on the same page professionally and with family."

"Family?"

"Will you marry Chloe?"

Michael nodded. No qualms there.

"What about Alison? How will you take proper care of her?"

Harold was right. There was stuff he wanted to talk to his father about. He'd hidden his mother and her needs for years, and now was a good time to make some crucial decisions. And best of all, now he had not one, but two fathers—Harold and Russell—who could be a sounding board and source of encouragement.

***

Chloe loved this. She loved the venue. She loved the band. She loved the food, and most importantly, she loved that everyone was celebrating her engagement to Michael. A real, sanctioned by parents, Facebook official engagement.

"Your dress is lovely." Esther came to speak to Chloe, carrying her newborn in her arms.

"Thanks for coming, Esther." Chloe pulled the wrap back from the baby's face. What was this shower of warm and fuzzies that shot through her?"

"You getting clucky?" Esther asked, a wry smile on her face.

"I must be," Chloe replied. "Who'd have thought?"

Esther smiled again. "You'll make a great mum."

This was crazy. Esther was deliberately poking her independent-career-sensibilities, and Chloe didn't care a bit. Bring on motherhood. She was ready.

"You want to hold the baby?" Esther asked.

Chloe didn't hesitate and held out her arms. Clucky was entirely the appropriate word for what she was feeling and she didn't care who saw it.

"Here come the boys. You wanna hand off?" Esther held her arms out to retrieve her infant.

"No fear." Chloe held tighter.

"Hope you're ready for kids, mate," Daniel said to Michael as they approached. "Looks like Chloe's got the bug."

"Don't tease her," Esther said. "Who wouldn't get the bug with such a gorgeous baby?"

"So, I hear Michael has cleared your name in reference to your traffic offenses?" Daniel said to Chloe.

"I was not speeding."

Michael and Daniel laughed.

"See, I told you," Michael said. "No one is gonna push my girl around. If there's justice to be had, she will fight for it."

My girl. How Chloe loved the sound of that. Totally crazy how love could change one's perspective on life.

"Can I have a hold?" Michael asked, holding out his hands towards the baby.

Chloe gently transferred the placid child to his arms and stood back to admire. Who didn't love a man with a baby in their arms?

"That's a really sexy look," Chloe whispered in his ear.

The corners of Michael's mouth pulled up in a knowing smile.

"I could kiss you," Chloe said.

"Please do," Michael replied.

***

"I bet you're proud of yourself," Russell whispered in Louise's ear as they stood watching the party going on around them.

This was a dream come true.

"I don't mind telling you, there were moments when I thought this whole situation would crash and burn—and I was terrified of being responsible for having connected them in the first place."

"It's turned out well this time, but Louise …" Russell turned and gave her a stern look. "Don't do this again. Please. My blood pressure can't take it."

"What are you talking about? You're as healthy as a mallee bull and, if you're honest, you were as instrumental in helping Michael find himself as I was in introducing him to Chloe in the first place."

"I know. I'm fond of the boy. But there has been so much that could have exploded, possibly still is, when you consider Alison's state of health."

Louise kissed him on the cheek. "They will manage. We're here to support them and so is Michael's father."

Russell took a deep breath and raised his eyebrows. "Speaking of which, I'd better compare notes with him to see who is going to give a speech first."

Louise squeezed her husband's hand before he moved off through the mingling group of guests. This cocktail engagement party was in full swing—canapes and drinks being handed around the room to guests dressed in colorful formal wear. It was wonderful, but Russell was right—there had been so many moments of tension when everything could have turned to custard, and one of those moments was brewing before her eyes. Harold Ainsworth was approaching Alison Sullivan, who was currently standing alone. Was that a good thing? Before she'd had time to think about it, Louise took the five steps that separated her from Michael's mother and assumed the position of guardian angel.

"Are you enjoying the party?" Louise asked, fully aware that the conversation was about to be interrupted.

"It's like a beautiful dream," Alison replied. "I don't know how I can go back to normal life after this."

Louise didn't have time to formulate a sage platitude before Harold inserted himself into the discussion.

"Good evening, ladies."

My, but he was a suave gentleman. Full of charm. Louise cast a nervous look towards Mrs Ainsworth. How was she responding to this awful social faux pas? Thank goodness Chloe had gone to stand guard over her future step-mother-in-law.

"Hello, Harry," Alison said. Louise did a double take. Far from being cowed by the man, Alison stood upright and confident.

"I just wanted to thank you for allowing me—us …" he waved his hand towards his wife. "…to be part of Michael's life."

Alison didn't speak for a few seconds, which seemed like an eon to Louise. She had scrambled through her thoughts and compiled several remarks she thought might be witty or poignant, but had abandoned each one in turn. Alison had to respond to this, not her.

"I'm not going to pretend that our association in the past did not cause me a great deal of pain, but I have never seen Michael so happy."

"I think Chloe may have something to do with that, don't you, Louise?" Harold looked at her for confirmation.

At last, she was being asked for an opinion—and right on cue, all sensible thought fled.

"Well … he seems … I mean … Chloe is very happy with him. And from my point of view, that's a wonderful thing."

Harold offered a tight smile and turned his focus back to Alison. "Thank you for forgiving me."

Alison nodded and took a sip of punch from the glass she'd been holding, white-knuckled.

"Michael tells me you're investing in a unit in a retirement village."

"Really?" Louise had missed this piece of information in all that had been going on.

"Yes." Alison gave Louise a quick smile. "It's too posh for the likes of me, but he's insisted."

"When you're living on your own, you'll appreciate the maintenance team and the security services," Harold said.

"Which village?" Louise asked.

"It's near the city and is a multistoried development."

"Does it have the usual social programs and services?"

"It has a pool, spa, tennis court, music room, library, chapel, and a slate of social activities for the residents to engage in." Harold delivered the information but still looked tense.

"I've never had any of that before, Harry. I'm not sure I'm going to fit in."

Louise watched her. What was she feeling? Alison sighed and continued.

"I will do my best, for Michael's sake. I know he worries about me and my mental health, and they do have social workers who support people like me."

"It sounds wonderful," Louise said. "If you're happy to have visitors, I'd love to come and have a hit of tennis with you."

Alison laughed. "You'd have to teach me how to play first. And I'm so unfit."

"We could try bocce. Do they have bocce there?"

"I've never heard of it."

"It's the Italian version of bowls," Harold said, "and I'm pretty sure I saw that on the program."

Alison stilled and looked straight at Harold. There was fire in her eyes.

"Harry, I know we are going to have to share Michael, but you don't have to—actually you shouldn't—concern yourself with me. You have your wife and I don't mean to make trouble for you."

At that point, Michael came up wearing a worried look. That was understandable, given his father and mother were talking, in public, with Harold's wife looking on.

"Everything OK?" he asked.

"We're just testing the waters," Alison said. "Having your father back in your life has changed everything for me. I just need to learn how to navigate life in this new context."

Harold nodded. "Well, thanks again Alison. Bernice and I couldn't be more pleased." He smiled in Louise's direction and returned to Bernice.

"Are you all right?" Michael asked his mother.

"I'm going to have to learn to live with it, aren't I?" It was said more as a statement than a question.

"The village sounds lovely," Louise couldn't help saying something.

"Honestly, Louise, it's beautiful. I just don't think I deserve anything so grand."

Michael opened his mouth but was cut off.

"Don't go on about it, Michael. We've been over and over it. If you're going to feel settled with me there, I won't say another thing about it."

"Thank you, Mum. I appreciate you making the sacrifice."

Louise could not detect any sarcasm in his tone. They really saw this massive change in her life as a sacrifice.

"Can I tell you something, Louise?" Alison said, after Michael returned to Chloe's side. "There is also a magnificent rose garden with beautiful shady trees. Do you know how long I have dreamed of having a rose garden?"

Louise took Alison's hand and gave it a squeeze. "We're all very happy for you and wishing you every blessing."

Alison nodded and then smiled. "Let's be honest, Louise, when those two start producing grandchildren, then we'll be swamped with all the blessings in the world."

"Amen to that." Louise cast her eye in the direction of her daughter and future son-in-law. They were holding hands and stole a kiss. When all the evidence was in, Louise felt she'd done a good job. A handsome, honest lawyer was in want of a wife, and despite Russell's gloomy predictions, her meddling had paid off. Again.

Before you go:

If you enjoyed this story, would you mind taking a few minutes to pop a review on the site where you purchased *In Want of a Wife*, or on the Good Reads website. Every review helps me, as an author, to get new readers involved. Thank you for spending the time with me and my Luella Linley family.

Meredith ☺

Coming soon - 2021

Book 3 in the Luella Linley – License to Meddle series

All Arranged

By Meredith Resce

Regency romance author, Luella Linley (AKA Louise Brooker), should feel satisfied she has helped her two daughters marry happily. However, her successful meddling came at a price and her husband has advised she leave the children to their own devices.

But her eldest, Pete, is thirty-five, living back at home and dejected after having been jilted days before his wedding. Her responsible, hard-working and handsome son would make a good husband and father—but he's given up after three failed relationships. He's a good catch, but unlikely to be fooled by his mother's scheming and meddling.

This situation calls for a direct approach. Just like in her novels, Louise decides the parents should do the arranging and sort out the wheat from the chaff.

Carrie Davis is a dedicated career woman and hasn't had time for relationships. However, her sister, Ellen, is now happily married with a delightful little girl and for the first time, Carrie finds loneliness stalking her. Ellen want's the best for Carrie, so when she comes across an odd advert in the classifieds, she wonders if it is a prank or an opportunity sent from heaven.

"Wanted. For a social experiment. A family arranged marriage."

Have you read Book 1 in the Luella Linley – License to Meddle series

<u>Organized Backup</u>

By Meredith Resce

Regency romance author, Luella Linley, arranges her characters' lives, making sure that they weather all storms and live happily-ever-after. Her characters are putty in her hands, but her 21st Century adult children are not so easily organized. When her daughter, Megan, asks for support with an inappropriate situation at work, Luella decides Megan should get a boyfriend to intimidate her boss. The cop who just pulled Luella over for speeding is a likely candidate.

Cam Fletcher is expecting to be interviewed by a famous author. Instead of sharing insights into his job working in the police force, he is sharing a meal with the famous author and her daughter, Megan. When left alone with Megan, Cam wonders when the interview will begin. The parents' extended absence gives him a clue, which Megan confirms. Luella Linley is playing matchmaker, but is he willing to play the game.

Also by Meredith Resce

The Heart of Green Valley series

(Period drama romance set in Colonial Australia)

Book 1 – The Manse

Book 2 – Green Valley

Book 3 – Through the Valley of Shadows

Book 4 – Wallace Hill

Book 5 – Beyond the Valley

Book 6 - Echoes in the Valley

The Schoolmaster's Bride (Period drama romance)

The Schoolmaster's Daughter (Period drama romance)

Mellington Hall (Murder mystery)

Cora Villa (Period drama romance)

For All Time (A time slip novel)

How Sweet the Sound (Fantasy Allegory)

The Greenfield Legacy (Contemporary romance)

Falling for Maddie Grace (Contemporary romance novella)

Where there's Smoke (Contemporary romance novella)

Four Short Stories (paperback of four novellas)

Mortal Insight (Contemporary political crime under pen-name E.B. James)

Thank you

Thanks to you, the reader, for engaging in this story. I hope you have enjoyed it and will get an opportunity to read the other two books in the *Luella Linley – License to Meddle* series.

I would like to thank some of my writer friends who encouraged me to keep going. I was considering packing it in after having released eighteen other titles, but there were some writer friends who gave consistent encouragement to keep at it. Iola Goulton – who suggested I turn one book into three (Book three was written first). Carolyn Miller – who consistently tells me she loves these stories and I *must* get them into the hands of readers. Narelle Atkins – who takes every opportunity to support and promote this series (and many other authors as well). Penny Reeve – who showed care and concern when I was ready to give up, and who gave solid feedback on this manuscript.

Thanks to my children, who also encourage me to continue. Thanks to my husband for helping me set up a new work space, and though he doesn't love it, is helping me get a library arranged. You know how writers love to have libraries.

Thanks to those readers who take the extra time to review. It is encouraging to an author, and it helps to tickle the algorithms to do something useful.

Thank you, God, Creator, Saviour, Healer and King – who is the genius behind anything that is particularly brilliant. I pray that something of his grace and peace is infused into these stories, and that they will bring inspiration and encouragement.

About the Author

South Australian Author, Meredith Resce, has been writing since 1991, and has had books in the Australian market since 1997.

Following the Australian success of her *Heart of Green Valley* series, they were released in the UK.

In Want of a Wife is Meredith's 21st published title.

Apart from writing, Meredith teaches high school students. She is an avid reader, particularly Christian fiction. She is a fan of British costume-drama television series, and British murder mystery shows. Jane Austen, L.M. Montgomery and Charles Dickens are favorite classic authors. Meredith is a country-girl at heart, and takes every opportunity to visit the farm where she grew-up.

Aussie rules football and cricket are her choice when following televised sport. Come on Aussies!

Meredith often speaks to groups on issues relevant to relationships and emotional and spiritual growth.

Meredith has also been co-writer and co-producer in the 2007 feature film production, *Twin Rivers* now available on Amazon Prime.

With her husband, Nick, Meredith has worked in Christian ministry since 1983.

Meredith and Nick have three adult children.

www.meredithresce.com

www.facebook.com/MeredithResceAuthor

www.ingramcontent.com/pod-product-compliance
Lightning Source LLC
Chambersburg PA
CBHW050034120726
47903CB00006B/2037